Samuel M. Smucker

The Yankee slave driver, or,

The black and white rivals

Samuel M. Smucker

The Yankee slave driver, or,
The black and white rivals

ISBN/EAN: 9783337889609

Printed in Europe, USA, Canada, Australia, Japan

Cover: Foto ©ninafisch / pixelio.de

More available books at **www.hansebooks.com**

THE

YANKEE SLAVE DRIVER;

OR, THE

Black and White Rivals.

WITH ILLUSTRATIONS.

'TIS STRANGE, BUT TRUE; FOR TRUTH IS ALWAYS STRANGE;
STRANGER THAN FICTION.—BYRON.

New-York :
H. DAYTON, 36 HOWARD STREET
INDIANAPOLIS, IND. : ASHER & CO.
1860.

PREFACE.

THE subject of slavery is one in which no American can take too great or too permanent an interest. Whether it is viewed as a single item in the great sum of human affairs; or as an important development in human history; or as a prominent ingredient in American society and government; or as a fruitful source of strange forms and habitudes of human thought and action, nowhere else to be discovered on the globe; in any case American slavery is a theme of imperishable interest and concern. And it will remain such, not only while this remarkable institution continues to exist, but for ages after it shall have happily become a thing only of history and of retrospection.

What other subject addresses itself so powerfully to the attention of the statesman, the philanthropist, the man of letters, the student of political history and economy, the moralist, and the observer of human character and society? None! It has no parallel in this

respect, in the whole range of human thought and inquiry.

Hence it is that the literature of slavery has assumed,
during its brief existence, various phases; but it has in
these latter days, achieved a new development, which
seems to possess greater power, and to gain a stronger
hold on public interest, than any it had previously displayed. We mean the department of slave-novels;—
works of imagination, based upon facts, as they are constantly exhibited and developed by the operation of
slavery. Several works of this class, possessing great
power and merit, have already appeared; and it is to
be hoped that the supply is not yet exhausted.

We contend that every American citizen possesses an
unquestionable right to speak boldly of slavery. If not
residing in a slave State, he has no right directly to interfere, either in its suppression or in its preservation.
But as a citizen of this confederacy; as one who, at
home and abroad, must bear a part of the universal ob-
loquy and disgrace which negro bondage brings upon
the American name in every clime; as one who, if
slavery should finally dissolve this Union, must endure
a portion of the social and political calamities which
that fearful catastrophe would inevitably inflict upon the
nation; in view of all these reasons it is undoubtedly
right, that every American should use moral suasion, if
he will, and the force of argument and narrative, if he

can, to aid in the suppression of the most monstrous and gigantic evil of modern times.

In the exercise of this privilege, the following pages have been written by an author, himself the native of a slave State. The reader may rest assured that nothing is contained in them which has not had its counterpart in real fact. If there is any distinctive feature belonging to this work, which distinguishes it from the other publications of a similar character which have already appeared, it is this: that while they all have *confessedly* softened down some of the most offensive attributes of American slavery, and in mistaken charity, have thrown over them a borrowed and unnatural hue of benevolence and moderation, which did not really belong to the subject, but are, in truth, actually incongruous and foreign to it; *this* book presents a picture of slavery, in which its *worst* features are as boldly and as unsparingly portrayed, as its best. There is nothing in American slavery worse than some things to be found here; and there is nothing better. It is therefore hoped, that in this book will be found a true, because it is an unmitigated, portraiture of the subject.

CONTENTS.

CONTENTS.

PLANTER'S VICTIM:

OR,

Incidents of American Slavery.

CHAPTER I.

TWO YOUNG SLAVES.

> " Heaven from all creatures hides the book of fate,
> All but the page prescribed, their present state;
> The lamb, thy riot dooms to bleed to-day,
> Had he thy reason, would he skip and play?
> Pleased to the last, he crops the flowery food,
> And licks the hand just raised to shed his blood."—POPE.

IT was the 5th of September, in the year 1840. Brightly gleamed the evening sun, when shedding its last golden radiance over the fertile plain, which formed the large and rich estate of Major Dudley, in Louisiana. At this moment two persons, seated alone on the turf, at some distance in the rear of his stately mansion, were gazing with silent rapture on the scene; for it was

2

indeed a picture adapted to excite the admiration of every beholder. The god of day was about to plunge behind the western steeps, and bid the world farewell; but ere he left it to darkness and silence, he shed upon hill and dale, and cotton field, a parting lustre, a glowing beauty, which no pencil could reproduce.

It was Sunday evening. During the day, the busy work of the plantation had been suspended. The slaves were for the most part unoccupied. Among the one hundred of these, who were owned by old Major Dudley, two were preëminent for intelligence, personal beauty and amiability.

These two were the persons already alluded to— George Sanford, and his betrothed and beloved Caroline. We will endeavor to describe both of them.

Sanford was a bright mulatto youth, of tall and muscular proportions, about twenty-four years of age. His complexion was scarcely a shade darker than that of his aristocratic owner. So faultless and perfect were the proportions of his figure, that he might well have served as a model for a sculptor, from which to mould some youthful and majestic Apollo, in the full glow of masculine beauty and splendor.

His countenance, too, was as remarkable as his figure. His features exhibited nothing of the distinctive characteristics of the negro; his eye was large, dark and expressive; his forehead was high, prominent and expansive; displaying a dome of thought, indicative of mental superiority. He had pearly teeth, and the long silken hair of an Italian.

As they quietly gazed on the scene, he placed his arm around the slender waist of his companion, who seemed in truth to be the counterpart of himself. Caroline was the illegitimate daughter of her master, old Major Dudley; the fruit of an illicit passion for one of his female slaves; who, some years before had died, and left her hapless child behind her in the world, an orphan and a slave.

Caroline had inherited all her father's intelligence and native dignity of deportment. She was a beautiful girl, possessing the same fair complexion as her lover. She exhibited the characteristic traits of all the beauties of the sunny South, whether bond or free; dark eyes and hair, a soul full of burning passion, and great ardor of temperament. Her features were classical in their outline; and her head was gracefully poised on a magnificent bust, of full and swelling proportions. Her slender waist and delicate foot might have emulated those of a countess; while all her movements possessed a native charm and grace, which were very captivating to the observer.

She and Sandford, living on the same estate, had early learned to love; and they loved, as only the children of a common misfortune can love, when a southern clime adds intensity to emotions created by mutual beauty and attachment.

"How happy this glorious sunset makes me," said George, "I feel that I can almost forget our toils, and imagine myself, for a moment, what I ought to be, *a freeman.*"

"As long as we are happy together, we must forget that we are slaves," Caroline responded. "Our lot is not, indeed, worse than that of thousands of others, and in some respects it is better."

"Yes, but while I am grateful for what we do enjoy, I feel an unquenchable desire for that which I know the great Creator intended that we should possess, that is— ourselves, our freedom."

"Yet, George, I hope you would not try to run away; the attempt would be full of peril to you; and beside, you would leave me behind you, and that would make me perfectly wretched."

"Oh no," replied George, "I never would think of running away; my plan is a very different one."

"What is it?" eagerly inquired Caroline.

"It is not to run away, nor to defraud my master of what he supposes to be his lawful property. I have been dreaming and hoping to secure this great blessing of freedom, by earning it myself; I intend to make a proposition to master."

"What is it?"

"I intend to ask him to hire my time out to some of the planters in our neighborhood; and then, without his knowing it, I will work extra, and save up my earnings, till they amount to something handsome; and then I will ask master what he will sell me for, and if I hav'nt enough I will work on, and save up more, till I get enough, and then I will buy myself. Oh, I will then be free! Carry, it must be a glorious thing to be free; to feel that no living being is your master, your tyrant, or your superior!"

Caroline did not receive this announcement with the approving ardor which George had anticipated. She seemed lost in pensive thought, and appeared to be sad.

The silence of a few moments ensued.

"Why are you so gloomy, my love?" asked George. Caroline raised her large dark eyes to George's, and said sadly, "Why should I feel happy at this declaration of yours? When you are free, the day that proclaims your liberty, will be the hour of my desertion and loneliness. You will not stay long after that in this land of slaves, and stripes, and tears. I know you won't. You will go to Canada, or to some other free and happy land, and I must remain here in solitude, in servitude, and in despair." And she began to weep.

"No, never, never, Carry!" said he, enthusiastically. "Wait till you have heard all my plans. When I attain my freedom, then every day and night, and every hour,

2*

will I toil, until I buy your freedom too. I can earn
eight or nine hundred dollars in several years, at most,
and I will not spend an idle moment till I buy your
freedom."

"Ah! that would be a happiness almost too great to
be imagined," replied Caroline, smiling.

"Yet we will some day enjoy it, I hope. That part
of our happiness will all depend on master; but he is
so stern and resolute, that I sometimes fear he will never
listen to my request, and may refuse to hire me out."

"Let us hope that he will not refuse," rejoined Caroline.

"If he does refuse me, I know not what I will do. I
will give up in despair. I know, Carry, that you and I
were never intended for slaves. We were born to be
free. I feel a mighty impulse in my soul, whenever I
think of the galling chains I wear, which seems to give
me strength to tear those chains in a thousand pieces,
and step forth upon this beautiful, bounteous, and fragrant earth, a freeman! one whom God has made in his
own image; capable of enjoying and of appreciating his
freedom, and his powers and faculties, which are human
and noble; and for using them for great and noble purposes."

Caroline listened to her lover in silence. He continued, reflectively, "I am a slave, owned by another
human being, no wiser, no better, no nobler than myself.

I have as much right, by the laws of God and reason, to command his fate and actions, and destiny, as he has to command mine. An unholy law, made by the base and grasping passions of the strongest, has sanctioned his authority over me; but no other law, and no other law-giver has sanctioned it.

"Nor is our present misery the sum of all that we must suffer. Our existence now is crushed. But look at the darkness and uncertainty of the future. We may at any moment be sold to another and more cruel mas-ter. We may be separated from each other for ever You, especially, would then be unprotected in the world. I may be compelled by some other master to endure still worse stripes and chains, and toil and buffetings, than I now suffer. The present with us is wretched; but the unknown future hangs over us like a dark cloud. Yet far beyond the confines of this gloomy land of chains," said he, smiling, "I know and have heard that there is a brighter land of hope and freedom, under other laws; where slaves become men, and where despairing beings, such as we are, become the possessors of, to us, an unknown happiness."

During the delivery of this burst of feeling, the expressive and intellectual features of Sanford became wrought up with intense excitement, and his eyes glared around him in calm and self-possessed defiance.

He proceeded after a pause, "Oh, it must be glorious

to be free! as glorious as it is ignominious to be a slave, a serf! I *will* be free, Carry, and so shall you! But I will not rob my master. I will not cheat him of what is not his own. I will buy myself, and I will buy you, too, if I die in the attempt. That would be a much more noble, ay, glorious triumph, than to run away! Don't you think so, love?"

During this speech, Caroline had gazed with silent rapture and admiration on her lover. The shades of evening had gradually settled, unperceived by them, over the wide and tranquil face of the landscape; and the sleepy sounds which are usually heard on a large plantation, when the lowing herds and the once clamorous servants are gradually sinking into rest, and are dispersing to their several quarters, reminded them that it was time for them to separate for the night.

"I will hope for the best," said Caroline. "I know you are capable of making noble exertions, George."

"How long will it be before you can obtain Misses's consent to our marriage?" said he

"I know not, love, but very soon, I hope." With this remark, George impressed a fervent kiss upon the lips of his betrothed, which was returned with equal ardor. The poor girl felt happy in her love, and in the hope of a better future.

At this moment the shrill voice of Mrs. Dudley, her mistress, was heard resounding from the back door of the mansion, calling for Caroline, whose duty it was to prepare Ada, her youngest daughter, a child of five years of age, for bed. Hearing the summons, she hastily rose, and went toward the house, bidding her lover good night.

George, silently and thoughtfully wended his way to his own rude quarters; where, on his humble wooden couch, he revolved in his mind, until a late hour, the restless thoughts and aspirations which had already taken possession of his soul.

The reader may imagine, that the description we have here given of these two quadroon slaves, is exaggerated and unnatural; that the language and ideas ascribed to them, indicate a degree of intelligence which is never found among the slaves of the South.

This is a very great error. We draw the picture of the thoughts and feelings of these two unfortunate beings from actual life. There is a class of negroes in the South, generally the children of white men and mulatto women, who possess and display a degree of natural intelligence, refinement and delicacy of feeling, fully equal to any thing exhibited by the white race. They, of course, want the finishing touch, which education alone can give, to natural qualities of that kind. Their minds, naturally gifted, and apt to receive impressions and accessions of knowledge from without, are not polished and adorned with the various graces and beauties

which learning bestows; which a knowledge of history
and science, and antiquity, and poetry imparts. But so
far as their own inherent and natural impulses and conception of things are concerned, they are as gifted and
as elevated as the whites; and often, indeed, far superior to those rude and savage wretches, in whose hands
their own fate sometimes happens to be unfortunately
placed.

It is two persons of this class,—their history, their
struggles, and their fate, which we propose to portray
in this work. Of course, the reader should bear in
mind, that while this class of slaves exists, and toils,
and suffers, it is a comparatively *small* class; yet their
career is often one of melancholy interest, surpassing
even the greatest marvels of fiction.

CHAPTER II.

A FAMILY GROUP.

'THE family of old Major Dudley, the owner of George Sanford and Caroline, were representatives of a very large and distinguished class of Southern planters.

Major Dudley himself, was a bald headed, dignified, portly old gentleman, of very florid complexion and robust health. He was a descendant of an ancient and aristocratic Virginia family, of English origin, who, two or three generations since, had emigrated from the Old Dominion to the cotton fields of Louisiana, and there purchased a large estate, of which the Major was now the sole inheritor.

He had spent his whole life on his estate; and the long familiarity with wealth and local consequence, which he had enjoyed, had given him a proud air and manner of command, which, to a stranger was somewhat marked and offensive. He never travelled, except once in several years to New Orleans, to make purchases for the ladies of his family; and occasionally he would ride about to neighboring plantations, to spend a day with their owners, with whom he was on terms of friendship and intimacy.

The Major's ideas respecting his slaves, were those of the wealthy planters of the South generally. He regarded them as little better than his cattle; he had no particular pleasure in punishing them, or in making them miserable; he did not, in fact, punish them unnecessarily. But if they were ever so unfortunate as to excite his wrath, he inflicted upon them terrible evidences of his vindictiveness. Then they were punished with great severity. Then he knew neither pity nor humanity. The slaves on the Major's plantation were generally well provided for; they had sufficient to eat and drink; good, though coarse clothing; and were not, in general, overworked. Their master acted on the sagacious principle, that it was much the best policy for slaveholders not to overwork their slaves; they made more out of their property, if they took good care of it; their slaves then brought better prices, and lived much longer.

Then, too, the Major and his family took great pride in the thrifty and sleek appearance of their slaves. They loved to make a show of all their fine cattle to their opulent visitors, of whom there was generally some one or other lodging in the house. They took pride in their large oxen; in the superior appearance of their horses; in the excellent breed of their sheep and hogs. They took equal pride in the excellence of their crops of sugar, rice and cotton; and even the thrifty state of their farming utensils was not a matter to be overlooked by them; the condition of their barns, corn-cribs, stables, wagons, carriages, and slave-huts,—all served to heighten their family pride, and feed the sense of their opulence and prosperity.

While these things were so, of course the condition and appearance of his hundred slaves were a matter of vast importance to the Major, and a source of great pride to his family. These slaves generally worked well; all things went forward quietly and harmoniously on the plantation. Sometimes a slave was very severely whipped; sometimes another was handcuffed; sometimes a third was confined for a day in the rude stocks, which their master had provided for the purpose. But for the most part, the overseer's task on Major Dudley's plantation was an easy one. It was, in fact, a model plantation in every respect.

Mrs. Dudley, the Major's wife, was a person of great dignity of deportment, and managed quietly to divide with her husband the sceptre and the dominion which he held over this little empire.

She was descended from an ancient, though somewhat reduced family of Tennessee, and had been in her youth a celebrated beauty; now, advancing age had considerably diminished her charms, though not her pretensions.

She was a good housekeeper, so far as housekeeping is requisite in the wife of a Southern planter, and kept every department of the establishment which came under her observation, in excellent order. She, too, was not unnecessarily strict or severe with her servants; though when they were guilty of disobedience or neglect, she could punish with great severity.

Mrs. Dudley was a professing Christian; she attended a church some five miles distant from the plantation, as often as the weather permitted. What her ideas of slavery were, it would indeed, be difficult to tell. Her intellect was one of narrow compass and feeble power; hence she did not, in any of her meditations, probe very profoundly into the absolute and fundamental nature of things, or of moral relations.

It is probable that Mrs. Dudley had no very distinct ideas respecting the nature of slavery, or of slaves. As a Christian, she could not deny that her slaves were human beings, and consequently had immortal souls. But as a slaveholder, she could not admit that they were her brothers and sisters, possessed of the same rights, hopes, fears, duties and destinies as herself. As a Christian, she must have admitted that Christ had died to redeem them; yet, as a slaveholder, it must have puzzled her to conceive why the Son of God should die to redeem such cattle, any more than he would have died to redeem the fat horses, or sheep, or oxen, with which the estate was stocked.

Mrs. Dudley had several favorites among her slaves, who had won her regard by their ready obedience to her whims, and by their general intelligence and amiability. One of these was Caroline. To her she entrusted the care of her wardrobe; and the neatness, taste, and aptitude displayed by the poor girl in the performance of her duties, had secured her mistress's good-will and kindness toward her.

The other members of Major Dudley's family, whom it may be proper here to mention, were his son Richard, his pride and heir; Julia, his eldest daughter, and Ada, an interesting child of five years.

Richard Dudley was a fine-looking, handsome young man, twenty-five years of age, who had been reared almost entirely upon his father's plantation. He had occasionally been absent from home, at New Orleans and other Southern cities, where he had spent a few weeks at a time, in those pursuits and pleasures congenial to youth and an ardent temperament.

He possessed rather more than an average amount of talent. His education had not been neglected, and he had gone through the course of elementary and polite learning, usual with young gentlemen of the South. He had also learned all their fashionable vices, and ardently indulged in them, without restraint.

His disposition was by no means as attractive as his person. In truth, his nature was one of unusual and extraordinary fierceness, bitterness, and resolution. He had ever been a spoiled and petted child, and when he grew up to man's estate, his passions had also grown with great power and intensity; and in the gratification of those passions, he knew neither restraint, nor law, nor reason.

The large amount of money which he could always command, had generally enabled him to attain the end of all his wishes. When not irritated in any way, Richard could be gentle, manly, and courteous enough. At times, even, when in a good humor, his great personal beauty would render him often attentive and fascinating. But when crossed or disturbed, he became fierce, vindictive, and implacable.

His sister Julia, had inherited her mother's beauty, and more than her father's intelligence. Accustomed from infancy to be constantly waited upon, she could do little or nothing for herself, without the aid of her servants; yet she treated them with great kindness.

This young lady was a type of the highest and best class of Southern heiresses. The charms of her person were very great. Her education had been carefully attended to. There was no accomplishment which adds a higher charm to beauty, nor grace which increases the attractiveness of wealth and station, which she did not possess in an unusual degree.

Julia was honored or annoyed, by a large number of suitors. Of one of these, her favorite, and finally her husband, we will speak hereafter. She made no profession of anything like religion. It is not customary or fashionable for the unmarried daughters of southern planters to do so. The usual routine of her life was alternated between her music, her books, her embroidery, and her visitors. Yet many of the impulses of her soul were benevolent, humane, and generous. Her passions were strong and impetuous; but as is generally the case with women, they were mixed with more than the usual gentleness and amiability of the sex; and she had sometimes a heart open as day to emotions of generosity and pity, when objects calculated to excite them were presented to her attention.

We have said enough about the Dudley family to convey to the reader an idea of the principal personages of whom we shall hereafter speak. Shortly succeeding the conversation described in the preceding chapter, events began to develop themselves which clearly illustrated the attributes which we have ascribed to the several members of this family; and constituted the moving spring of the misfortunes and destinies of those under their power—their slaves, and eventually their victims.

3*

CHAPTER III.

THE ATTEMPT AND FIRST FAILURE.

"I'll have her—but I will not keep her long."—RICHARD III.

THE quiet and uniform routine of life on a Southern plantation, is well calculated to engender habits of luxury and dissipation in the young inheritors of large estates.

Richard Dudley, the heir of this immense property, had a short time since returned from a visit to New Orleans, and had brought with him a beautiful mulatto girl, whom he had there purchased at a very high price.

During some weeks after his return, he seemed to be quite enamoured of her charms. The connection between them was, of course, known to everybody on the plantation; but neither in the house of the master, nor among the slaves, was any allusion made to it. These *liaisons*, if they may be dignified by such a term, where brute-lust, without any affection or esteem between the parties, is the only attraction, were matters of such repeated occurrence among persons of the class to which Richard

Dudley belonged, that they excited no surprise and occasioned no remark.

Soon, however, Richard began to weary of her attractions, and especially did he grow more indifferent to her,
as the ripening beauty and graceful manners of Caroline
came more closely under his observation and scrutiny.
A keen, vulture-like passion began to grow within him.
His eye, from time to time, gloated upon her matchless
figure and her attractive proportions.

It was not long indeed, before he had come to the deliberate determination to ravish the charms of the girl,
and subject her to the indignities of a permanent or
transient concubinage, as it might suit his fancy. One
day, with this end in view, and watching his opportunity,
when he observed her alone, at a short distance from
the house, he approached and addressed her. Caroline
was in a remote corner of the garden, weeding her patch
of flowers. The situation was favorable to a retired conversation; the heavy foliage screened them from immediate observation.

"What pretty flowers you have here," said Dudley,
to her, as he approached.

Caroline rose from her knees, and gazed with surprise
at the person who addressed her. She immediately
curtsied gracefully to Richard, and replied: "Yes, master Richard, mistress gave me the seeds. I planted them
here, and they have grown up into beautiful flowers."

" You love flowers, I suppose," said he.

"Very much, master. Whenever mistress lets me have a little time to myself, I come here, to weed and trim my flower-bed, and I enjoy it very much. I *do* love flowers."

" But these do not occupy all your thoughts, do they?" inquired Richard, as he ran his eye over her full and graceful figure, and took a fresh impression, as it were, of her attractions.

"I do not understand you, Master Richard," said she, inquiringly.

"Do not understand me? If you love flowers, you can surely love something else, or somebody else," said he, with a sarcastic and significant smile, and leer of his eye.

Caroline blushed deeply, as the thought of his base meaning rushed upon her mind.

"Oh yes," said she, trying to avert the impression which his remark had made upon her mind. "I love my mistress, and Miss Julia;—everybody. Indeed, I hate no one."

"Ah, then, perhaps you can love *me*," said Richard, as he approached Caroline, and slowly placed his arm around her waist, and gazing at her.

Caroline was terrified at her position. She saw at a glance its dangerous and unhappy nature. She knew the power which Richard possessed over her. She knew that it was almost omnipotent. She also recollected the violence and fury of his temper, of which she had on former occasions witnessed various demonstrations, too terrible to be easily forgotten.

Caroline blushed deeply. She trembled from head to foot. Gently removing his arm from around her waist, and turning her large and beautiful eyes imploringly to those of Richard, she said: "I hope, Master Richard, you will not think of such a thing."

But Richard was not so easily to be despoiled of his prey. Controlling the rising sensation of anger which her manner and reply had occasioned, and resolving to play the lover rather than the ruffian, he said: "Why not love me, Caroline? If love is a stranger to you, let me be the subject of your attachment: let me teach you to love. I will be an expert master, I promise you."

At this moment, the thought of Sanford, her absent and betrothed friend, rushed upon her mind. At first, the recollection of him whom she so truly loved, created a sickening sensation, when combined with a consciousness of her dangerous position.

A moment's reflection however enabled her to recover her self-possession, and she replied with some determination: "The love you propose to me, Master Richard, you must know, is not an honorable love; it is a base, a degrading one. I cannot be your wife, and I am sure, you cannot expect me to be anything else to you."

"Indeed!" said Richard, sarcastically, and standing away from her several yards, and regarding her with an expression of intense hauteur and scorn, "Indeed! if you cannot be my wife, you cannot be anything else! Of course you cannot be my wife. But are you certain that you cannot be anything else?"

"Never, Master Richard, never!" and the poor girl burst into tears.

Richard Dudley gazed upon her, as the vulture glares upon his prey. No pity nor relenting emotion took possession of his soul. What! should he regard the tears of a slave—of his own property? Could his favourite horse *Selim* weep, he would have paid more regard to his irrational tears, than he would to those of Caroline, when the black surges of the sea of lust within his soul were dashing to and fro tumultuously.

He gazed upon her; but her flowing tears, and the supplicating attitude to which she had knelt, and which displayed yet more fully the fine points of her proportions, but excited his passion to an intenser pitch.

"Do you say, you will never yield? Have you the hardihood to refuse and reject me?" said he, fiercely. "Know you not, that I have the power to compel you? I can do with you just as I please;" and he took hold of her arm rudely.

Caroline did not resist him. The nature of the place shielded her from immediate outrage, and seeing that the mingled passion and resentment of Richard were aroused, she stood motionless, and wept.

Silence ensued for some moments. "Make up your mind not to oppose me, Caroline," said he; "I like you, and admire you, and you must obey me."

"Oh, Master Richard, pity me. Do not ruin, do not disgrace me. You will break my heart, and break the heart of another, too."

At this allusion Richard released her arm, and said, with surprise, "Ah! there is another person then, in the case, is there? Who is that? I have a rival, have I?"

Caroline had unwittingly made this disclosure in reference to her lover, and she shuddered to think that her indiscretion had involved him also in the misfortune of opposing the passion, and exciting the hatred of her young master.

She, however, thought it was best not to disguise or hold back the truth.

"You have no rival, Master Richard; but I am engaged and promised to—to George Sanford; he loves me, and I love him. Oh, pity me—pity us, master; do not, I beseech you, ruin me!"

At this declaration, Richard Dudley stood silently regarding her for a few moments. It took him quite by surprise; he knew not at first what to say.

But Richard was a man who was never accustomed to

listen to the voice of reason or of pity, whenever his
passions were excited. In this case, the information
Caroline had just given him, instead of teaching his
reason the propriety of regarding the purity of the
plighted love of these two young, innocent beings; it
only added another ingredient to the raging passion
within him; and that was an intense hatred for the
unfortunate slave, who happened thus unconsciously to
stand in the way of the gratification of his desires.

To men of the temperament of Richard Dudley, opposition in the way of their pleasures, does not discourage
nor deter them; it only serves to whet the appetite,
which is thereby temporarily deprived of its food; and
renders their pursuit of the desired gratification the
more resolute, desperate and determined.

Such was the feeling produced in the mind of Richard
Dudley, in the present instance.

Instead of regarding with any sort of delicacy, the
plighted love of these two young slaves; instead of
viewing it as something sacred and noble, approved of
by heaven, and to be cherished and protected by all intelligent and rational beings, he esteemed it no more
than he would the instinctive passion of brutes. In his
soul he determined to thwart their attachment, or at
least to defer it, until it should no longer interfere with
the gratification of his own temporary lust.

Said he to Caroline, rudely and fiercely, "I tell you,

girl, that you shall not marry Sanford; or, at least, you shall not marry him until you have first gratified my wishes, as much and as long as I may please. If you yield and obey me, then afterward, you may marry George, but not otherwise. Do you hear me? I am resolute and determined in my purpose."

Caroline made no reply; she stood, looking upon the ground, in mute misery and despair. A full consciousness of her wretched position come over her; she saw the ruin which impended. She could make no reply; she stood still, and wept.

"What answer?" rudely demanded Richard.

"Oh, pity me, Master Richard, pity me!" said she.

"I have told you my purpose. I shall not change it. I will give you a day or two for reflection. You have resisted me now, but as I am your master, I will conquer you;" and turning to leave her, with a significant glance of the eye, and threatening movement of the finger, he added, "I will yet compel you to obey and gratify me!"

Having uttered these words, Richard Dudley slowly withdrew from the garden.

Caroline stood long and sadly ruminating over the new miseries and dangers of her position. She well knew the fierceness of Richard's purpose. She was a religiously disposed girl; and aside from her pure attachment for George Sanford, she would have recoiled with

4

disgust from the moral contamination to which she was invited.

Common as such connections were, between the young slave masters of the South and their favorite female slaves, she had received sufficient religious instruction to know that they were degrading and sinful. Hence, her mind was in no sense reconciled to such indulgences. Besides, she knew her own origin, and who her father was. She felt a still greater abhorrence at the thought, as she well knew Dudley to be her half brother. Yet, even this consideration, familiar as it was to him, did not deter him from his purpose.

With a sad heart, and eyes swollen with weeping, Caroline sought her own room as quietly as possible, to reflect in secret upon the novelty and danger of her position.

CHAPTER IV.

THE WHITE AND BLACK RIVALS.

"A rose, by any other name, would smell as sweet."—SHAKSPEARE.

BONDAGE cannot eradicate the inherent attributes of
the human soul. In youth, there burns an ardor and
brilliancy of hope in the human breast, which sheds a
radiance over all nature. The future becomes invested
with a thousand gaudy and glittering hues, rendering
each expected joy far more intense in the anticipative
state, than the cold and faded reality afterwards possesses.

It was thus with the ardent natures of George and
Caroline. They looked forward to their life of wedded
love, as human beings have a disposition to do, when
ever pure affection unites their destinies. Indeed, the
only redeeming and cheering portion of their future
existence, they knew to be centred in their union; and
amid the raptures of their true love, they hoped to forget, for a time at least, the miseries attendant upon
their state of bondage.

Richard Dudley and George had grown up together from their infancy, on the same plantation. There had even once been a boyish attachment between them; but that had become weaker and weaker, as Richard approached to man's estate, and began to be more fully conscious of the vast superiority of his social position, over that of his former playmate and slave.

In place, therefore, of his whilom attachment and familiarity, there had sprung up in the breast of Dudley a spirit of hostility to George, intended as a sort of retributive punishment for the ingenuous friendship which he had enjoyed with his young master, at that halcyon period of life, when the happy innocence of childhood makes us all feel as brothers and equals together.

As soon as Dudley discovered that George was the impediment which stood in the way of the gratification of his passion for Caroline, his hatred to George became still more intense than before. At the same time, his determination not to be foiled in his purpose, became more resolute and unflinching.

Upon the next meeting of George and Caroline, which occurred the day after her interview with Richard Dudley, the poor girl, as might well be supposed, was very sad. They met, as before, a short distance in the rear of the mansion,—their usual place of meeting.

Tears began to flow from Caroline's large, dark eyes,

as she gently reposed her head in silence on George's shoulder.

"What do you cry for, Carry," at once he inquired, as he detected the pearly drops falling over his breast upon the ground.

"Oh, George, I am so wretched," said she.

"Not more wretched than usual, I hope?"

"Yes, more miserable than ever!"

"What has made you so? what has happened?"

"Oh, I fear to tell you," said she, raising her head, and looking intently at him.

"Come, let me know the worst."

"I shudder to think of it; much more to speak of it," said she.

"But let me hear it at once. Do not torment me longer with this suspense."

George had not the most remote conception of what was to come, or he would not, perhaps, have invited the dreadful revelation. He thought that probably Caroline had received some rudeness and insolence from her mistress; probably another outburst of passion from old Mrs. Dudley.

"Well, then," continued Caroline, "I must tell you, and I will tell you all. Yesterday, when I was weeding my little patch of flowers in the garden, Master Richard came to me, and after some pleasant talk, he—he—"

4*

Caroline blushed deeply, and could proceed no further; she burst into a flood of tears.

By this time, George's apprehensions had been thoroughly aroused. Raising himself up, and gazing at her, he impetuously demanded, as he took her hand, "What, my love—he did what?"

"Oh! I cannot tell you," said she.

"But you must tell me. I must hear it. I cannot longer bear this suspense."

Blushing more deeply than before, Caroline, thus impelled, proceeded, "Master Richard gave me to—to understand that he—wished and determined—to make me his—mistress, his concubine. Oh, misery! misery!" and her tears flowed afresh.

Had a thunderbolt from the angry heavens struck George, it could not have produced a greater shock upon him than the poor youth experienced at this announcement of Caroline.

His strong frame shook with agony, and despair was depicted on his countenance.

"Of course you told him that it was impossible, did you not?" he inquired hastily.

"Yes, I told him it was impossible; but he declared that he would not be denied nor resisted," said she.

"Infamous wretch!" exclaimed George, as he rose from his seat on the green turf, and raising his eyes to heaven with an expression of despair. "Infamous wretch!"

Both seemed lost for several minutes, in deep thought upon their common woe.

"But you did not tell him that you and I were engaged to be married—that you were to be my wife? You could not have told him that, else he would have desisted and relented?"

"Yes, I even told him that; told him that I could not do such a thing; that it was wrong, and that we were to be married. But he only laughed at my tears; he became only more violent when I opposed him, swore and raved at me, and left me with the words that he would give me a few days to consider whether I would yield to him willingly or by force."

"And he despised our engagement!" said George, abstractedly, looking intently on the ground. "Master Richard would trample on my bleeding heart, my broken heart, as he would upon my whipped and bleeding body. He would dishonor me and my wife! He would heap ignominy and scorn on our love!" He continued thus reflectively to grasp and appreciate the full extent of the wrong which his young master proposed to inflict upon him.

At length, looking upward, he said, "Righteous heaven, can it be possible that we must endure this, too! What can we do to avert this dreadful calamity? Alas,

I know not how to avert it. We are his slaves, his victims. He can do with us as he pleases."

Silence, tho silence of utter hopelessness and despair ensued for some moments. The two young slaves were lost in that deepest woe, which finds no utterance in words. Their mutual sobs and tears alone gave proof of the unfathomable depth of their misery.

At length Caroline said, "Alas! what is to become of me? I know I am his half sister. We have the same father, though he looks upon me as he would upon a horse or a dog. Yet I know it is hateful. Such things are vile, as well as sinful; and the curse of God follows all such things. Beside, think that I am to be your wife, too. Alas! alas!"

George Sanford was one of those negroes who had picked up, during the course of his life, a considerable amount of religious information. He had been taught to read by old Uncle Jesse, a preacher on the plantation, to whom the reader will be introduced in due season. He had attended camp-meetings and church for some years; and these advantages, combined with his strong natural powers of mind, had enabled him to attain to considerable religious intelligence. He even preached occasionally to the slaves on the Dudley plantation, and to the slaves on the neighboring estates; and though he had great natural spirit and vivacity, he was at heart religious and moral.

Viewed in this light, Caroline's revelation to him places his feelings, in this emergency, in a new aspect to us. While he fully appreciated the wickedness of the act to which the unhappy Caroline was invited, and might, perhaps, be compelled; he was well assured that any demonstration of revenge on his part toward the person who contemplated inflicting upon him, knowingly, the greatest wrong which one human being can perpetrate upon another, was improper, and in any case, unjustifiable, as well as futile.

But, at first, desperate thoughts of resistance and revenge did come surging up within his soul, like a mighty and resistless flood. He asked himself, what right had his young master thus to step in between him and his pure and heaven-born love, to defile his marriage bed, and perhaps even tear away from his grasp entirely the prize which his love had won, to be defaced and destroyed upon the impure altar of wanton and cruel lust.

But then again, several considerations withheld him from any demonstrations of that sort. The first was the fact, that his master possessed absolute control over the person of his slave, and could compel her to any act he chose, however sinful or degrading it might be.

The next consideration was, that resistance was not only impossible, but flight from the savage sway of the master was out of the question. Their home was in

Louisiana, a thousand miles distant from the confines of the free States; and several thousand from Canada, the land of liberty for the slave. To pass through so vast a territory, securely and successfully, was utterly impossible, and he well knew it to be so.

The last consideration was, that resistance and revenge were sinful, and not, in any case, justifiable; and his moral sense was so strong, and so well instructed, that he was capable of at once suppressing all his uprising emotions of that kind.

At length, after a long pause, he said: "Well, Carry, we must trust in God. He may preserve you from this great calamity." She wound her beautiful arms tenderly around his neck, and rested her head upon his breast, in silent grief. She had no answer to make. George drew her, in a warm embrace, nearer toward himself.

The lovers were aroused from their revery by an approaching footstep.

"What you do da, honey?" said the intruder, a coal-black, good-natured looking negro, known on the place as Uncle Ben. "Ha! I spose you'se makin lub, is you?" Uncle Ben was one of those easy-natured creatures who, in the midst of their ignorance, had always regarded the attachment of married negroes for each other, much in the same light as he regarded the attachment of the brute creation. He had himself possessed some four or five wives, who had been successively sold to distant plantations; and his heart had become somewhat accustomed to the process of yielding up its treasured affections, as a thing to which he himself possessed no inalienable right.

He, therefore, was very different in his feelings from his two young friends, upon whose disconsolate *tête-à-tête*, he had thus suddenly intruded. He was a great favorite with all the slaves on the plantation, in consequence of his general good nature.

"Uncle Ben, come here," said George; "we have something to tell you."

Uncle Ben hobbled up to the two, and sitting down, tailor-fashion, upon the ground before them, prepared himself to hear the forthcoming communication.

"What is it, honey? what you got to say to Uncle Ben, eh?"

Thus invited, George felt disposed to relieve his own misery, by communicating the nature and the cause of it, to his humble friend. In this respect, strange as the fact may appear, George possessed the universal principle of human nature within him, by which grief is always lessened by communicating it to others. To shut up the dark and bitter emotions of the soul within the breast, to admit no communion or intercourse of sympathy with others, renders the pain of endurance more intense. Such is human nature, white and black

George, therefore, having full confidence in Uncle Ben, informed him of the nature of their trouble; he told him what Master Richard had threatened to do, and expressed the agony of their minds at his cruel determination.

Uncle Ben consoled them as well as he could. After a moment's reflection he added, thoughtfully: "Honey! I'll tell you what to do. Go and git married rite away; Uncle Jess 'll do it for ye. Master Richard darrent tech you arter dat. Git married rite away!"

CHAPTER V.

THE YANKEE SLAVE-DRIVER.

"I have often heard my mother say,
 I came into the world with my legs forward;
 And so I was, which plainly signified,
 That I should snarl, and bite, and play the dog."
                                        RICHARD III.

MEANWHILE the usual work of Major Dudley's plantation moved on. The Major had employed, as his slave-driver, a man named Robinson   combined great energy and activity of mind, with unrelenting cruelty toward those who were placed beneath him.

Robinson, a tall, raw-boned, awkward fellow, had been born at the North, in Vermont; was consequently a full-blooded Yankee, and had travelled to the South, some years before the date of our narrative, peddling wooden clocks.

He was the son of an honest mechanic, in the land of pumpkin pies and steady habits, who had received in his youth some English education, but no trade. At home,

5

anterior to his peregrinations southward, he had been a general "operator" in his neighborhood, on a very small capital. He had dealt in horse-flesh, cattle of all kinds, and bought promissory notes of people who were in pecuniary straits; until by dint of skinning, shaving and cheating, and extensively riding over the country in pursuit of these mercantile adventures, he had accumulated about one thousand dollars, which he had invested in the clocks aforesaid, and travelled with them toward the land of the sun.

After selling off, to some advantage, this valuable stock, he had leisure to look about him, and determine what was next to be done.

He had disposed of his last clock on the plantation of Major Dudley. This event threw him into connection with the old gentleman, who having nothing on his hands to do, was generally disposed to be talkative and friendly to any chance stranger who might visit his house.

Robinson was naturally intelligent and witty. He had now seen something of the world; and his conversation had some charm for the old man, tired and weary with the quiet monotony of his life on the plantation.

The Yankee described at length to his host, the various peculiarities of his native state, and of New England. The planter listened with attention, while the other soon discerned, that he was growing gradually and rapidly in the old man's graces, and that there would probably be

but one obstacle to some connection, or ground of difference between them, and that was the matter of slavery.

But the Yankee had already learned the first and greatest lesson of social policy and economy; and that was to
know *where his interest lay.* He thought to himself,
that possibly here might be an opening of some sort for
him, much better than peddling clocks, and wandering
about, a vagabond over the earth. He had heard that
the old planter's slave-driver had died, a short time previous to his visit, and that his successor had not yet been
selected.

Why might not he aspire to that high function?

Would not the sovereignty over a few slaves, even
though it be second-handed, and delegated from another,
be a vast improvement on his former dependent state?
The eminence was well worthy of his ambition. He,
the poor Yankee, who had been a homeless adventurer,
to whom the language of submission had ever been
much more familiar, than that of command, might possibly now assume the tone of high authority. But one
obstacle alone might impede the realization of this sudden
dream of high, vaulting ambition in the Yankee.

That subject, as we have said, was slavery. In one of
those familiar talks with which the Major condescend-
ingly favored the Yankee peddler, one afternoon, when
sitting together in the shade on the portico, the latter
adroitly introduced the subject.

"What a great fuss people do make, whar I cum from, about your slavery," said he initiatively. "They say thar, that the slaves is wuss off here, than any other kind of people any whar," he added, emitting a whiff of cigar smoke.

"Oh yes," responded the Major, "people in the North lie about us, and misrepresent us, most outrageously. There is no truth in what they say about us and our slaves."

"Not a word of truth; I sees your slaves here, and I thinks they are much better off than the free blacks whar I cum from, and many of the poor, beggarly whites too," answered Robinson.

"That is my opinion from all that I can learn," responded the Major, who had never set foot beyond Masons and Dickson's line, in his life. "Our slaves are much happier, better provided for, and more contented than they ever would be, if they had their freedom."

"Jes so, jes so," said Robinson. "Abolitionism and the abolitionists are a great cuss to the country. They unsettles everything; and they does the niggers more harm than good. I could hang the half of them, if I had 'em in *my* clutches."

This last bold declaration of sanguinary opinion, on the part of the Yankee, at once elevated him to a high position in the estimation of the Major, who inquired of Robinson if he ever had had anything to do with slaves?

Robinson catching a remote glimpse of the import and tendency of this question, answered that he had not, but that he would have no objection, nay rather, would be happy to come to closer connection of some sort with them.

"Ain't you afraid your earlier prejudices might make you feel unhappy, if you had anything to do with such unfortunate creatures?" asked the Major.

"Not a bit of it! not a bit of it," responded Robinson. "I never was led off by them ar foolish noshuns, as prewails whar I cum from. I thinks slavery is right. It's necessary for the South; you could not possibly get along without 'em; and as for the slaves the'selves, they could'nt possibly get along no how without having masters and miste'sses over 'em. They'se jes like chil'ren, and must have some 'un to perwide for 'em, and make 'em do for theirselves."

"Well now," continued the Major, who thought the thrifty and industrious habits of Robinson might be turned to good account for himself, "Well now, how would you like to be my slave-driver and overseer? My old driver is dead, as you know, and I have not yet got a substitute."

"I shoud'nt keer much," said Robinson, quietly.

Thus encouraged, the Major proceeded, and the two worthies at length, after some friendly disputing and

5*

conference, as to the wages the Yankee was to receive, struck the bargain.

Robinson, the Yankee, becomes slave-driver on a well-stocked Louisiana cotton plantation, with a comfortable salary, and with despotic sway over the actions of seventy-five human beings.

What a position for the Yankee clock peddler! In fact Robinson, at the time of this transaction, was completely adrift for any thing. Whatever offered that seemed feasible, he was fully prepared ' to go in.'

Behold him, then, as he exercises this new dominion. On the cotton-field, wielding his heavy slave whip, with its immensely long lash, a new nature seemed to be developed within this adventurous and unworthy son of New England. He now no longer seems to be the same person, or to possess the same nature which once actuated him.

As is generally the case with those whose dispositions naturally are unfeeling, selfish and brutal, however much their position in life may serve to conceal these attributes,—as soon as circumstances exist which are favourable to their display, their inborn traits show themselves with augmented and aggravated intensity.

It was precisely thus with Robinson. Naturally of a coarse nature, as soon as he found himself invested with a little brief authority, the love of command, and the tendency to cruelty amazingly displayed themselves.

The cotton field was his favourite arena. There he exhibited without restraint, the innate brutality of his nature; and there he, who all his life had been taught to regard a negro as a fellow mortal, as a human being as good, though not quite as fortunate, as himself;—there, he treated them with more than the average cruelty of slave-drivers,—as if they were lower than the brutes of the field, born only to be whipped, kicked and crushed.

His stentorian voice might be heard all over the widespread cotton fields, commanding here and there; sometimes cursing and threatening; at other times laughing, jeering, and yelling; every where he would range abroad among the toiling and trembling multitude around him, as a tyrant to be feared and shunned. Whenever any of the slaves would excite his special hostility, he would whip them with the most unflinching and heartless severity.

Such a person would undoubtedly make an apt instrument in the hands of such a man as Richard Dudley, to aid him in the accomplishment of such a foul purpose as that which he had conceived in relation to Caroline.

Tyranical toward his inferiors, Robinson, like all other men of similar natures, was most obsequious and cringing toward his superiors. The immorality of a thing never stood in his way, when his interest prompted him to advance to its attainment. All the orthodox sermons which he had heard in his youth, in the meeting-houses among the Green Mountains and thrifty vales of Vermont, had long since been *burnt out* of his memory, by the corroding canker of selfishness and avarice.

One day Richard Dudley rode out to the cotton fields of the plantation, and after surveying the busy scene before him for some minutes, drew up his horse under the shade of a large tree and called to Robinson, who happened to be not a great way off.

Robinson walked up hastily to Richard, and inquired what was wanted?

"Robinson," said Richard, "I have a job for you to do."

"I'm on hand for anything, sir, you may want me for," responded the ex-Yankee.

"I'll tell you now what it is," lowering his voice and looking suspiciously around him; "You know that handsome quadroon of mine, Caroline?"

"Yes, I know her; oncommon hansome she is, too," the driver responded.

"Well, I've taken a fancy to her; she is the prettiest girl I have seen for many a day. But she is so damnably virtuous and religious, that I have not been able, as yet, to do anything with her. Now, I'm determined not to give her up; I won't be baffled in any purpose I may have, I warrant you."

By this time the Yankee had gained some glimpse of what was to come; and alert to render an obsequious service to his master, he at once responded: "May be I can help you in some way; if I can, jest name it—don't be shy."

"Well, I tell you what I have been thinking of, Robinson; she has repulsed my advances once; I'll soon try her again; if she is as stubborn and as impudent as before, I swear I will have her whipped half to death!"

"Good! the very thing," hastily chimed in the driver. "I'll fetch her to, for you, I'll warrant!" And he swung and cracked his formidable lash around him, as if practising for the *chef d'œuvre* of professional skill, which he expected soon to be called upon to achieve.

"Only think of the provoking stubbornness of the hussy!" said Richard. "She cried, and talked of the sinfulness of the thing, and her love for another, (and that, too, one of our slaves on this very plantation,) and blubbered, and implored, and resisted, until I desisted."

"Instead of thinking it a great honour, as she ought to have done!" said Robinson. "She ought to have been very proud of the honor of attracting the admiration of her young master!"

"Now, Robinson, I tell you what, if she persists in her refusal," said Dudley, changing his position on his horse, and leaning over lazily and as comfortably as possible, "I'll have you whip her, and you will know what it is for; so you must lay on well."

"I'll do it! I'll do it!" said the driver.

"And at every stroke," continued Dudley, "you must say, 'Will you obey Master Richard, in what he orders you?' And you must lay on the lash, until she promises to do it; she'll know your meaning. Do you hear me?"

"Yes, I do, and I'll do it, too;" said Robinson.

"Lay on till she answers, yes; if you have to give her five hundred lashes. You must break her down for me—you understand?"

"I will—*I'll* break her down for you."

"I want you to make her promise, because these religious wenches have great regard for their word; and when they promise, they are apt to keep to it. That's the reason I want you to make her promise."

"It shall be done, sir," said Robinson, resolutely. After this conversation, the thoughts of the worthies turned on something else.

Richard Dudley rode leisurely homeward, over the fields, thinking of his future conquest.

Robinson roared and swore away, among the wearied cotton pickers, and his harsh voice, and the cracking of his whip, echoed loudly over the plain; nor did they cease to reverberate, until the setting of the sun, and the thickening shades of twilight gave the signal for a general return to the slave-quarters.

CHAPTER VI.

THE RELIGION OF SLAVES.

AFTER the preceding conversation between Richard Dudley and Robinson, respecting the fate of Caroline, they held another private interview for the purpose of more maturely settling their plans for accomplishing their purpose.

The next Sunday after the preceding events, the slaves on Major Dudley's plantation assembled as usual, for religious worship, in the hut of Uncle Jessy, the religious teacher of the establishment.

Silence reigned over the Dudley mansion, the slave huts, the outhouses, barns, cattle, and over all the attendants and attachees of the place.

The church of the negroes resembled, in its primitive simplicity, the temples of God wherein patriarchs and prophets preached and worshipped in those primeval ages of the world, when worldly grandeur and architectural splendor, were things unknown to the services of religion. It was a log hut, on the outskirts of the straggling row of huts in which the negroes lived. In the single room it contained were a low bedstead, made of pine wood, covered with a bag of straw and several blankets, and a rude bolster at the upper end.

There were six or eight three legged stools in different parts of the room. One large fire-place, made by a chimney stack of rough logs, occupied nearly the half of one end of the room, and was floored with several very large, smooth stones. A rude cupboard occupied the wall on the opposite side of the room. There was a loft overhead, which was reached by a ladder.

The religious services of the negroes were all held in this hut, because, being the most remote from the mansion of Major Dudley, the noise and loud singing of the negroes, who sometimes reached an alarming degree of frenzy and fanaticism, did not annoy the family or their master.

As soon as the audience was assembled, which consisted of several dozen negroes of all ages, of both sexes, and of all shades of color, Uncle Jesse gave out a hymn. He had learned to read from some one on the plantation; although it must be admitted that his literary attainment was a very limited and humble one indeed. After the hymn had been sung in the loud and frenzied manner so prevalent among the slaves of the South, Uncle Jesse prayed; and then proceeded to preach.

Taking a very small Bible from his coat pocket, which bore the unmistakeable evidences of being well thumbed and handled, he proceeded to turn over the pages. He evinced considerable difficulty in discovering either the book or the chapter in which his "text" was to be found. He seemed to be confused by the multiplicity of leaves and pages. He seemed to know that his text was to be found somewhere in the middle of the book; but he was a long time searching before he was able to discover the part in question. He was looking for, and doing his best to find the Psalms of David. At length he lit upon one of the pages of that great book of songs; and knowing the number of the Psalm in which his text was contained, he had but little further difficulty in resting his eye upon it.

Being sure that he had at last found his text, Uncle Jesse read it over first carefully to himself, to see if he was perfectly right as to its identity. Having satisfied himself on this point, he hem'ed and haw'ed once or twice, in order to clear out his throat; and then slowly and deliberately read the following words from the 107th Psalm 8th, 9th, and 10th verses: "Oh! that men would praise the Lord for his goodness, and for his wonderful works to the children of men. For he satisfieth the longing soul, and filleth the hungry soul with goodness. Such as sit in darkness and in the shadow of death, being bound in affliction and iron."

Uncle Jesse knew enough to know that these words originally applied to the Jewish people. He told his

6

audience so; who received this announcement, and evidence of superior erudition from Uncle Jesse with gaping mouths, and countenances expressive of the utmost astonishment. Uncle Jesse then proceeded to apply the words to all Christians under affliction everywhere; and finally, declared that the "language of the tex" had special reference to poor slaves like themselves, who were in the shadow of death, and were bound in affliction and iron. He urged upon his auditors to remember that God would eventually bring them out of all their afflictions.

After Uncle Jesse had concluded his discourse, the singing of a hymn followed, and George Sanford arose in one corner to address the audience. Every observer must have noticed how the multitude of men differ from each other in their desire for mutual improvement, and their apathy on the same subject. This distinction holds among all the races of men, whether high or low, bond or free. Some feel and exhibit no inborn desire to elevate themselves; but are content to drone away their lives in whatever condition they may at first have been placed, without ever conceiving one aspiring- thought. Others again, possess and display an innate and irrepressible impulse to rise, to improve, and to ascend in the scale of intellectual, social, and sometimes, moral elevation.

Such an one was George Sanford. Gifted with very

considerable natural talent, ho had ever felt a yearning
desire after improvement. While he despised no one
around and beneath him, he was proud of the mental
superiority which ho had already attained. Consequently, he was studious in his leisure hours. He possessed a few valuable books, which he carefully read.
His library consisted of the Bible, the Methodist Hymn
Book, Doddridge's Sermons, Rise and Progress, Baxter's
Saint's Rest, the Life of Washington, the Declaration
of Independence, and an old Gazeteer of Geography and
History.

Furnished with this literary apparatus, meagre as it
was, it was surprising how much information and culti-
vation George had obtained. The fruits of his studies,
unpropitious as were the circumstances under which
they were carried on, were to be especially seen in his
homilitical performances.

George was a natural-born orator, and had been gifted
and furnished with all the qualities requisite for the
exercise of that high function;—a commanding figure, a
melodious and flexible voice, a graceful delivery, and a
great readiness of utterance. On a more favourable field,
he would have made no contemptible figure as an orator;
and when the wrongs of his race excited his enthusiasm,
he would often diverge, in the course of his sermons, as
much and as far as ho dare, into fervent and powerful
invectives upon those who were the causes of their misery

and ruin. Yet he would ever temper these excursions, with appeals to his auditors, to exercise the noble quality of patience; as the Lord in his own good time would assuredly bring all things right.

"My brethren," said he, "you have already heard an explanation of the words of Holy Scripture, which have been read to you. That explanation is correct, and need not be repeated. In every age of the world, there have been instances of human persecution and cruelty; and it has ever been the unhappy lot of some one portion of the human family to suffer as the victims of the greater strength and superior power of their fellow men. Sometimes God has permitted this unhappy state of things, as a punishment for the sins of those who are thus held in bondage. At other times he has permitted it, in order that the oppressors may be allowed to act out, to their full extent, the cruel and unholy propensities of their nature; to accumulate by their iniquities upon the feebler and the down-trodden, wrath against the day of wrath.

"Under all these circumstances and conditions, whatever may be the reason which induces the wise ruler of the universe to permit such suffering and misery, on the part of one portion of the human family, one great truth is certain and undeniable. Our duty in the circumstances under which we are placed, is clear and self-evident. In God's providence *we* happen to be the victims of affliction and of chains. Whether we suffer this misfortune on account of our own sins, or the sins of our forefathers; or because God permits our masters to fill up the measure of their iniquities, in order that the amount of their punishment may be the greater—it does not become us now to inquire. One thing is certain. Our duty is to submit to the decrees of Providence without resistance. God is infinitely wise, and great and good. Our holy religion teaches us to believe that all the events of life, even its worst calamities, will be promotive of the best interests of those who obey and love the truth. The slavery which surrounds us, and of which we bear a wretched part, is but one chapter in the great book of human history and fate; and that one chapter has its true interpretation, like all the rest, perfectly consistent with the divine wisdom, power, and benevolence. Submit then, I pray you, in silence and resignation to your unhappy fate. Even give thanks to God, that your condition is as fortunate as it is, for it might have been much worse. You might this day be benighted heathen, on the dark shores of Africa. As it is, among your temporal and physical miseries, you possess one inestimable boon, which the cruelty and selfishness of your masters can never tear from your breasts, —a knowledge of the true religion; faith in the Redeemer of men; and a bright hope of future immortality,

6*

when the trials and sufferings of this present life, shall all have passed away forever!"

George's discourse was interrupted from time to time, by the ejaculations of his auditors, approving of his doctrine, and expressive of the comfort which it gave them. The evident effect of such rational discourse upon their minds was good; it accustomed them to think of the better future; and encouraged them to endure, without repining, the misfortunes of the present.

CHAPTER VII.

THE RELIGION OF MASTERS.

"There is no power in the tongue of man
To alter me. I stay here on my *bond.*"
SHYLOCK.

WHILE the scene was in progress, which we have described in the last chapter, another of a very different character, was taking place in the mansion of Major Dudley.

It being Sunday, religion and church-going must be attended to by all respectable people; and could not, therefore, be overlooked in so genteel a household as that of the Major.

Several days previous to this Sunday, an event of considerable importance had occurred on the plantation, which now requires to be mentioned.

This event was the visit of Mr. William Stanley, a young lawyer of distinction, from New Orleans, to Julia Dudley, the rich and accomplished daughter of the Major.

In their last visit to a watering-place of celebrity in

the South, Mr. Stanley had become acquainted with Miss Julia. He was a tall, handsome, and well-formed person, of good family in New Orleans; and an advocate of rising talents, and increasing celebrity in his profession.

His ideas on the subject of slavery were precisely those of aristocratic Southerners; especially of those who, to fair social position, add the intensified haughtiness of supposed intellectual superiority.

At the Springs, he had been much fascinated by the charms of Miss Julia, which, to say the truth, were of no ordinary character. Where a field favorable for the display of her various attractions was presented to her, such as a large and fashionable watering-place, she had few-equals, and no superiors. She reigned supreme. Possessing not only wealth, family station, and great personal beauty, unlike most Southern young ladies, she consisted of something more than a mere bundle of caprices and stupidities, encased in a handsome person, and gilded over with considerable fortune. She had intelligence; was naturally a woman of superior mind; had wit, vivacity, and humor, as well as gracefulness and amiability. She was a queen among the vapid, languid and common-place coquettes, who usually throng such places of fashionable resort as that we have just referred to.

Stanley had been charmed with her at their first

meeting; he at once discerned her superiority over all her rivals; he saw that she had mind, soul, heart, intelligence and passion. The impression which he made upon her was equally favorable. He was, in truth, as much superior to the brainless, mustachioed, perfumed, and mouthing snobs who surrounded him, as she was to the rest of the female part of the company.

Their intercourse soon ripened at the Springs, into familiarity and friendship. They were admirably suited to please each other. It was not, therefore, strange, that when the company separated, Stanley should receive a polite invitation from Major Dudley to visit his plantation, and that the invitation had been eagerly accepted.

Stanley came before three months had elapsed, and his arrival is the event to which we now refer. He was cordially received; for no race on earth are more hospitable than Southern planters toward the stranger, and even the penniless beggar and pilgrim; provided he have not one great and irredeemable curse stamped upon him,—provided he is not *black*.

Stanley found, in the family and station of his inamorata, every thing which could be desired. He and Richard Dudley soon settled into terms of close friendship, and even intimacy. They rode together, hunted together, fished together, played cards together, and smoked together; in fact, they very soon became attached friends.

Meanwhile, Stanley's attention to Miss Julia became daily more marked and expressive. When not engaged in some way with Richard, he was sure to be chatting with her. A large portion of his time was spent in her society. Time flew by on golden wings. The ultimate issue of the affair, was no longer in the least degree problematical in the minds of the Dudley family.

Sunday came, and the party prepared for church. The place of worship was five miles distant from the estate of the Dudley's. Old Major Dudley and his wife led the way in the family carriage, Julia and Stanley rode on horseback behind them, while Richard, who was not ready when the rest of the party started from home, followed on horseback, at his leisure.

It was a beautiful morning in Autumn. All nature seemed fragrant with sweets, and the animated creation, as they passed along the road through woods, and corn-fields and cotton-fields, appeared to be humming an universal song of joy and contentment. Julia and her lover kept up the usual tenor of their conversation, a mixture of sage remark and witty repartee.

Richard, as he quietly rode along, thought of Caroline, and the conquest he determined to make over her charms and her virtue.

The two elder Dudleys, who preceded in the carriage, conversed in a low tone, so as to be unheard by the coachman, Uncle Ben, upon the issue of Stanley's suit to Julia, and the arguments pro and con, in case he should make a proposition of marriage.

At length the party arrived at the church. This was a plain brick building, without spire, of moderate proportions, situated upon a rising ground, in the midst of an ancient wood. Next the church was a graveyard, where many slanting white gravestones reared their heads to mark the eternal resting place of many of the old planters, and wealthier inhabitants of the neighborhood.

Both church and graveyard were inclosed together by a low brick wall, which was overgrown with vines, and in some places was broken and tottering to its fall. Around the church were scattered under the trees the carriages of the richer worshippers, and the horses of many others were tied here and there to the lower branches of trees, by the bridle. The woods were full of these several modes of conveyance, with here and there straggling negro drivers, lounging and chatting together. The grassy spaces in front of the church, and the graveyard, were filled with the people who had not entered the church, as the time of commencing the service had not yet quite arrived.

Some were talking in groups about their crops and cotton fields, some speaking of runaway slaves, and the virtues of certain bloodhounds, whose last greatest achievement in negro-catching had lately occurred in

tho neighborhood. Others were strolling among the
gravestones, carelessly reading the inscriptions, a thousand times read before, and examining the shape and
structure of their gravestones. A few were gazing
mournfully upon the last silent resting places of beloved
friends, shedding tears upon their crumbling dust below,
and trimming the vines and flower stems which they had
planted around their headstones. Thus, everywhere,
the voice of our common nature speaks, in all climes,
and in all languages, eternally the same !

Presently the clergyman arrived, and this event became the signal for everybody to enter the church.
Soon the congregation became seated, and the services
began.

The preacher who thus comes before the reader, was
the Reverend Thomas Pimp.

This gentleman was a New Englander by birth and
early association. He had been educated at a New
England college of celebrity. His theological training
he had received at an ancient institution of eminence,
in one of the larger Middle States. While engaged in
these preparatory studies for his great mission of preach-
ing the riches of Christ to man, he had been remarked
as a very violent opponent of slavery, and was ever loud
in his denunciations of those, especially Christians, who
dealt in the purchase and sale of the bodies and souls
of their fellow men.

After finishing his theological studies, and being admitted into the clerical office, he had expected an invitation to settle over some church in New England. In this he was disappointed. But an eligible vacancy occurring at this juncture, in the church in Louisiana, to which the Dudley's belonged, and he receiving a call thereto, through the instrumentality of a Southern friend and fellow student, whom he knew at the theological seminary, he accepted it, and was settled.

Behold, now, Mr. Pimp, contrary to all expectation on his part, established as the pastor of a slave-holding church. He who had been reared and educated in holy horror of slavery; who had ever spoken of the slave-holder as one who violated every principle of humanity and religion, what will he now say and do? Will he adhere consistently to the doctrines which he had so frequently inculcated previous to his arrival in a slave State, and his acceptance of a church of slave-holders?

We will see. The text, on the occasion in question, happened to be very appropriate to the inquiry we have just propounded. It gave a fair opportunity to the preacher to express his whole mind on the subject of slavery. It was the first occasion after his settlement upon which he had spoken freely on that dangerous topic.

The Reverend Mr. Pimp took his text, appositely enough, from Paul's epistle to Titus, second chapter
7

verse 19. "*Exhort servants to be obedient to their own
masters, and to please them well in all things, not
answering again.*"

He began by saying, that the text was one of a series
of precepts, of the most important and valuable description, which Paul, in the epistle before him, imparted to
his favorite spiritual son, Titus, the first bishop of the
church of the Cretans.

After alluding at some length to those other precepts,
Pimp returned to the one which formed, on that occasion, the special subject of his remarks.   He dwelt first,
in an explanatory and exegetical way, upon the important word "*servants*," as used in his text., He insisted
that this word did not mean servants, in the present
sense of that term, nor even in the exact sense which
that word possessed in the times of King James's trans-
lators.   Pimp held, strongly and positively, that the
word *servants* meant *slaves*, and not servants; and he
endeavored to establish this hermeneutical principle, by
showing that slaves existed in the times of Christ, and
that too, in the region where Titus lived, and in which
the principles of Paul's letter to him were to be carried
out and illustrated.   Pimp drew largely upon his critical
learning on this occasion, and he succeeded in exciting
the admiration, as well as confirming the opinions of his
audience, on the subject before him.

Having settled at great length, that the servants

referred to were identical in character and position with American slaves, the reverend gentleman proceeded to the next important inquiry, as to what their duty consisted in. Here he seemed perfectly at home. He had triumphantly established the first and most important premise; the conclusions came thereafter quickly, easily, and naturally.

"Exhort servants," said Pimp, "to be obedient to their masters. Here we have the great law of obedience to masters and *owners* (for they are in the *original* the same thing) clearly enjoined and enforced. Masters have a right to the undivided obedience of their slaves. It is God's law, and it is man's law. None dare resist an authority so supreme and so universal."

But Pimp was not satisfied with this bold declaration. Proceeding with his subject, he became animated, excited, and warmed with holy enthusiasm against the slave. He thumped the cushion of the pulpit before him. He sawed the air with his right arm. His kindling eye ranged over his congregation, and communicated by his glance his own enthusiasm to them. "Further, brethren," said Pimp, "the apostle in the text not only teaches that obedience is due from the slave to his master, but he goes further. He declares that slaves must be obedient to their masters in *all* things. This obedience must be universal; there is no restriction whatever. A proper interpretation of the passage, according to the *original*, will not allow of any restriction. Slaves have no right even to think for themselves; for thought necessarily leads to action, and thus disobedience and conflicting purposes would take the place of that universal and harmonious submission which God enjoins upon the slave.

"Slaves must please their masters in *all* things," Pimp continued, "not answering again, not purloining, and showing all good fidelity. These, my brethren, are the duties which you are justified, as Christians, in exacting from your slaves. It is God's law, man cannot and dare not gainsay it. The master possesses absolute power over his slave; for what else can be inferred from language so plain and so emphatic as that of the text?"

At this stage of Pimp's sermon, could the reader have seen and perused the countenance of Richard Dudley, he would have discovered that one of Pimp's auditors, at least, heartily approved of the preacher's exposition. Seated in one of the front pews of the church, Richard was a prominent person in the congregation; and at the utterance of the last words which we have quoted from the sermon of Pimp, an approving smile passed over his countenance; and he gave his head a decided nod, when he thought how admirably the preacher's doctrine chimed in with his own principles and purposes.

If the unrestricted obedience of the slave to the master, be just and obligatory, then his demand upon Caroline, tnat she should accept his impure embraces, and become his paramour, was a just one, a righteous one—the Reverend Thomas Pimp himself being the judge.

Richard could not help thinking to himself, whether, if Pimp knew the application of his doctrine which his hearer was then secretly making, he would still approve and justify it. Richard's mind was, in doubt on that point; he felt within him, that his purpose in reference to Caroline was so brutal, and so cruel, that no law, possessed of any tone or degree of moral education, could possibly approve and justify it. Yet Pimp had been so positive and so sweeping in his assertion, that slaves must obey their masters in *all* things, without any reserve, as he insisted the passage must be rendered, if rendered aright, and "according to the original;" that he had some hope that Pimp might sustain him, even in the practical application which he intended to make of the preacher's text and doctrine.

Pimp having concluded the services to the satisfaction of himself and the congregation, both dispersed. The Dudley family returned home in the same order which they had preserved in the morning. Richard Dudley said nothing to the family of his reflections upon the sermon, which happened to be so congenial to his feelings. But whether his intention was in accordance with Scripture, or not, according to Pimp's scandalous inter-

pretation of it, he determined soon to accomplish his
purpose with reference to the unfortunate Caroline.

Nevertheless, Pimp was a fair representative of very
many New England clergymen, who, while at home,
condemn slavery from principle, and when they become
residents of the South, uphold it from interest.*

---

* The following choice morsel is taken from political Parson "Brownlow's Whig:"

"There is a great deal of Abolitionism in East Tennessee, and with it
a fearful increase of insolence and hellish daring on the part of negroes.
Negroes take more liberties in East Tennessee, and display more insolence
in their intercourse with white people, than anywhere we have ever been,
and we have travelled extensively. Many of the negroes can read, and
they keep themselves posted up on the subject of the controversy between
the North and the South, touching the Slavery question. They can be
heard relating matters of this sort to other negroes who can't read, at any
time. To the disgrace of East Tennessee, we must admit, that white men,
everywhere, play cards, fight chickens, drink whiskey, and Sabbath-break
it with the negroes. Abolitionists meet with more favor in East Tennessee
than anywhere else in the South. The scoundrels fill our pulpits; preside
in our schools; sell us goods; marry into our families; serve us as clerks
and attorneys, and figure in every other way! The true-hearted citizens
of East Tennessee, and property holders, ought to enter into a *league*, and
whip, black, and ride on a rail, irrespective of age, calling, or family associations, every preacher, citizen or traveller, who dares to utter one word
in opposition to Slavery, or who is found in possession of an abolition docu-
ment. These are our sentiments, and we are willing and ready to help
others carry them out."

The Rev. Robert N. Anderson, also a member of the Presbyterian
Church, says, in a letter to the Sessions of the Presbyterian Congregations
within the bounds of the West Hanover Presbytery:

Consider, O Pimp! when thou comest to render up thy last account to God, of the stewardship wherewith thou had'st been entrusted, how wilt thou justify thy-

"At the approaching stated meeting of our Presbytery, I design to offer a preamble and string of resolutions on the subject of the use of wine in the Lord's Supper; and also a preamble and string of resolutions on the subject of the treasonable and abominably wicked interference of the Northern and Eastern fanatics with our political and civil rights, our property and our domestic concerns. You are aware that our clergy, whether with or without reason, are more suspected by the public than the clergy of other denominations. Now, *dear Christian brethren*, I humbly express it as my earnest wish, that you *quit yourselves like men.* If there be any stray goat of a minister among you, tainted with the blood-hound principles of abolitionism, let him be ferreted out, silenced, excommunicated, and left to the *public to dispose of him in other respects.*

"Your affectionate brother in the Lord,

"ROBERT N. ANDERSON."

The Rev. Dr. Hill, of Virginia, said, in the New School Assembly:

"The abolitionists have made the servitude of the slave harder. If I could tell you some of the dirty tricks which these abolitionists have played, you would not wonder. Some of them have been lynched, and it served them right.'

"Some few persons have expressed their disapprobation of the turning of the negro who murdered Moore, his wife and sister-in-law, above Dandridge. We have to say in defence of the act, that it was not perpetrated by an excited and infuriated mob, but by one thousand citizens—good citizens at that—who were cool, calm and deliberate, who informed him of their purposes the day before, and gave him one day and night to prepare to meet his God.

"When we consider the kind treatment he had ever received, the cold-blooded and inhuman butchery of three innocent and virtuous citizens, in the dead hour of night, all to enable the demon to commit violence on the person of a virtuous young lady, we unhesitatingly affirm that the punish

self, that thou did'st thus "prophesy smooth things" to
cruel and bloody men, against thy own conscience and
clearest convictions !

ment was unequal to the crime. Had we been there, we should have taken
a part, and even suggested the pinching of pieces out of him with red-hot
pincers—the cutting off a limb at a time, and then burning them all in a
heap. The possibility of his escaping from jail, forbid the idea of awaiting the tardy movements of the law. And let gentlemen who are shocked
at the "outrage," as they are pleased to call it, fancy to themselves that
their sisters or daughters were the sufferers, and they will conclude burning was too good for the villain."—*Brownlow's Whig.*

c.

CHAPTER VIII.

THE RIVALS AGAIN.

"Look here upon this picture, and on this;
The counterfeit presentment of two brothers."—HAMLET.

IT was but a very short time, before Richard Dudley
took occasion to sound George privately, in reference to
his attachment to Caroline. He anticipated that immediately upon his broaching the subject, and giving George
an intimation of his own wishes, the latter would instantly
withdraw his claim, and quietly acquiesce.

"George," said Richard, one evening after the day's
work was done, as he sauntered along the line of huts, in
which the negroes lived, " George, what is there between
you and Caroline."

George at first did not seem to comprehend him, or
at least was slow to take the unpleasant import of his
meaning. But after a moment's pause, he answered,
"nothing, master Richard, nothing particular."

"Ai'nt you engaged to one another? come now, no
deception, be honest, and tell me the truth."

George at once comprehended the answer which he

ought to make to this direct question, and replied hesitatingly, "well yes, sir, Caroline and I are engaged, and as soon as she gets Mistress's permission, we hope to get married."

"You do? do you?" said Richard sarcastically, slightly coloring, and angered at the honest announcement, which interfered so directly with his own plans. "Well now, I may as well at once be honest with you, George; I don't want you to marry Caroline. In fact, I positively forbid it."

A blow smote the soul of George at the utterance of these words, as if the hand of a Titan had fallen upon him. His countenance indicated his dismay and despair. His eyes dropped to the ground, and for a moment he could command no utterance.

Richard, knowing his advantage, surveyed George with a sullen and defiant look, waiting for a reply. At length George said, "Oh! master Richard, I pray you not to say so. Do not forbid us to marry; Caroline and I have loved each other for many years. We have grown up together; and now we hope to be happy together. If you forbid us, we shall be perfectly miserable." And the large tears were forced from his manly eyes, at the thought of losing all that was dearest to him in life.

"Well now, George," said his master, "there is no use in your begging and whimpering in this way; I should not object to your marrying Caroline, if it did not interfere with purposes of my own. Do you understand me?"

George too well understood his master, and the allusion only added a more deadly pang to the agony which was piercing his soul.

"Yes, I understand you well, master; but can you not pity us? Can you not forego a purpose of your own like that, when it destroys the happiness of two beings who love each other, even if they are slaves?"

"Nonsense, George, nonsense, you can soon forget her; marry somebody else: others just as handsome as Caroline. There is a fine Mulatto wench over on Major Richard's plantation; I saw her there the other day when I rode over to his new mill, and you can get her, I'll give you a pass to go whenever you want, eh?"

"Oh, master, I cannot. To me there is no one in the world like Caroline. I never could love another, or marry another. Please master, do not forbid me to have Caroline."

These words were uttered with such earnestness, with such a tone of plaintiveness and despair, that they might almost have moved a rock to tears.

They had no effect on Richard, who continued unconcernedly to smoke his cigar, alternately looking at George, and gazing around him at the slave huts, and the stables in the rear.

"No, boy, I can't and won't oblige you by disobliging myself. If I could I would, but I can't. You stand in my way, and I warn you to get out of it."

When George saw how hopeless entreaty was in the case, his manly nature was aroused, and he felt like appealing to his young master in a higher tone.

"But, Master Richard, do you not know that what you purpose is wrong, is sinful in the highest degree? You would sin yourself, and you propose to compel an innocent being, because she is helpless and in your power, to commit sin too."

"Get away," said Richard contemptuously. "How dare you talk to me about sin? Don't I know what sin is, as well as you? And what do I care for sin, or whether a thing be sinful or not? Don't you know that I am your master? Ain't you slaves bound to obey your master in *all* things? At least, so says the Reverend Mr. Pimp,—if you talk of the sinfulness of a thing; but sinful or not sinful, I am determined to have my way about this matter."

"Master," said George, solemnly, drawing himself up to his full height, "God says, that for every impure act, he will bring us into judgment; and what you demand, would destroy both the body and the soul of your helpless victim."

"Enough, enough of this!" said Richard, hastily, and turning upon his heel, was about walking away. After a step or two, he turned back and said: " Now, George, if you persist in this purpose of yours, I shall punish you most severely. Recollect that!"

"But, Master Richard, Caroline and I are already promised and betrothed. We are united by Heaven, and what God joins together, let no man put asunder, is what the Bible teaches us," said George.

"Damn the Bible and what the Bible says. What care I for the Bible? If you don't keep entirely away from Caroline,—if I hear of your being together again, I'll have you both whipped till you are half dead. Now remember this; I will not be trifled with." This was uttered by Richard with so much ferocity of manner, accompanied by so violent a thrust of the fist into George's face, that he was quite intimidated and silent. His heart was broken, and tears began to flow over his manly countenance.

Both were about to separate, one to enter his desolate hut, now more desolate than ever, the only ray of hope and joy which had illumined its gloom forever excluded and shut out; the other to return to the mansion-house.

After George had entered, he heard the voice of his master calling to him. He immediately answered the summons. Richard had apparently assumed a more friendly and cheerful aspect toward him as he approached. He had resolved to try another stratagem.

"George," said he, "do you want to be free?"

8

The abruptness of this question somewhat startled the poor fellow, who could scarcely realize that it was addressed to him.

"Yes, master, I should be happy to be free," was his very natural answer.

"Well, then, I promise you, that if you abandon Caroline, and never speak to her again, you shall have your free papers in six months from this time. I promise it positively!"

"Master Richard," said George, solemnly, "listen to me. I am a slave; I am your slave. I long for liberty as eagerly as the most wretched captive who ever pined in a lonely dungeon. I work for you now faithfully; yet I would be too happy to be free. But I cannot and must not promise a thing which my heart tells me I cannot fulfil. I freely own to you that I love Caroline. She is kind, amiable, and affectionate. We are promised in marriage now. If you tear her from my cheerless bosom, you will make my life to me insupportable. I have looked forward to the hour of our marriage, as the brightest, fairest, happiest moment, which it will be my lot ever to enjoy in this world. With her society, I could endure all my fate, for she would sympathise with me, and pour the oil of true love into my heart. But if you tear from me this one and only consolation which I hope to have; if with an iron heel you crush this single joy which blooms for me in this vale of tears, I am undone forever!"

After the delivery of this passionate outburst of feeling, Richard, who at first had begun to be somewhat affected by it, but afterward recovering his wonted severity and indifference, gave vent to a loud burst of laughter.

"Away with you! away!" said he; "none of your damned sentimentality with me. Niggers must not deal in sentimentality. I tell you once more, and for the last time, that if you have any thing more to do with Caroline, I will have you both whipped 'till you are half dead. Dam'me if I'll be thwarted by you. Mind your work, and keep away from Caroline, that is all I have to say to you," and he passed on.

George turned again into his cheerless hut, threw himself upon his bed, and burst into a fit of uncontrollable grief.

CHAPTER IX.

THE MOONLIT MARRIAGE.

"Hail! wedded love, mysterious law, true source
Of human offspring, sole propriety,
In paradise of all things common else,
Founded in reason, loyal, just and pure,
Perpetual fountain of domestic sweets,
Whose bed is undefiled, and chaste pronounced."
MILTON.

IT was not long before the lovers met again. Both
of them had become fearfully conscious of the dangers
which impended over them. To them, the sky of their
existence had now become suddenly darkened o'er, by
lowering clouds and blackening tempests. Despair was
about to ascend the throne, where bright Hope had
heretofore reigned, and whence it had diffused some
glimmering light over their gloomy way.

George and Caroline met one evening, after their
day's work was done, at their usual trysting place, a
short distance in the rear of the mansion house.

"I have seen Master Richard yesterday," said George,

and he spoke of you to me. He forbids us to see each other again.

"Is it possible? Can he be so cruel?" said Caroline.

"He can indeed. He declares that we must break off our engagement—he forbids it. He says we shall never marry."

"Alas! alas!" she replied, "how cruel! how heartless. But did you appeal to him, did you ask his pity and generosity?" inquired Caroline.

"Yes. I used every means in my power to change his unfeeling purpose. I told him I loved you, Carry, and that without you, I had rather be dead. I told him, that his purpose in reference to you, was sinful,—that it was incestuous. I urged him to pity you,—to pity me.—But all my appeals were of no avail. He threatened the greatest severity if I persisted."

"Oh! how unfortunate!—how miserable!" and the poor girl bursting into tears, laid her head on her lover's shoulder and wept.

George continued: "He even offered me my freedom, if I would consent to give you up."

"What did you say to that?" inquired Caroline, looking up intently at him.

"I answered, that while I loved freedom better than my life, even freedom itself could not tempt me to consent to a separation, which would make life to me an unchanging curse. Oh, I should kill myself, had I to think, that I, even for freedom's sake, had consented to your degradation, your infamy, your ruin!"

The lovers paused, and seemed lost in deep reflection. At length Caroline resumed.

"George, what will Master Richard do to hinder our marriage?"

"He will have us whipped, if he sees us together, or learns that we have ever met. Beside, he will soon, I fear, attempt some violence with you."

"Oh, horrid! horrid!" exclaimed Caroline.

"You know the fury of his temper, his unbending and unyielding purpose," said he.

"Alas! I know it too well," she replied.

It is often said, that the blackest hour of night precedes the breaking of the dawn. It is ever thus with the vicissitudes of human suffering. After the soul has reached the lowest depths of despair, and can no deeper plunge amid its rolling, fœtid shades, then the reactionary forces of man's nature begin to operate, resolution takes the place of despondency, energy succeeds instead of apathy, and an upward tendency is felt and exhibited. Men then hope against power, and smile in defiance of despair.

After the silence of a few moments, George suddenly aroused himself, struck his hand upon his knee, and said, "Caroline, let us defy our tyrant; let us thwart his fiendish purpose in reference to you. Let us go this minute to Uncle Jesse, and get married. We will see whether our master will prevent our marriage!"

Caroline was taken quite aback by this sudden proposition. A tempest of mingled emotions raged within her. On the one hand rapture filled her heart at the thought of being so soon the wife of the man she idolatrously loved; while on the other, apprehension of her future fate, and of the additional retribution which the act might bring upon them both, was mingled with the joyous emotion which she felt. She was for a time quite undecided. She expressed to her lover her feelings, without restraint.

But George, who possessed more energy and elasticity of mind than she, gave way to his enthusiasm. He would hear of no delay. He had just then made up his mind positively to defy and to defeat their common foe. Worse it could not be for them, than it would be, were Richard Dudley successful; and it might perhaps be better. Hope still whispered in his ears charming words of encouragement, and conjured up delusive phantoms of unwarranted felicity.

"Come," said he, "Come my love, let us go to Uncle Jesse, and put an end to this sad uncertainty."

"Well, George, let it be as you say—I hope Heaven will protect us;" and she arose, trembling from head to foot, to take the great turning and decisive step in her lifetime,—the source indeed, of transient rapture, but the fatal cause of innumerable woes and miseries.

They passed noiselessly around the house of Major Dudley, went to the hut of the old preacher, Uncle Jesse, and knocked at the door. Harriet, his wife, answered the summons, and opened it.

"What does ye want, child?" said she, as soon as she perceived and recognized the person of George.

"We want Uncle Jesse. Where is he?"

"He isn't to hum, now, honey. He's gone to weed his corn-patch, back on the creek. He's thar; thar you'll find him."

George knew that Jesse had, like all the elder negroes on the plantation, a small corn-patch allotted him, which he could cultivate out of work hours, and raise broom corn and a few other things, the proceeds of which he was allowed to appropriate to himself. But George did not know the precise locality of Jesse's patch, and might have trouble to find it.

"Come with us, aunt Harriet, and show us the way. We want to see Uncle Jesse, particularly," said he.

"Shure I will, honey, certain. Why, Carry, you here too!" she said, as for the first time she obtained a glimpse of Caroline's face. Both of these were great favorites with Jesse and his wife, and the true state of the case flashed at once on the mind of the old woman. "Yes, I'll go 'long wid ye. Maybe ye may want a

witness, eh ?" and she began to laugh and giggle as she
shut her door, and led the way around the corner of the
hut, and struck directly across the fields towards a large
creek, the serpentine shores of which were lined with
long grass and tall walnut trees; which creek ran about
three quarters of a mile in the rear of the buildings of
the plantation. They walked rapidly, and said but little
on their way. The hearts of the two lovers were too
full, their emotions too intense, for the utterance of
words.

It was about nine o'clock when they reached the patch
of Uncle Jesse, which was situated on a rising ground, a
short distance from the water. He was about returning
from his work, and had begun his quiet pathway homeward, when met by the wedding party.

It was a glorious moonlight night in autumn. The
wide and fruitful face of nature was silent, and buried in
repose. The tall trees on the borders of the creek waved
their leafy branches gracefully in the evening breeze,
which was wafted from afar, refreshingly over hill and vale,
over the rippling water, and the waving corn and sugar
fields. The starry sky was studded with a few light-
flitting clouds, while the moon, as if rejoiced to witness
so pure and holy a scene as was about to occur below,
sailed majestically and triumphantly along among the
shifting vapors.

The hearts of the lovers were glad. They were happy

in the present. The apprehended shadows of the future
they shut out wholly from their thoughts.

"We want you to marry us, Uncle Jesse," said
George, boldly and abruptly, as they reached the old
man, just beginning to trudge homeward.

Jesse stopped short, and looked searchingly upon the
three, who had thus unexpectedly met him.

"Why George, why Carry, is dis you!" said he.
"Yah! yah! yah!" the old man loudly cachinated, as
he discovered the nature of the job before him. "You
wants to get married, does you, eh?" The old man
little knew the mental struggle through which the lovers
had passed, in order to arrive at the purpose which they
were now carrying out, else he would have treated the
affair with more solemnity.

"Well, I reckon I must, den," said Jesse, laying
down his hoe, and trying to assume something of the
gravity suitable to the important function he was about
to perform. "I must, I reckon. Berry well, I'so
ready."

The spot was favorable to so solemn a scene. It was
a grassy knoll, somewhat elevated above the surrounding
grounds. Harriet stood at one side, a little in the rear
of Uncle Jesse. She was the sole witness on the important occasion.

George and Caroline stood up before the preacher
George held Caroline's hand in his. He looked brightly,

boldıy, happily up at Jesse's good-natured face, and anon over the surrounding scene, so quiet, so beautiful, so serene. Caroline's breast heaved with emotion. Her feelings were too deep for utterance, and she trembled.

Uncle Jesse began solemnly.

"We are 'sembled here in de presence of God, to jine togedder dis man and dis woman in holy matrimony, which was ordained of God as a holy state, and is not to be entered into lightly and unadvis'dly, but reve rently, discreetly, and in de fear of de Lord."

Looking then at George, he continued slowly.

"Does you take dis woman to your wedded wife, to live togedder after God's ord'nance, in the holy state of matrimony? If so, answer yes."

George responded with a full tone, "Yes."

Turning to Caroline, he said,

"Does you take dis man to your wedded husband, to live togedder after God's ord'nance, in the holy state of matrimony? If so, answer yes."

Caroline answered audibly, "Yes."

"Den jine your right hands," said Jesse.

"Inasmuch as dis man and dis woman have consented togedder in wedlock, and acknowledge de same before 'Mighty God, I pronounces dem man and wife. Them who God has jined togedder, let no man put asunder. Let us pray."

Jesse concluded the ceremony by a feeling prayer.

All the party knelt down upon the soft grass. Jesse raised his hands towards heaven, in a patriarchal manner, as he invoked the divine benediction. The young couple joined heartily in the prayer for their future happiness, which the old man so fervently uttered. When he had concluded, they arose.

"Salute de bride," commanded Uncle Jesse, good naturedly, and in a somewhat authoritative tone, addressing George.

George turned and impressed a fervent kiss upon the beautiful lips of Caroline; whose heart was too full of emotion to return the affectionate pressure of her husband's salute, but received it in silence.

Instantly, old Harriet was trudging forward to take her turn at the bride's handsome countenance, when Uncle Jesse, forgetting the appropriate dignity which became his late ministerial function, pushed her aside, and said: "Go 'long wid ye, it's my turn next;" and gave Caroline a loud whack of a kiss. "Now you may," said he, turning to Harriet, who quietly awaited her opportunity. The party then joyfully returned to their quarters.

Thus ended this moonlit wedding. Thus were united together, by an eternal and heaven-born bond, two loving hearts, whom God had created for each other, and for each other alone. Here was enacted one of those unions which the Creator approves, because they are, in truth,

a union of pure hearts; a union which no human power
can rightfully dissolve. That was an interesting scene.
The temple in which it was enacted, was the vast dome
of nature, erected by the infinite and eternal Architect
of all things. The mighty etherial concave above them
spanned that humble group with far more grandeur and
sublimity, than ever "long drawn aisle or fretted vault,"
or gothic dome could have done. The witnesses were
attending angels, who sped from their heavenly homes
to chaunt melodious strains upon the evening air, unheard, indeed, by mortal ears, in honor of the happy
event. The priest—no titled, robed, or mitred digni-
tary, with heart full of worldly passions, ambition, pride
and envy; but the priest of nature, a simple MAN, the
created, though marred, image of a God; alone standing up to speak in that dignity, which the Infinite had
impressed upon him by his own plastic and omnipotent
hand.

It was a silent, solemn wedding. The marriages of
negroes are usually attended by much noise and Ethio-
pian merriment. The fiddle and the banjo are called
into active requisition; and the boisterous festivities
usually continue to a late hour of the night.

But in this case, the circumstances in which George
and Caroline were placed, required great secrecy and
caution. They intended to deprive their great foe of
his coveted prey. They intended to execute their own

9

just purpose, in being united as one, in heart and soul, at least, forever. They might hereafter be separated, far, far from each other. The iron hand of their master might strive to crush their budding loves; but wherever in the future sad journey of their lives they might wander; wherever and whatever they might suffer; though they might toil, and at length, perish hundreds of miles apart, yet they would forever enjoy thenceforth one cheering and blissful recollection, and that was, that their loving and bleeding hearts had once been united together by the strongest, holiest, noblest, and sweetest tie, of which human souls are capable.

> "Oh love! young love! bound in thy rosy band,
> Let sage or cynic prattle as he will,
> Those hours, and only those, redeem life's years of ill!"

CHAPTER X.

CHANGES AMONG THE "UPPER CRUST.

An event occurred at this time on the Dudley plantation, of considerable importance; which withdrew the
attention of Richard Dudley, for a period, from the impending fate of Caroline.

This event was the death of Major Dudley. The old
gentleman had lived a long life of luxury and opulence.
During several of the last years of his career, he had
suffered considerably from dropsy, and now the resources
of medical art failed to alleviate his sufferings, and to
postpone the period of his dissolution.

As his end approached, his conscience became more
and more tender; and as the arrogant and imperious old
man drew nearer to the presence of his final Judge, in
spite of his usual self-complacency, he began to feel certain qualms and twitchings of conscience, which sadly
disturbed his repose. Several matters troubled him,
but, strange to say, his principal perplexities arose from
the subject of slavery.

He began to entertain doubts as to the justice of that

peculiar institution.   He had often, during the course of
his life, been cruel and unrelenting in the punishment
of his slaves; his unquiet memory wandered back over
a long series of years, and conscience reproduced in his
ears the groans and sobs, the stripes and the pangs of
many poor unfortunate human beings, who had long
since laid down in the rest of the grave, and rendered
their account to that God before whom he was now summoned soon to appear.

In this emergency he could do no better than send for
his spiritual adviser, the Reverend Mr. Pimp. Remorse,
—that inexorable scourge of bloody and tyrannical
men—was lashing his departing soul without mercy;
and he would now gladly avail himself of the balm
which religion was able to bestow upon the troubled
mind.

Pimp was accordingly sent for.   He came; and was
introduced into the bedchamber of his anxious parishioner.

After the usual preliminary inquiries in reference to
himself and his family had been made, the pastor approached the main subject of their interview.

 The Major told Pimp, that his mind was ill at ease—
he was unhappy.

"What troubles you, my dear sir," asked Pimp.

"Well, I am disturbed on the subject of my slaves

I fear that I have done some things in reference to them, which are of questionable propriety.'

"What things do you mean?"

"Well, as to the holding of slaves at all. I fear I may have been robbing my fellow-men all my life of their toil, their wages, and their freedom."

"Pooh!" said Pimp; "Nonsense! All that is perfect nonsense. The laws of your country declare your property in slaves, lawful; what then need you fear on that head?"

"Yes, but the law of God; does Christianity and the Bible justify the act? That law is plainly a higher and greater law than the law of the land."

"Well, my dear sir, I have often said, and preached, that the Bible justifies slavery. Slavery existed during the ages of the Old Testament. It existed at the time of Christ in Judea; and Christ did not lay down a law to his followers, that they should abolish the relation of slaves among them in that age."

"Yes, but Christ teaches certain general doctrines, which, if carried out, must forever condemn slavery. He commands us to do to others, as we would have others to do to us. Now, we have only to ask ourselves one question: would *we* wish to be held in bondage? and the opposition of slavery to the spirit and letter of Christianity, is most clearly and indisputably seen."

"You trouble yourself unnecessarily on that subject,"

9*

said Pimp. "Christians are not compelled to achieve impossibilities. We find slavery already established here, and as we cannot remove it, we must make the best of it, that is all that is required of us."

"Yes, but I could have set my own slaves free. I could have washed my own hands of their blood," said the Major, as he turned uneasily in his bed, and directed a calm glance on the preacher.

"This would have been unnecessary," replied Pimp, "for that reason. Had you set your slaves free, you might have encouraged others to do the same thing, which they might not have been able to do, without great pecuniary loss, and even ruin to themselves. Thus, your example would either have made your fellow-slaveholders do an impolitic thing, or have made them unhappy from their not doing it."

"Ah! my dear sir," sighed the Major, "I fear God will not listen to the argument from policy, when the bodies and souls, the rights and happiness of my one hundred human beings are concerned."

"Yes he will! yes he will!" hastily answered Pimp. "You have done the best you could under the circumstances, I dare say; and you have nothing to fear. Depend upon the infinite goodness of God, and you will not be disappointed."

It was thus that the Reverend Pimp administered treacherous consolation to his dying parishioner. The

rest of his clerical performance need not here be narrated. Suffice it to say, Major Dudley died; the Rev.
Thomas Pimp officiated at his funeral, and spoke long
and feelingly of the piety, patriotism, benevolence, and
moral worth of the deceased. His family deeply felt
the bereavement. Even many of his ill-used slaves,
being an impressible and sympathetic race, also shed
tears, as the funeral cortege slowly departed from the
mansion house, carrying the body of their late master
to the tomb.

As a matter of course, after Major Dudley's death,
the plantation came under the complete control of his
only son and principal heir, Richard Dudley. The first
few weeks after his father's death were spent by Richard
in the arrangement of the affairs of the estate. There
were but three heirs; himself, his sister Julia, and his
mother. No present division was made of the property.
Richard soon settled down into the position of the
acknowledged and absolute master of the whole estate.

This new position effected little or no change in his
habits. It only gave him a wider field and more unre-
strained scope, for the indulgence of his passions and
propensities. If he had been violent and brutal toward
the slaves of the plantation before, he was much more
so now. His usual severity and arrogance assumed a
still more intense degree. He was in a short time feared

and dreaded, as well as hated, by every slave on the estate.

It was not long before his thoughts returned to his contemplated victim, Caroline. Three happy months,— months of wedded love and rapture, had quickly fled away, during which she had by stealth frequently enjoyed the society of her husband. Oh! happy hours for the poor slave, never, never more to be repeated by her on earth! Soon she discovered from unmistakeable proofs, that her great tormentor was again about to begin his persecutions. It became necessary for her to be much more reserved in her visits to her husband's cabin; and, indeed, their intercourse for a time became almost entirely suspended.

Richard watched his opportunity, and came upon Caroline one day suddenly, in her own apartment, in one of the slave cabins. Caroline occupied a neat little room. It was furnished in the rude manner, in which all the rooms of the slaves were furnished. But her superior taste and neatness were exhibited, in the more tidy and cleanly appearance of everything; and she had embellished her humble home, with various little cheap articles, which she had from time to time purchased, with what little money she could command.

Her toilet exhibited nothing of the splendor and luxuriance of a Parisian belle, indeed; but good taste and neatness, and certain proof of what she would and

CHANGES AMONG THE UPPER CRUST.

could have done, had she the means to do it, appeared upon the top of her rough bureau; while in her small mirror, framed in red pine wood, was reflected from time to time a face and form of natural loveliness, which many a Parisian belle would have died to emulate. A few books, several bottles of perfumery, the present of Miss Julia to her; one of Miss Julia's splendid hair brushes and combs, now considerably worn and broken; some handsome pieces of ribbon and head pieces, distributed over and around her glass, also her gift; several old fashion-plates from the magazines, pinned here and there upon the wall; these, and such as these, constituted the humble collection of the poor girl's *bijouterie*.

It was into this apartment that Richard Dudley suddenly intruded himself, at a moment when he knew that Caroline was there. As might be supposed, she was much startled at his entrance.

"Master Richard, are you here?" said she, retreating.

"Yes, Caroline," he replied, seating himself on a chair, by the side of the bed. "I believe I have not been here in your room before, for a long, long time," said he, looking round, and taking a cool survey of the apartment and its contents.

"No, it is the first time I have ever seen you here, Master Richard," said she, trying to speak pleasantly.

"I do not think it will be the last, now, since I have found the way," said he.

The poor girl colored deeply at this remark, and began to tremble.

"I hope you have thought of what I told you, when we last talked together, Caroline," said he.

By this time her emotions of fear and dread overcame her, and she was compelled to sit down on a stool opposite to him.

"What do you mean, Master Richard?" she inquired.

"I told you to think of my proposition. I admire you, Caroline. You know I am your master. I wish you to accede to my wishes. Come, now," said he, coaxingly; "none of your nonsense, none of your mock modesty. You are a pretty girl. It's not often I take a fancy, but I admire you, Caroline." With this, he reached over his hand and attempted to take hold of her arm.

Caroline pushed her stool back, and avoided his effort to seize her.

Looking at him solemnly, for a moment, she said to him: "Master Richard, I hope you will never speak of that again. I never can consent to such a thing; it is impossible."

"What! the same old story over again! I thought you had learned better sense by this time. I see now how it is. You are in love with that rascal, George. I'll sell him to New Orleans. I'll clear him off from the plantation. I suppose, then, you will soon forget him. That's what I'll do.'

At this announcement, Caroline's apprehension became the greater. This threat struck dismay to her heart.

"Oh no, Master Richard, don't do that, don't do that, I pray you!" and she burst into tears.

"Yes, I will do it; and what is further, I want no more of this nonsense; no more of it," said he, sternly, and gazing fiercely at her. "Come here to me," said he, holding out his hands toward her.

"No, I cannot, Master Richard," said she, sobbing. "If you knew all, you would not ask me."

"Knew what? What do you mean," he inquired eagerly. "Knew all what?"

"Well, then, I'm—I'm married, Master Richard!"

"You are, are you? to whom are you married?" said he, impetuously; "say, to whom?"

"I'm married to George; we have been engaged, you know, and we're married now," she replied.

The astonishment and rage of Richard, at these words, knew no bounds. He swore and stamped with extreme fury and violence. Caroline hid her face with her hands, and wept and trembled.

"You are married, are you? Did I not forbid you expressly to get married to that fellow? How dare you disobey me in this manner, you infamous huzzy?" and he gave her a blow which knocked her off the stool, and stretched her upon the floor.

After a moment she arose, and again seated herself, Richard still standing, and gazing at her with rage.

"How long have you been married?" he fiercely demanded.

"Three months, master," said she, weeping.

"You cursed huzzy, you, I'll punish you for this, enough, I'll warrant you. Married! three months, eh? And all so quietly, so secretly. And that scoundrel George; I forbade him, too, from marrying you. You have both disobeyed me, and trifled with me; you have disobeyed my most express order. I'll punish you for it, though. Married, eh!" he repeated to himself several times, thoughtfully; "well done!"

After an awkward silence of some moments, during which Caroline quietly awaited her fate, and Richard seemed to be maturing some deep plan of future vengeance and cruelty, and to be reflecting upon the contumacious conduct of his two young slaves, in getting married contrary to his orders, he said fiercely, "I'll remember you for this!" and took his departure from the room.

Caroline, overcome with her emotions, fell upon her bed, and wept in the bitterness of her soul.

Richard Dudley brooded gloomily and bitterly over this discomfiture of his amorous purpose, by the expert and precipitate ardor of the two lovers. As soon as he found himself alone in his chamber, he gave utterance soliloquisingly, to his deep mortification. The more his thoughts dwelt upon the irritating theme, the more intensely bitter did his animosity become. " Shall I," said he, " be thus thwarted of my wishes by the pertinacious lust of my own slaves ? Shall this daring black scoundrel, George, hereafter move around me, day after day, bearing within him the exulting consciousness, that he has plucked the fragrant rose I would have possessed ? Every time I see his cursed image, I will be reminded of his triumph, and of my failure. I'll be revenged! Yes," said he, fiercely stamping upon the floor, " I'll persecute them while I live!"

Richard paused, as he paced hurriedly to and fro, and bit his finger nails in deep abstraction, until they almost bled. Then he started forward quickly again. Then he paused and cursed once more in the bitterness of his soul. " Yes, I'll do it, by the great Gods," said he, with fiendish exultation. I'll follow both of them with my insatiable vengeance as long as they live ! I'll persecute them to their graves, I warrant that! I'll throw a bitter pill into their cup of sweets! It shall be th   'ain purpose, the greatest pleasure of my life, to torment and curse them to ' the death !' "

Thus raved and raged the handsome, vindictive, and dark-souled Richard Dudley. Nor will the seeming violence of this rhapsody, appear absurd or extravagant, when we remember the iron qualities of his nature,—a nature which was haughty, inflexible, and implacable to the last degree. Of the terrible reality of his purpose, the unhappy victims of his rage soon felt the most deplorable evidences; and they continued to experience them, as the sequel will show, even until the friendly grave at last closed over their sorrows, and shut them out forever, from the light of day.

CHAPTER XI.

VENGEANCE.

RICHARD DUDLEY very soon took occasion to put his threats of vengeance into execution.

He had now given up all idea of accomplishing his brutal purpose in reference to Caroline. He could not degrade her in the way which his lust had dictated; but he could abase and crush her in another manner, and that was, by the cruelty of his punishments. He had only despaired of accomplishing his former purpose, because he saw in Caroline's virtuous conduct, such proofs of insurmountable opposition and repugnance to his wishes, as rendered her willing acquiescence forever hopeless and out of the question.

Beside, George, his own slave, had stepped in defiantly between himself and the attainment of his purpose; and now the conquest had lost all its charms. Another passion wholly took possession of his fiery and malignant soul; no longer lust, but revenge, reigned within him, and kept up a continual storm and tempest of conflicting emotions, which gave him no rest.

He looked about him for a fit instrument of his wrath, and he had not long or far to look. Robinson, the ex-Yankee slave-driver was at hand, and had even already been aptly tutored to his will.

He sent for Robinson, and reminded him of their former conversation; he told him what had occurred since that interview; how Caroline had resisted him; how George had refused to give her up; how the two had afterward married in despite of him; how Caroline has since then persisted in her obstinacy; and how he was now determined to gratify his rage and revenge.

"I'm on hand, Richard, for anything," said Robinson gaily, as soon as Dudley had ended his statement of the case. "I'm on hand, and wide awake!"

Richard reflected for some time, upon the best way of punishing both his disobedient slaves. Several modes of torture suggested themselves to him. Indeed, the resources of the slave-owner are abundant in this respect.

Robinson suggested several different kinds of punishment, either of which, one would suppose, would have been sufficiently severe. At length, after some deliberation, it was resolved that both of the offenders should be publicly and severely whipped. It was also determined, that it should be openly announced to all the slaves on the plantation, that the punishment about to be inflicted on George and Caroline, was the penalty of

their disobedience, in getting married without the permission of their master.

Thus, an opportunity was taken to impress upon the
minds of the slaves, a salutary lesson of obedience to
his orders. Richard determined that all his slaves
should learn that they should not marry hereafter,
without his express permission. Such, indeed, is the
general law of slave-owners on this subject; but it had
never been made the subject of such general and public
attention before, on the Dudley estate, as it was now to
become. But the assignment of this reason for the
penalty to be inflicted, was merely a sham, an excuse;
for the real reason was the bitter hatred felt by Richard
toward his successful rival, George, and his anger at
Caroline, for her virtuous obstinacy and disobedience.

Richard informed Robinson of the conclusion to which
he had come.

"Whip 'em both, eh? Whip 'em both together?" he
inquired. "Wall, I'll do it for you, and do it right,
too!"

"Yes, I want no mercy shown them, Robinson; none,
whatever. I want these two obstinate miscreants soundly
and thoroughly whipped."

"When do you want the job done, sir?" inquired
Robinson.

"To-morrow afternoon—Saturday; let all the hands
come home from work an hour before sun-down, so

that they may all see it done;" Richard sullenly answered.

"Very good; it shall be done. I'll show the rascals
a few scientific touches with my lash, I warrant them.
To-morrow afternoon, eh? They won't want another
taste of my whip in a good long time." And Robinson
went about his business, leaving Richard in a state of
fiendish exultation, at his anticipated gratification.

The announcement of the approaching punishment of
Caroline and George, filled every soul on the plantation
with sorrow and dismay. Beloved by all the poor slaves
on account of the innocence and amiability of their deportment, it was to each one, as if a beloved brother and
sister were about to suffer the pangs which the lash of
the driver would inflict upon them. Every one sympa-
thized with them.

But what good did the sympathy of their fellow slaves
do the unhappy victims of Richard's fury?

Alas! nothing. It could but aggravate their misery.

They could but be silent and unwilling witnesses of a
horrid and cruel scene, which would harrow up their own
feelings; while they possessed no power to alleviate or
help the sufferers.

George and Caroline heard their sentence with terror
and despair; Caroline, in consequence of her apprehension of the severity of the punishment; and George,
from tender sympathy for the agony which she must

endure, who was dearer to him than life itself. He cared but little for his own sufferings; he was strong and vigorous; he could bear what his master would inflict upon himself; but oh! how could he endure to see his beloved torn, scathed and scarred, by the bloody thong of the relentless slave-driver.

Happily, the two victims did not know their cruel fate till the morning of the day on which it was to be inflicted. Richard took the precaution not to communicate any thing to them on the previous day, fearful lest they might attempt to escape during the intervening night.

At length the hour arrived at which this horrible scene was to be enacted. Richard ordered two large stakes to be driven deep into the earth in the barn-yard. This yard was at some considerable distance from the house; so that the screams and groans of his victims might not reach the ears of the ladies of his family.

Tom and Jerry, two of the strongest and stoutest slaves on the plantation, were compelled to perform this task. When the stakes were well driven, he ordered George and Caroline to be tied fast, one to each post. The stakes were about five feet apart, and about six feet high, above the surface of the ground. The victims had their hands tied together fast to the top of the post, so that they stood on tiptoe; and their feet were tied fast to the stake just above the ground. In this way their whole bodies were exposed to the keen lash of the slave driver.

Richard ordered Robinson to give each one a blow alternately.

The barn-yard was filled with the sad and unwilling spectators of the infamous scene; some slowly sauntering about, others looking gloomily on, and others still turning their faces away from the scene.

While the preparations were being made for the execution of this sentence, Richard continued to curse and upbraid his victims with their obstinacy and disobedience. "I'll put an end to your fun," said he; "I'll make it a dear job for you," he continued.

Meanwhile, poor Caroline, unused as she had always been to such severe treatment, was overcome with terror. Every now and then her unhappy husband would address to her, in an undertone, words of consolation and encouragement; but he dare not speak so as to be heard by his master, else his sympathy would but excite his rage still more.

The delicate form of Caroline was strung up high against the post, with her back to the slave-driver. Her light cotton dress presented little protection to the heavy blows of his stout whip.

"Begin now," said Richard, in a loud and authoritative tone, while he stood back some yards, placing his arms a-kimbo, and leisurely taking a survey of the scene.

Robinson stepped up, took his stand at the requisite distance from his victims, raised his whip, swung his long and heavy lash scientifically around him several times, and finally brought it down with such tremendous force upon the back and shoulders of Caroline, that it seemed to jar and shatter her whole frame.

Instantly the blow extorted from her a loud and long scream of agony, which rent the air, and appalled every listener; and her slender body writhed in intense pain.

But Robinson was well used to such things. Her awful scream did not engross his attention for an instant, and he turned to repeat the exploit upon the more vigorous frame of his other victim. He cut and carved his broad back and shoulders scientifically, and exerted his utmost strength to make the blow tell upon him.

George did not move from his position. Yet he could not but utter one deep groan of suffering, forced from him by the pain which the blow inflicted.

Next came Caroline's turn. The same blow, and the same scream, so heart-rending and affecting, were repeated. But Robinson paused not in his work. He had no time to lose. It would be night before his task was ended; and he had to hurry himself.

Fast and thick the blows fell upon the two young slaves. George gave but little sign or proof of his sufferings. Caroline, long before a hundred blows had been dealt her, had ceased to scream, or to wail; but hung insensible by her hands to the post which sustained her lacerated body. And long before her two hundred and fifty lashes had been bestowed, not only her dress had been riddled and cut to pieces by the thong of Robinson's whip, but her whole back was cut into deep gashes; blood flowed plentifully down her back, and every time the lash touched her body, it sunk deeply into the soft, mashed and lacerated flesh of his victim.

Caroline had already ceased to feel. She was for a few moments beyond the power of her master's rage. She had fainted. By Richard's orders, she was untied from the stake, and several of the elder slaves carried her insensible body back to her hut, where they left her to recover as best she might; as they were afraid to offer her any assistance, lest they themselves might excite the wrath of their master

George still remained tied to the stake. He had yet one hundred and fifty blows to endure.

As Robinson resumed his bloody task, the poor wretch could endure it no longer, and broke out into earnest supplication.

"Oh, Master Richard, don't, don't whip me any more. I'm most gone!" said he, frantically.

"Lay it on the scoundrel, lay it on," Richard peremptorily commanded Robinson; who obeyed him with alacrity.

Blow fell after blow. The body of George was by

this time covered with scars, and cuts, and welts. The blood flowed freely. His sobs and groans alternated with the heavy blows of Robinson's whip. By the time his allotted four hundred lashes had been inflicted, his shirt had been cut entirely away, and the flesh of his back actually hung in strips from his bones. George too had fainted. His nature, strong and vigorous as it was, had sunk beneath the mighty agony of that fierce struggle between fiendish wrath on the one hand, and enduring constancy on the other. The four hundred stripes had been told, and Robinson's execrable and damnable work was done.

George's body was covered with blood. Richard Dudley approached him, and examined his wounds, while Robinson stepped back, to sit down upon a log, and rest himself from his long toil. Richard, seeing the loose flesh hanging in strips from George's lacerated back, took out his jack-knife from his pocket, and amid the screams of his victim just returning again to consciousness, he actually cut off the strips of flesh, and threw the pieces from him away to the hogs in the barn-yard; which ate that human flesh with avidity.

When this had been done, he commanded George to be untied. The poor wretch fell immediately to the earth. He could not stand, and groaning and moaning in his great agony, he too was carried, by the orders of Richard, to his quarters among the slave-huts.

Thus ended the first dark scene of Richard Dudley's vengeance against his unfortunate victims. And for what was this terrible penalty inflicted? Why was humanity thus outraged in the person of these two unhappy beings? Why was the utmost tyranny, and the most fiendish cruelty inflicted on them, by one who happened to possess irresponsible power over them? Why were the most terrible punishments known in the long catalogue of human woes, perpetrated on these two creatures, and not only present anguish, but also future and long-continued pain entailed upon them? Why?

Because they loved each other, according to the behests of nature, and of nature's God, and had in so doing, thwarted the base and impure purpose of a most godless and brutal reprobate, who, to gratify his passion, would have trampled under foot all rights, human and divine.

The slaves slowly dispersed to their several quarters, as the shades of night fell upon the horrid scene, to tremble at the recollection of what they had just witnessed. Dudley returned to his house, to forget, in the fumes of intoxication, the exhilirating exhibition he had just enjoyed. And his two victims lay in agony upon their hard couches, racked with pain, and tortured with despair.

CHAPTER XII.

THE LIGHT OF REASON IN A DARK PLACE.

SHORTLY after the occurrence of these bloody scenes, an event of more amiable and pleasing interest happened at the plantation.

Richard Dudley had gorged his vengeance with a full meal, and for a time his bad passions, like a boa-constrictor which had devoured an ox, lay dormant, inert, and passive.

Some months having elapsed since William Stanley's last visit to Julia, he now again visited her. During the interval between his first and the present visit, they had regularly corresponded, and their attachment to each other had become more and more confirmed.

The match was one every way suitable and desirable. Both Julia and her lover were noble specimens of Southern chivalry; handsome, graceful, accomplished, and rich. Upon this second visit, the manner of each toward the other was more cordial, and less formal than before; and but several days elapsed before Stanley

11

made a direct offer of his heart and hand to the fair and accomplished Julia.

The proposition, however agreeable to her feelings, could not at once receive an answer; but propriety dictated that she should allow at least a short time to elapse, during which she should seem to reflect upon the important offer made to her, and prudently determine upon the course she should adopt.

Stanley anticipated such a delay, and was prepared to await it. His time was spent agreeably, in the usual amusements and diversions of young gentlemen; and with bright hope to cheer him, and the occasional solace of the society of the fair Julia, time hung by no means heavily upon his hands. He had spent the interval between his two visits in attentive devotion to his professional business in New Orlea. 1ad risen higher still in the scale of distinction and excellence; and the present relaxation from labor was not unwelcome to his own feelings.

While affairs remained thus, as it were, in suspense, however certain the issue might finally be, who should make his appearance on the plantation, and at the mansion of the now defunct Major Dudley, but the Reverend Mr. Pimp?

There was nothing very peculiar in the manners or appearance of Mr. Pimp. He was clothed in the sombre and genteel black suit, in which clergymen usually dress;

with a white handkerchief of very fine texture tied around
his neck. His manners were agreeable and pleasing,
like those of most educated men. His person was one of
medium height and size, and possessed nothing remarkable. His countenance indicated considerable intelligence; and a dash of shrewdness was perceptible in the
quick twinkle of his small gray eyes. He was atten've
to his pastoral duties; and was especially industrious in
visiting his parishioners, particularly those who seemed
disposed to neglect the duty of regularly attending public worship.

Pimp was received with cordiality by the members of
the Dudley family. His conversation to the widow of
the old Major was edifying and comforting. She acquiesced in all his sage counsels and wise consolations. But
he found in Julia a less pliable and docile hearer.

When Julia Dudley was at boarding school, several
years before, she had had as a classmate and roommate,
a young lady who had been partly educated at the North,
and had imbibed some decidedly anti-slavery principles.
She had, beside, carefully examined the whole subject,
and was at home in all the arguments and aspects of the
question. She had held long and frequent conversations
with her on the subject, and the inquiring and well-
balanced mind of Julia, soon penetrated the true state
of the case, and had arrived at some very clear and
rational views in reference to it.

Pimp and she were, as usual, soon engaged in conversation in reference to the only matter upon which they
differed in opinion.

"My dear Mr. Pimp," said she, playfully, "I never
can possibly get over or reconcile the absurdity and the
monstrous contradiction, of human bondage existing in
this free nation."

"Why, what is there so wonderful in that," said Pimp,
raising his eyebrows at such a bold declaration on the
part of Julia.

"Our government and our constitution are based,"
said she, "upon one great principle, one cardinal doctrine, that all men are born free and equal, and that all
are entitled to the uncontrolled possession of life, liberty,
and other pursuit of happiness. Now, how in the name
of reason can Americans, in the face of such a declaration, hold three millions of men as slaves, depriving
them of that very freedom, and of that very pursuit of
happiness, for which they themselves contended in the
Revolution?"

Pimp was somewhat bothered at this rather positive
and direct appeal of Julia; but after a hem and a haw
or two, he replied, "Yes, but Americans are born freemen, and the blacks are born slaves."

"That makes no difference," she replied; "and
beside, that cannot be true, my dear sir; pardon me for
saying so; because the Declaration of Independence

declares that men cannot be born slaves, that all men are born free and equal; and though tyrants may claim that certain persons are born slaves, that claim is false and atrocious. Men cannot be *born* slaves, though they may be reduced by a stronger power to slavery, immediately after they see the light."

"But we find slavery already among us, and it is impossible for us to remove it," said Pimp, hesitatingly.

"Yet so great a violation of the principles of our government," replied Julia, ought to be abolished at all hazards; because its existence is an everlasting stigma on our nation. Only think of it, Mr. Pimp! Think of the freest nation on the globe,—America,—the home of the free, and the refuge of the exile from foreign bondage; a country, whose very birth and beginning were nursed amid the-storms and thunders of a revolution, intended to throw off a foreign yoke, simply because our people had no representation in the assemblage which decreed their taxes. Think of that same nation holding three millions of human beings in the worst form of slavery! 'Tis monstrous, Mr. Pimp! 'tis very monstrous!"

"Yes, but money is invested in this property. Our citizens cannot afford to lose all this money," said Pimp.

"If they have invested money in that which they had no right to buy, and which no one had a right to sell,"

11*

replied Julia, " they must bear the consequences,—the loss, if necessary, which may ensue. Suppose I were to buy your wife and your child, from an uncle of yours, and pay him two thousand dollars for the bargain. Would that fact give me a good title to the possession of your wife and child? Would the fact that your uncle undertook to sell to me that which did not belong to him, convey or communicate a good title to him, to that which he never possessed. I can't make that out, Mr. Pimp," said she, quizzingly. "If all men are born free and equal, nobody ever had a right to buy, and nobody ever had a right to sell these slaves; and whoever bought, and whoever sold, did it without the slightest show of right or reason. And if they who did it in the beginning, did it without any right so to do; whoever does it afterward, as their successors, and under their authority, does it with no better claim to right than they who bought and sold in the first instance. Is not that so, Mr. Pimp?"

Pimp was sorely put to. Aside from the fact that he was on the wrong side of the question, and really had no answer to make to the shrewd argument of Julia, he he did not wish to offend his opponent nor any of the family; he rather would, on the contrary, have courted their favor at all hazards, and that for a reason which we will presently mention to the reader. He was therefore very mild in his reply, which was a sort of half-and-half answer, and meant nothing.

Julia continued: "When we hear of such slavery existing in Russia, in Turkey, or in Morocco, we are not at all surprised; because such monstrosities would be perfectly consistent with the principles of their governments, to say nothing of their religion. But in a Christian land like this, with many thousands of Christian preachers; the whole people professing to believe in a religion which commands us to do to others as we would that others should do to us; and in a free country, where it is continually proclaimed that all men are free and equal, and where we hear everlasting plaudits and praises everywhere sung to the blessings of liberty; and hearty thanks are continually ascending to heaven for the possession of it on our part; in such a land, to see flourishing the most cruel and widely extending example of slavery existing anywhere on the whole globe; all this is to me most monstrous and unaccountable. What do you think of it, Mr. Pimp?" said she, inquiringly and seriously.

"It is much to be lamented, no doubt;" said he, driven to the necessity of saying something apologetically. "But I do not see any way by which the evil can be remedied. Do you?" he inquired, adroitly endeavoring to throw some difficulty in the way of Julia's intellectual attack upon him.

"Certainly I do," said she. "Slavery could be easily removed, if American citizens and slaveholders would just go back to first principles. If they would set their slaves free—all of them—absolutely and at once, give their slaves what is their own, that is, their full freedom; make them amenable to the same laws as the white people; let them stay upon the soil to which they are acclimated, and which is now their native country, and where their labor is absolutely indispensable; and then *hire them* to do their work at reasonable wages, and pay them for their toil; if the whites did this, I believe that, in one year's time, the free black labor of these slaves would give a new birth to Southern enterprise, commerce, agriculture and wealth, and turn these rich, but now wasted realms, into a very paradise on earth. That is my opinion, Mr. Pimp, and I speak it boldly," said Julia, rising and walking majestically across the room.

"Where in the world did you get such ideas and notions into your head?" said Pimp. "You astonish me beyond all measure; one would imagine that you were a red-hot, blazing, burning abolition lecturer from the North—from Maine, Vermont or Boston!" said Pimp, good-naturedly.

"Oh, at school I had a lady-friend from the North, who gave me some light upon the subject, and I became quite convinced of the truth of her opinion, though I never say much to any one. I thought, however, that you might have convinced me of the error of my sentiments; but I must say, Mr. Pimp, you have not convinced me," said she, laughing.*

Pimp was not much flattered at this declaration of the young lady. After a moment, he said, "Every one must entertain their own opinions; it is a free country, you know,"—slightly blushing, however, at the monstrous absurdity which the prevailing custom and cant of speech had unintentionally seduced him to utter.

At this juncture Richard entered the parlor, in which the preceding conversation had been held; and his presence suggested to Pimp the main purpose of his visit.

Pimp had observed that since his father's death, Richard had not once attended church. Several of the Dudley family had, at different times previously, held office in his church, and had been men of prominence and importance in the congregation. He had conceived the idea of getting Richard to join the church; and as he was a young man of wealth, was now the sole head of the family, and was therefore a person of consequence in the community, the acquisition was very important.

* Shortly after the preceding conversation occurred, Pimp was surprised with the honorary degree of *Doctor in Divinity*, from one Southern college, and with the degree of *Doctor of Laws* from another; but for what reason, or on account of what superior mental quality, no one has yet been able to discover, unless it be that he is a Northern man with Southern principles. But the titles sound well and look well, at any rate—The Rev. Thomas Pimp, D. D. & L. L. D.!

An election of officers was soon to take place in his congregation, and if he could only get Richard elected a
deacon or a trustee, Pimp thought he would thereby
bind the Dudley family closer to his interests, get the
support of their great wealth and influence; and at the
same time, of course, be doing much *good!*

It was with such an ambitious scheme that Pimp had,
on the present occasion, visited the Dudley mansion.
Julia retired, and the reverend gentleman was left alone
with the young planter.

After some preliminary observations, he at length
introduced the subject of his wishes. Richard was at
first much surprised, but he listened with respect to what
Pimp had to say. Pimp dwelt upon the importance of
his becoming a member of the church, and the usefulness
and honor which would result from his accepting an
office in the vestry, and trying to do something to build
up the cause of religion and morality in the world.
The Dudley family had long been prominent and useful
in the church, and now he was the head of the family,
it became him to step into the shoes of his worthy pre-
decessors, and take their honored places.

But the eloquence and logic of Pimp were utterly
useless. Richard had neither taste nor ambition for the
task he was so unexpectedly invited to assume. His
habits and disposition were dissolute and licentious in the
extreme; his spirit was overbearing, haughty and cruel.

He was the last man on earth to assume even the outward moral restraints of religion, much less to cultivate
anything of its inward spirit or temper.

After a decorous parley on the subject with Pimp, he
gave him a flat denial. Pimp was much mortified and
disappointed; he had counted on getting young Dudley
into the church; but all his arguments were of no avail.
He at length gave the matter up in despair, only reite-
rating his injunction, that Richard and the family should
not wholly neglect the church of their fathers, but attend
upon its services as often as they possibly could.

Meanwhile Stanley and Julia came to a final under-
standing in reference to the interesting matter between
them. Julia accepted his suit. He placed upon her fair
finger a diamond ring, as a pledge of their mutual and
plighted love. In a day or two he took his departure
for New Orleans. The marriage was to come off in three
months from that time.

On his return to New Orleans, Richard Dudley, to
alleviate the monotony of his life on the plantation,
accompanied Stanley, to spend a short time amid the
pleasures and fascinations of the Crescent City. The
slaves on the plantation were left under the control of
Robinson, who received strict orders as to what was to
be done, during Richard's absence of several weeks'
duration from home. Old Mrs. Dudley rarely went out
of her chamber; her health was feeble, and she passed

her time for the most part alone, taking no share in the management of the affairs of the house. Julia became the virtual mistress of everything, and she was well qualified in every sense to discharge the duties which devolved upon her in her new position.

CHAPTER XIII.

MERCY.

"The quality of mercy is not strained;
  It droppeth as the gentle rain from heaven,
  Upon the place beneath. It is twice blessed;
  It blesseth him that gives, and him that takes."

                MERCHANT OF VENICE.

JULIA DUDLEY heard of the terrible cruelty which Richard had inflicted upon George and Caroline, several days after its occurrrence. She immediately inquired into the circumstances of the case, and her anger was very much excited at the details. But she knew that Richard was now their absolute master, and that remonstrance and expostulation would be of no avail. It would but excite his rage still more. She well knew the brutal severity of his disposition.

But she determined to do what she could to alleviate their sufferings, and make their condition as tolerable as possible.

She immediately went herself, to the apartment of Caroline, and addressing her in tones of sympathy, said: "Caroline how are you now; have you much pain?"

12

Caroline was lying on her hard couch, stiff from suffering, and weak from the loss of blood. She raised herself slowly on the bed, and said in a feeble and scarcely audible voice: "I am better now, mistress Julia, I thank you."

Her mistress sat down beside her on the bed. Caroline had been her favorite servant, in consequence of the superior neatness of her person, and tidiness of her habits. She had allowed Caroline to dress her hair, and to perform other little duties about her toilet; and she had really esteemed the poor girl, and would sometimes bestow upon her a cast off dress or bonnet. As soon as Julia began to examine the wounded and bloody back and shoulders of the poor girl, she almost fainted at the sight and proof of so much cruelty, and such fearful suffering. She immediately sent for proper medicines, and soothing and healing appliances, with which she ordered Aunt Harriet to dress her wounds; after which she felt better.

Julia also sent to the house for better food for the sufferer. She had a better and softer bed made for her; and indeed did everything which a kind and generous heart could do to alleviate the miseries of the unhappy victim of her brother's rage.

"Thank you, mistress," said she, "thank you; you are too kind," said Caroline to Julia, after her orders had all been complied with, and the other slaves had quickly and eagerly obeyed her. "You have always been kind to me," she continued, "and I will ever be grateful to you for it."

"I am sorry for you, Caroline, that you have been so cruelly abused; but this is one of the misfortunes of being slaves," said she.

After a pause Caroline added, "There is one thing, Miss Julia, which troubles me."

"What is it?" she said.

"You know I am now married to George. He has suffered worse than I have. I would like to be near him, and to nurse him. May I go to his cabin and attend to him?"

The propriety of this request at once struck the attention of Julia, and she hastily replied, "Certainly, I give you permission to live with him altogether. Here, Harriet," addressing the old woman, who still stood by the bed, "Move all Caroline's things to George's cabin, immediately."

Caroline grasped the fair hand of Julia, and passionately kissed it. "Thank you, thank you, Mistress Julia," she said warmly, as her tears flowed.

"And take some medicine and wine along for him; and Harriet, do you nurse him, and dress his back for him as well as you can."

"Yes, Missee, I will. Golly, I'se too glad to do it;"

and the old woman bustled around in a great hurry, to fulfil the benevolent orders of her mistress.

"Are you strong enough to go now to George's cabin?" said Julia, addressing Caroline.

The thought of being near her husband, and of alleviating his sufferings by the tender offices of her affection, had given new strength to the poor heart-broken creature, and she seemed possessed of unwonted vigor. She answered, that she thought she could soon go; that she felt much better, and would be too happy to be at once the companion and the nurse of her husband.

"Then go at once," said she. "He needs your assistance. Poor fellow, he must have suffered badly enough. I pity him very much."

And Julia left the house of the poor beaten slave, and returned to her own sumptuous mansion, enjoying the noble and exalted consciousness of having ministered to the misery, and lessened the suffering of an unfortunate human being.

Caroline required no urging to induce her hasty removal to the quarters of her husband. The condition of his back was indeed awful. His sufferings were intense. Deep ruts, whence the living flesh had been cut in strips by the whip and knife, were perceptible. Nature had endeavored to repair the ravages of the cruel hand of his master; but her work was only just begun. He had himself, without a friend to aid him, tied some greased cotton around the gashes of his back, which served to stop the flowing of the blood; but his sufferings were still almost beyond endurance.

When George, who was laying down on his side, heard the soft voice of Caroline, as she slowly tottered into his cabin, he opened his eyes, and a sad smile of affection played upon his wan features. She went up to him and kissed him. Both began silently to weep; for nature will ever speak when the springs of affection and sympathy within the soul are stirred. And human nature is the same in all lands and ages, whether it sit in splendor on a throne, or whether it grovel in poverty and want in the beggar's hut, or in the cheerless cabin of the slave.

Caroline soon communicated to George what her kind mistress had done for them, and all that she had said. She comforted him with soothing words of love and commiseration. She immediately applied the remedies her mistress had sent him, and dressed his still bleeding wounds. She did all that the most tender affection could do to diminish his sufferings.

Caroline and Harriet immediately set to work to arrange the apartment which was now to be their common home, so as to make things as comfortable as possible. While they were engaged in this task, the provisions and little delicacies arrived, which Julia had sent them, and to which they had long been strangers. As

12*

several large baskets were set down inside the door by
Jesse, who added that they came from " Missus Julia,"
tears of gratitude arose in their eyes, and they could
not find utterance for their overflowing feelings.

May blessings descend on that fair and noble head,
which thus pitied the miserable of earth, and contributed
to the alleviation of their cruel sufferings!

Left alone to themselves, the two unfortunate lovers
could commune in sympathy of feeling, and administer
comfort to each other. George's religion had not de-
serted him in this trying hour. He had prayed to
heaven for consolation and support, and heaven had
granted his prayer. During the lonely hours of the
day, when all the hands were out in the rice and cotton
fields, and they were left behind alone, as both were yet
too weak to perform any work, they would engage in
devotional exercises. George read from the Bible
cheering words of consolation, and offered up his prayers to heaven for himself, his wife, his master, and his
fellow slaves. And often, as he sang the songs of Zion,
with which he was familiar, with the fine full-toned voice
which he possessed, a thrill of rapture would pass through
him as he thought of his eternal home, where he and the
wife he loved so well, would one day, as he hoped, enjoy
everlasting repose, their sins washed white in the blood
of the lamb, and they reigning with him for ever and
ever.

CHAPTER XIV.

ROUGE ET NOIRE.

"The gods are just, and of our pleasant vices,
Make instruments to scourge us!"

UPON his arrival in New Orleans, Richard Dudley
plunged without restraint into all the dissipations of
that voluptuous city.. Having taken with him a considerable amount of money, there was no excess nor
gratification, however expensive, in which he did not
indulge.

William Stanley, although given to the usual amusements of young gentlemen, did not long remain the close
companion of Richard in his adventures. He had his professional affairs to attend to; and soon Richard was left
alone to make such acquaintances, and to engage in
such pursuits as best pleased his fancy. Richard needed
no one to introduce him into the *penetralia* of New
Orleans life and dissipation. He made acquaintances
easily. Having plenty of money, and being fond of the
society of young men like himself, being also jovial and

agreeable as a companion, and handsome and pleasing in his person and manners, he became, in a short time, the favorite of all his acquaintances of both sexes Among the latter, he soon numbered several of the most celebrated and fascinating beauties of New Orleans, whose reputation for virtue, unfortunately, was no better than it should be.

One day, Richard was dining at a Café in Bourbon Street, one of the most fashionable in New Orleans, when he accidentally sat opposite, at a side table, to a handsome and exquisite young man, evidently a French man, who however, spoke English with much fluency, and indeed without any foreign accent whatever. A conversation soon sprung up between them, then a familiarity; and before they left the Café, so congenial had they proved to each other, that they departed together as future friends, and intimate associates.

This young gentleman, the Count de Clermont, was a native of Normandy, in France, but had spent most of his life in Paris. He was descended from a noble but reduced family; had long since spent the small patrimony which he had inherited, and had for some years lived only as a *chevalier d'industrie.* His long residence in Paris had made him perfectly familiar with all the fashionable vices of that great centre of the profligate civilization of the world. He was an adept in everything; there was no game nor play, no art, no trick, no sort of gentlemanly dexterity in raising money, with which he was not quite familiar ; and there was no luxury, indulgence, or gratification, which he had not fathomed and exhausted to the last dregs of pleasure. Gifted with a vigorous constitution, this young adventurer bore little evidence, in his outward appearance, of the ravages on health, which dissipation such as his, usually entails upon those who indulge in it. He was familiar with all the most secret and select *arcana* of Parisian life ; and his recollections of his adventures in that capital were not only treasured by him in his own mind, but he possessed the art of describing these things to the uninitiated in such a way, as to invest them with the most exciting novelty and interest.

Such a man, with such accomplishments, and with such experiences, would of course be a most attractive associate for Richard Dudley. He was a treasure to be prized and cherished. Clermont sometimes had plenty of money, and at other times he was almost penniless. Richard's purse was always open to him. Under Clermont's guidance, he was introduced to the various dissipations of New Orleans, and especially to those most ruinous and destructive of them all, the gambling houses.

One evening, as the two friends were strolling together along the most fashionable part of St. Charles Street, they arrived in front of a house of disgraceful celebrity, which was brilliantly lighted up, and presented a very attractive appearance. Elegantly dressed gentlemen were passing in and out of it, and occasionally a fashionably attired female would enter a side door, or private entrance, by inserting a private key, and disappear within.

In that house were collected and perpetrated all the fashionable vices which attract, engage, and ruin human beings. On the first floor was a drinking saloon, filled with half-drunken men, who were destroying bodily health and vigor, by frequent libations of the poisonous cup.

On the second floor were the large gambling rooms, filled with all the various appliances necessary to the several desperate games of chance which were there played,—faro tables, rouge et noir, roulette, dice, and the rest. Here were collected together a considerable number of persons engaged in play; but before we describe the scenes which occurred here, it will be proper to finish our catalogue of the purposes to which the rest of the building was appropriated.

On the third floor was a harem. Unlike the two lower stories, which were occupied by one large saloon in each story, this third story was subdivided into some fifteen small apartments, elegantly furnished, which were occupied by as many fair though frail daughters of pleasure, the mistresses and paramours of the usual frequenters of the gaming and drinking rooms below.

On the fourth story were to be found a pawnbroker's shop, and a gunsmith store. On this floor, the unfortunate victims of the gaming-table, who had lost all their money, might raise small sums, by pledging any articles which they might still possess about them. And here, too, should they lose their last penny in the world, even the products of their pawn-tickets, they had not very far to go, in their desperation, to obtain the means of putting an end to their wretched and ruined existence. Here, luxury, pleasure, hope, poverty, despair, and death itself, were all congregated together under one single roof.

On entering the sanctuary of vice and ruin, on the second floor, Dudley was at first struck with the solemn silence which reigned, in the numerous assembly before him. He heard only the monotonous voice of the banker at intervals pronouncing the mysterious words; "*Make your game, gentleman! The game is made! All is done!*' that is to say, the stakes are on the table, and cannot be withdrawn; and soon after proclaiming the decrees of Chance; *Number* 25, *black, odd, and wins; No* 12, *red, even, and loses;*" according to the number, color, and combinations, which had turned up. One particular group attracted Richard's special attention

The altar erected by the worshippers of Chance, was an oblong table, rounded at the ends, in the centre was fixed the *roulette,* a sort of hollow cylinder, turning on an axis, and fitted with alternate red and black divisions, each marked with a number.

This cylinder having been previously set in motion, the *tallieur* threw from his hand in an inverse direction, an ivory ball, which, after bounding several times from side to side, lodged in one of the divisions, and thus decided the successive chances.

At the four corners of the *roulette* facing each other, after the fashion of the cardinal points, were four *tailleurs* or bankers, who presided at the game. Before them was a sum of from forty to fifty thousand dollars, in silver, gold, and bank notes; this was the *bank;* from it, the gains of the players were paid, and it was replenished from their losses, which were quickly gathered up by attendants armed with long maces.

The table was covered with green cloth, printed with various designs; first, came a pattern of red and black lozenges; then three longitudinal rows of twelve numbers, surmounted by *nought and double nought.* By placing money upon the devices of the numbers, any person secured a share in this lottery in action.

The players, or *pontes* as they were termed in the jargon of the place, crowded round the table in various attitudes, and displayed the most opposite emotions.

Some manifested a real or affected indifference, others laid no restraint upon their feelings and expressions; several tried to calculate chances, and followed with eager solicitude the capricious fluctuations of the game, pricking them down upon cards prepared for the study, and generously provided by the establishment; a few were seriously occupied with algebraical computation, by which they were *certain* to foretel the number to be drawn; others were gravely taking notes to establish an infallible system which they were on the point of discovering: and finally, some exhibited the strongest superstitions, such as stopping their cars with great care, so as not to *hear* the banker call out the numbers, which they nevertheless *saw* quite plainly.

Those who have not visited the haunts of gamblers, can have no idea how much their determinations are influenced by *round sums*. A player, having made large profits, feels inclined to retire from the table; but something is still wanting to complete the cypher he intended to attain, and, in pursuing this fraction, he loses all that he had before gained.

Another appears to be in a fair way of breaking the bank; he is in what is termed a formidable *vein;* nothing, neither his mistakes nor his address, neither his hesitation nor his boldness appears to affect it; he wins because he *does* win; that is the only reason. But he had settled in his own mind: "I will not exceed a certain sum;" and that sum is in his possession, he retires —thus evincing, doubtless, much wisdom and fortitude,

13

but missing nevertheless the fortune that was within his grasp.

Such a scene possessed an irresistible charm for so excitable and intense a nature as that of Richard Dudley; for a while he remained only a spectator of the scene before him, anxiously watching the fickle fortunes of the gamesters. At length one of them arose to withdraw from the game; and Richard took the vacant seat at the table.

At first his bets were moderate in their amount. But as he began to get more and more excited with the game, as he lost and won, and lost again, he became quite desperate, and placing a large amount of money in bank bills before him, he bet largely and heavily. At first, he was rather fortunate; but the fickle Goddess soon turned against him, and he continued unsuccessful until he had lost an immense sum. Clermont stood by, during all this time, without taking part in the game. He saw the vein of ill-luck into which his friend had fallen, and he at length succeeded in drawing him away from the table. During the course of an hour, Richard Dudley had lost the sum of three thousand dollars.

For several days after this unfortunate occurrence, Richard abstained from the gaming table. Clermont, however, remained his constant companion: and he solaced himself for his losses, by abundant indulgence in other forms of dissipation.

But he soon returned again to engage still more ruin-ously in this fascinating pleasure. He could not resist the temptation which allowed him to burn his wings at the lurid flame which had already scorched him. His general want of success did not deter him. He still hoped from day to day, not only to repair his losses, but to add largely to his gains. He was disappointed. The sharpers had discovered that he was a fat goose to pluck, and they plucked him well. During the course of two weeks, Richard had not only lost the five thousand dollars in cash which he had brought with him to New Orleans, but had lost fifteen thousand more, which he had borrowed on his own notes, from several merchants in New Orleans, who knew his family and the extent of his wealth. All this he lost, and at his last sitting, he even bet and lost his elegant span of horses with which he had travelled to New Orleans. The consequences was, that being thoroughly cleaned out of money, credit, and every thing else, he took stage to return home.

Before he left his noble friend, the Count de Clermont, in New Orleans, he detected sufficient evidence to con-vince him, that the fascinating and agreeable Count was an accomplice and an ally of the gamblers who had so completely fleeced him, and that he actually received his percentage on the amount realized from Richard's losses.

Under these circumstances, it may well be imagined

that the young planter returned home in r.o very amiable
humor. He had been completely "taken in, and done
for." But the principal thing which disturbed his equa-
nimity, was the fact that his notes for fifteen thousand
dollars were coming due in New Orleans, and that he
must prepare by some expedient to meet them.

The only means by which this end could be accomplished, was by the sale of some of his negroes. He informed his mother and sister of the facts of the case,
and they, of course, had to acquiesce in the necessity of
the measure.

In consequence of the wealth of the Dudley family, no
sales of slaves had taken place on their plantation for
some years. It was therefore, a new event both to the
master and to the slaves themselves. The announcement
of the fact that some of them were to be sold, created
quite a stir and a sensation among them.

While Richard was thinking of taking the necessary
steps to make a sale, an incident occurred which suited
his purpose exactly, and saved him all further trouble.
One day about noon he saw a chain-gang of some fifty
slaves coming down the public road at some distance
from his residence, and he immediately mounted his horse
and rode to overtake them. The gang consisted of a
miscellaneous collection of slaves of all kinds, of all
ages, and of both sexes, field hands, house-servants, me-

chanics, cooks, seamstresses, nurses, every thing that could be thought of or desired.

This assemblage of human beings was the property of one Simon Snapp, a regular slave dealer from St. Louis, who made his yearly migrations through the Southern States, for the purchase of slaves for the New Orleans market.

Richard rode up to Snapp and entered into conversation with him. As soon as a halt was ordered by the latter, the whole gang presented a most singular appearance. A large chain was passed along between the slaves, and they were fastened to it in couples, by handcuffs. A monstrous big negro led the van of this inglorious and inhuman march. The men were chained together on the forepart of the chain, and the women and young girls behind them. Some of the women carried their infant children in their arms; while among the number might be seen woolly-headed boys and girls, not yet fourteen and fifteen years of age. All were chained together, and compelled to travel along, frequently at a rapid dog-trot.

Snapp and several of his assistants rode behind and at the side of the gang, armed with long whips, with which they occasionally quickened the pace of those who seemed disposed to lag behind, or to drag upon the chain. The whole gang appeared to be run down with fatigue. When they stopped, they seemed almost out of breath.

13*

Some of them immediately laid flat down upon the
ground. Others sat down. Some engaged in sullen
talk with their next neighbor. A few had a word of
friendship or recognition for some old acquaintance in
the gang. But scarcely any sign or sound of cheerful-
ness was exhibited in the large and motley group of
wretches who were thus hastening onward to all the horrors of the slave market. Some were almost naked, and
others had a small portion of clothes upon them, while a
few were fortunate enough to possess something like
decent apparel. The women who had their infants with
them, embraced the opportunity to suckle them; and
what with the crying of the infants, the jabber of the
men and women, the groans and moans of the wearied,
and the cracking of the whips of the drivers to keep the
gang all in their allotted limits, the whole effect was a
most singular and miscellaneous one. Some of them
bore the marks of terrible stripes and lashes upon their
persons. The day before this, Snapp had knocked a preg-
nant woman flat down in the road, with his fist, for not
travelling along fast and willingly enough. Two large
negroes, who were the most refractory in the gang, and
had attempted once to run away, were placed the hind-
most in the row, and had heavy shackles on their ankles,
which had worn and inflamed their legs to a frightful
degree, so that the least motion inflicted on them intense pain.

"How many slaves have you here?" said Richard to Snapp.

"I've got about fifty now, but I want fifty more, if I can get them," he replied.

"Where do these come from you have got here?" inquired Richard.

"Oh! all over the South, some from Tennessee, some from Kentucky, some from Georgia. I'm a regular trader. I make a regular business of it, I do," replied Snapp. He continued, "I advertise for niggers all over. See, there is my card," said he, taking out a well-worn newspaper, and pointing out to Richard an advertisement in it, which read as follows:

500 NEGROES WANTED.

We will pay the highest cash price for all good negroes offered. We invite all those having negroes for sale, to call on us at our Slave Mart, opposite the lower Steamboat Landing. We will also have a large lot of Virginia, Alabama and Georgia negroes for sale in the fall. We have as safe a jail as any in the country, where we can keep negroes safe for those that wish them kept.

BOLTON & SNAPP.

"That's what we advertise for. May be, Mister, you've got some niggers to sell, eh? If you have, I'll give you as good price for 'em, as any dealer in the Southern country. What say you?" said Snapp, turning to Richard.

"Well, yes, I've a few I might sell, if you gave good prices for them," responded Richard. "Suppose you come down to my house. Perhaps we can deal together."

"Agreed!" said Snapp, "I'll go."

With that, both of them rode rapidly down to the house. Arrived there, Richard immediately summoned together from their cabins and from the fields, his whole complement of slaves, amounting to the neighborhood of a hundred. This process required some time, and during the interval, Richard informed Snapp, that he wanted to raise the sum of fifteen thousand dollars, for a certain purpose, and that he would be willing to sell him about fifteen slaves, averaging a thousand dollars each, for that purpose.

Snapp doubted whether he had so much money by him. Nevertheless, he would see what he could do.

The slaves were soon assembled in the large yard in front of the Dudley mansion. They seemed much surprised and frightened. Silence reigned among them. Snapp, a pot-bellied, short, fat, red-faced, and brutal looking fellow, on whose countenance the fire of brandy and whiskey perceptibly burned at all times, walked, or rather toddled in among the group of human cattle, to make an examination. He felt this one, poked in the ribs of that one, took hold rudely of the lower jaw of others, opened their mouths, and examined their teeth; handled the persons of the women coarsely and indecently, and knocked and kicked about inquiringly and indifferently among the whole lot.

At length he picked out some seven large-sized men, five likely and good-looking young women, and three boys, fourteen years of age, and told them to stand at one side. They did so, looking aghast at the fate which had so suddenly overtaken them, in being sold down the river to the New Orleans market,—the great Gehenna of misery in the dark imagination of the poor slave.

Richard carefully examined with his eye, the selection Snapp had made. "How much will you take for this lot?" said Snapp.

"Well," said Richard, after he had made some further observation on the selected negroes, "That is a likely lot you have picked out; about the best of the whole of them. I see you know what's a good stock, old fellow."

"It's my biz'ness, you know, and ther's few kin beat me in buying niggers, that's a fact. Yah! yah!" responded Snapp. "But say, what 'll you take for that ar lot? Let's make a bargain, and I'll be off."

"Fifteen thousand dollars, cash," said Richard, "is what I'll take for them, without any further parley or higgling about it; if that sum will suit you, take them; if not, not."

"Well, I dun'no; it's a good lot, to be sure," said Snapp, once more carefully inspecting the negroes, one by one. "But that's a big sum, too; av'rage of a thousand dollars a-piece. Howsumever, I guess I'll go it," said he, after a pause. "Make out your papers, and I'll pay the money."

With this Richard and Snapp retired into the house, to draw up the bills of sale. While this was being done, Snapp counted out his money. It happened that he had enough on hand—the amount demanded by Richard, and by the creditors of his gambling debts in New Orleans.

The papers were soon made out, and the money paid over. That done, the buyer and seller in human blood came forth from the house. Snapp told the negroes whom he had bought, that he was now their master; and rudely ordered them to get ready to travel. By this sudden sale husbands and wives, brothers and sisters, parents and children, were all unexpectedly separated, without a moment's warning, and that most probably forever! Now was to be their last embrace—now their last and sad farewell on earth!

"Ah! then and there was hurrying to and fro,
And gathering tears, and tremblings of distress;
And there were sudden partings, such as press,
The life from out young hearts, and choking sighs,
Which ne'er might be repeated!"

The sentimental reader, accustomed to associate these lines of Byron with all that is high-born, beautiful and chivalrous, in the glorious nobility of old France and

Belgium, will doubtless laugh outright at the application of them to a parting scene between the poor, down-trodden woolly-heads of a Louisiana plantation. Would that his laugh, so hearty, and perhaps so ironical, might alleviate the pangs of that sad hour of life-long separation!

The poor slaves immediately hurried to their cabins, to tie up in little bundles what clothes they possessed, or most needed; money and trinkets of any sort, they had none. Any small memento, however valueless—a knife, a comb, a handkerchief, anything—they quickly bestowed with a blessing, as a farewell gift to a beloved brother, wife, or sister, whom they were never more to see on earth. And then came the last hurried embrace, the last kiss of affection, and the last uttered benediction. Fathers said farewell forever to their children; husbands to the wives of their bosom; and brothers to sisters, whom they loved. Tears flowed—such bitter tears as the poor slave alone can shed, when his heart is forever desolated in its dearest affections, by the cruel and unrelenting tyranny of the master. The words, "Good-bye, honey! God bless ye!" might then and there have been heard over and over again, amid sobs and groans, which told of the heart-breaking agonies of the poor, defenceless, unresisting slave; even just such pangs as you, O! most high-born and accomplished reader, would feel, were you torn away by the decree of

some throned despot, from the kind mother who bore
you, from the revered father who reared you, from the
tender sister who cherished you with pride and affection;
—torn away, to be consigned forever to a life of distant
toil, ignominy and wretchedness. Our poor humanity
is ever the same, in all its hopes and fears, its joys and
sorrows, its affections and its impulses; beneath whatever sky it may dwell, however high or however low
may be its sphere, and whether the color of its outside
coating be white or black.

Snapp roared out to the slaves whom he had bought,
and who had not yet left their several cabins, to hurry
themselves: his gang was waiting on the road. He
mounted his horse and drove his new recruits before
him, along the lane which led out to the main road, and
there they were chained together, in the same way as
the other slaves were chained. After all had been
arranged in one continuous gang, and everybody safely
secured, the drivers cracked their whips; Snapp loudly
gave orders for the procession to advance; the slaves
all fell into regular line; and away the melancholy
company silently moved toward the still darker and
gloomier regions, of the great slave-market of the
Western world.

CHAPTER XV.

LIGHTS AND SHADOWS.

A FEW weeks after the return of Richard Dudley from New Orleans, his mother, old Mistress Dudley, became sick and died. Her illness was not of very long duration. During its continuance she received every attention from Julia, and even Richard displayed what little humanity remained in him, by his assiduous attendance upon her during her last sickness.

The Rev. Pimp, as a matter of course, was also called upon to render his professional attendance in the case. He embraced the opportunity to repeat his earnest solicitation to Richard to come forward and take a prominent position in his church. In vain! Richard's bad passions, were too fiery and impetuous to permit him even to be a good hypocrite. He steadily resisted all the seductions which Pimp brought to bear upon him. The Reverend Pimp at last gave him up as a bad job, and desisted.

As to Mrs. Dudley, she died at least in outward com-

14

munion with the church. What the real state of her
mind and conscience might have been, it is unnecessary
for us importently to inquire. She was at length borne
to her long home, and buried by the side of the Major,
her husband, beneath the grassy turf in Pimp's churchyard. .

By this time George and Caroline, the unhappy victims of Richard's vengeance, had recovered from the
effect of their late brutal whipping. At the time of the
sale of the fifteen slaves to Snapp, they were both still
unable to go abroad, hence they escaped the scrutiny
of that sagacious inspector of human cattle, and were
not sold. It is not improbable that had they been well
at the period of his visit, they would have been selected
by him at once for purchase before all others, in consequence of their superior physical advantages.

As soon as George left his bed, he was placed by
Richard's orders, at the very hardest work on the plantation. His drudgery was continual and extreme. It
was his young master's purpose to degrade him to the
utmost ignominy; and it seemed to be Richard's delight
to persecute the poor wretch, who was so completely in
his power, by every annonyance and degradation which
he could devise or imagine.

These things of course rendered the existence of
George one continual scene of misery to him. From his
superior intelligence and knowledge, he knew that he

was intended for, and adapted to, far better things. But he would have been content, had he been treated merely as the rest of his companions in bondage were treated; and if he had only to perform the same tasks to which they were assigned. But George was compelled by Richard's orders, to pick more cotton in a day, and to do a greater and heavier amount of work, than was required from any other slave on the plantation. He had, therefore, often to rise before the break of day, and go forth alone to the cotton field, long before the other slaves began their labors, and to work hard all day without intermission, in order to make up the requisite weight, when night came. During this drudgery his mind, naturally of a thoughtful and sagacious turn, could not but dwell with sad intensity upon the unequaled miseries of his condition and destiny, and had he ever read the mournful history of Jaffier, as portrayed by the powerful pen of the no less unfortunate Otway, he might well have said with him:

" Tell me why, good Heaven,
Thou mad'st me what I am, with all the spirit,
Aspiring thoughts and elegant desires,
That fill the happiest man? Ah rather, why
Did'st thou not form me sordid as my fate,
Baseminded, dull, and fit to carry burdens?
Why have I sense to know, the curse that's on me?
Is this just dealing, nature?"*

*Venice Preserved, Act. I. Scene I.

Nor was the condition of Caroline now much better than that of her husband. Richard's hatred of her was evinced in various ways; and though Julia Dudley endeavored to alleviate the severity of the treatment which she received as much as she could, it was not in her power to counteract the whole strength and intensity of her master's hostility to her.

By Richard's orders, she was degraded from her service in the house, and from her attendance upon her young mistress, to the labors of a field hand in picking cotton. Being unaccustomed all her life to such hard toil, she suffered under it much more than would otherwise have been the case. Another cause now also began to render such work almost unendurable. She was in a short time to become a mother; and her condition becoming each day more delicate, she was more overcome and prostrated by the excess and severity of her toil.

Richard, who frequently rode out to see the field hands at their work, could not fail to perceive the condition in which Caroline was placed, or to see that humanity and decency required that she should be relieved of the rude and heavy labor to which she had been condemned. But he was inexorable. She was kept in the field till within a day of the birth of her child.

During this long endurance of toil and misery, her unhappy husband did all in his power to cheer and

encourage her; but it must be confessed that the prospects before them were dark and gloomy in the extreme.   After returning from the field late at night, as
soon as their rude supper had been despatched, it was
their mutual solace and consolation to engage in those
religious exercises, those prayers and hymns which are
so congenial to the oppressed and the wretched.

At length her child was born,—a beautiful boy, the
offspring of love and misery.   At length the unhappy
girl, having become a mother, had new fountains of
affection opened within her; a new and almost only
source of joy or hope left to her in the world.   Her
child bore the lineaments of both its parents.   It had
their very light complexion, their dark eyes, and their
expressive features; but its constitution, in consequence
of the great and recent toil and lassitude of its mother,
was evidently weak and frail.

As Caroline fondled over her new-born treasure, as
she looked into its little dark and unconscious eyes, and
marked, as a mother only will mark, the movements of
her infant, its helpless innocent artlessness, her soul
was filled with sadness, at the thought of all the miseries
and misfortunes which would be his future inevitable
doom.   She knew and felt that the little unfortunate
had only been born to a cheerless heritage of wretchedness and tears.

Yet its presence, and the tender cares which its
14*

necessities entailed upon her, cheered her heart; and
George himself, though his own spirit had been already
so lacerated, that he felt as if he was friendless and
hopeless in the world, now felt that there was one more
tie to bind him to earth, and to the cheerless career
open before him upon it.   He would caress the little
stranger with affection; and the wounds which lacerated
his heart seemed to heal, as he felt his infant's caress
upon his lips:

> "The caress that falls as soft as snow upon
> The sea, and melts in the heart as instantly."

As soon as Caroline was able to carry her infant, she
was compelled to resume her work in the cotton field.

Sometimes she would lay it upon the ground, near the
spot where she worked, and watch it as well as she
could.   At other times she would carry it upon her
back, slinging it in a kind of sack made for that purpose.
She endured this extra toil cheerfully, for it was a
mother's burden which she bore; and that which would
have been irksome to others, to her was in truth a
pleasure.   And had her strength been equal to her task,
she would have derived naught but additional gratification, in her nearness to the little being whom she had
unfortunately brought into the world.

But the maternal joys and solicitudes of Caroline
were destined to be but of short continuance.   An event

soon occurred which, while it displayed more clearly the depraved attributes of her master, soon deprived her of her infant's care, and relieved that infant of the miseries which would have been its inevitable portion.

One afternoon Richard rode out to the cotton field, where all the slaves were at work. The heat was intensely great, and Caroline, overcome by the weather, had taken advantage of the shade of a tree, to sit down for a few moments and nurse her infant.

"What are you doing there, you lazy huzzy?" exclaimed Richard, as he rode up and discovered her position, and the task she was performing. " Get up and go to your work," he continued, getting off his horse, and approaching her in a threatening manner; "d—n you, I'll teach you to loiter around in this manner."

" But, Master Richard," said Caroline rising, terrified at his savage appearance, "it is so hot, and I am very weak. Won't you let me rest awhile?"

" Rest! no, not an instant, you worthless vagabond. Get about your work. Hurry yourself!"

But Caroline was too much exhausted to move rapidly, and the slowness of her gait irritated her master still more. "Get along," said he, as he dealt her a severe blow on the back, "you and the young dog you carry with you. The little hateful beast!" he continued, looking fiendishly and contemptuously at the unconscious infant. "There! see how it will like that," and he brought his fist quickly and savagely down upon the face of the babe, as it lay in its mother's arms, and before she had time to protect it.

The blow was a most violent one, perhaps more violent than Richard may have intended it to be. His muscular fist flattened the soft flesh of the infant's face, who instantly gave one spasmodic shudder or struggle, in the arms of its wretched mother,—and never moved or breathed again!

The agony of Caroline at the sight of this brutality, and of its fatal consequences, may be imagined, but it cannot be described. Her misery at the death of her infant, was mingled with a momentary rage at the fiendish wretch who had committed the infamous deed. But her rage would have been futile and harmless against her persecutor, and was soon absorbed in the greater emotion of wretchedness, such as a mother only could feel under such circumstances.

Glancing for a moment at her dead babe, laying now unconscious in her arms, and then looking at Richard, she said, regardless of his authority over her, "Oh, you cruel monster! you have murdered my child! Oh, God! what shall I do?" and she fell to the ground and fainted.

When she came to herself, she found several of the female slaves around her, trying to resuscitate her by such means as were in their power.

After she had entirely recovered, she took her dead infant in her arms, and kissed it over and over again, with passionate emotion. The poor little creature had been suddenly relieved from a future life of toil and misery; and already his innocent spirit, redeemed by the Friend of sinners, had winged its happy way to the land of eternal peace.

When Caroline swooned, Richard had given orders to the negro women, whom he had directed to attend her, that as soon as she recovered, she might return to her quarters with her dead child; and he then rode away, indifferently and carelessly, whistling a comic song. In accordance with this order, the wretched woman now began to trudge homeward with her dead burden in her arms; and oh, what a bitter journey was that which she now made! On the way she sat down upon the turf, to think of the horrid scene which had just occurred. She could scarcely believe it to be a reality, until she gazed again upon the little corpse in her arms, all unconscious, and bearing upon its little face the cruel marks and bruises inflicted by the savage blow of its owner; and then indeed she was convinced of its reality.

"My poor innocent babe, farewell! farewell!" said she, as she burst into an agony of tears. She wept long and bitterly. Her heart was indeed broken. She longed to die, and almost envied the happiness of her departed

infant, in that it was now for ever free from the miseries
of existence, and from the terrors of the taskmaster.

She arrived at her quarters but a short time before
the rest of the slaves; and her husband entered their
cabin soon after her arrival. He had not heard as yet
of the misfortune which had overtaken him. The few
slaves in the field who knew of the murder of his infant,
had refrained from communicating the sad intelligence
to him, out of sympathy for his miseries, which they
knew to be already sufficiently great.

As he entered their cabin, he had a kind word ready,
as usual, for his wife; but he was suddenly stopped in
its utterance, for he found Caroline laying on her humble bed, bathed in tears. She had laid her dead infant
down beside her on the bed, and her tears fell upon its
head and features. She arose as George approached,
and pointed in silence to their child.

"What is this?" said he hastily, "as he discovered
that the infant was dead. "Is he indeed dead?" he
continued.

"Yes, he is dead. Master Richard killed him with a
blow of his fist, in the field," she replied.

"Gracious heaven, is this possible!" and he took up
the lifeless form of his child, and kissed its mashed and
defaced features. "Oh, my God!" said he, "must I
endure even this! The cruel fiend! Oh, misery!
misery!"

For a moment, fierce thoughts of vengeance swelled up in his soul; but after an instant he calmly suppressed them; for his religion had taught him, as one of its sublimest truths, that vengeance belongs alone to God.

The next evening George and Caroline buried their murdered child, quietly by moonlight, in the remote spot of ground appropriated to the burial of the slaves of the estate. Two or three only of their fellow slaves were present at the sad ceremony. George himself dug the grave; himself placed the rude box which contained his infant in it; and then himself filled up the grave again.

It was indeed a sad, heart-rending sight, and the agony of the unhappy parents it were vain to attempt to describe. After the grave was filled, George and Caroline sat down beside it to weep. Long and bitterly they wept, when they thought of the unhappy fate of the little innocent, now sleeping calmly below them, in that long eternal slumber, which the judgment morn alone shall terminate. George prayed and sang, as was his usual custom, over the new-made, tiny grave; and then the company returned in sadness to their quarters. He and his wife were drinking the cup of Richard's vengeance to the very dregs.

About six weeks after the death of her child, the health of Caroline began perceptibly to fail. She could

not banish from her mind the dreadful circumstances of
ferocity and cruelty under which that event took place.
This fact,—the anguish of her spirit, combined with the
severity of the labor which she was compelled to endure,
in constantly picking cotton in the field, served to produce this effect upon her health.

She would often steal alone after nightfall to that
little grave, where slept the body of her murdered babe,
to shed a mother's tears upon it.   She uniformly returned to her humble cabin from these visits, still sad-
der, still more hopeless and depressed than before.

George beheld with agony the advancing strides of her
disease. Its ravages on her form and features were
clearly visible. Consumption had marked her for its
victim. As he gazed upon her fading beauty, and her
attenuated frame, his own misery was unspeakable,
when he remembered how soon he would be left absolutely alone and desolate in the world.

At length she could not rise from her bed, and George
was compelled by his tasks, to leave her alone during
the day. One evening, upon his return from the field,
he was startled to see the fearful ravages the disease
had made upon her. She seemed scarcely able to survive a week.

"My dear Carry, you seem much worse to-night,"
said he, as he sat down beside her bed, and taking her
hand, which had now melted away to a shadow.

"Yes, George, I shall leave you soon."

"Don't tell me that," said he. "I can't bear the thought of it," and his eyes were suffused in tears.

"I know I shall not live long;—my only regret in dying, is to leave you here behind me, in sorrow and misery, greater than what you now endure."

"Oh! I can't bear the thought of your leaving me," said George. "It's almost selfish, I know, to wish you to stay here; but how desolate and cheerless will be my condition, when you are gone! Life, even now, would be too great a burden for me to bear, if it was not that I am strengthened by your sympathy and society."

"I love you, indeed," said she, "and I would gladly stay here in this miserable world to cheer and comfort you; to sympathize with you, and to nurse you when you are sick. But I know and feel that is impossible. I'm going soon. And there I shall see our dear babe,— our murdered babe, in that better world!"

George laid his head upon his hands and wept bitterly. He knew it was no empty assertion of his dying wife, that she would fain remain with him, to share his joys and sorrows. But he also knew, that her wish of affection could not be gratified, and that she was soon to bid him a last adieu.

"You will soon follow me, I think, George," said Caroline, fixing her large dark eyes affectionately on her husband. "And we will be happy forever there," and

15

she pointed with her finger upward, and a sweet smile played upon her features, as she looked thither. "I will watch over you, my love, when I am gone."

"Yes, Caroline, I doubt not you will. But I shall still be wretched here, till I meet you yonder."

"Oh! I long to be in Heaven," said she, turning toward him on her couch. "Where is that happy place, George; and what do the blessed inhabitants do there?" said she, inquiringly.

George's religious ideas, as we have said before, were highly intelligent; and he at once answered her, happy to enlighten her views, and if possible, to be the means of preparing her for her last great change.

"Heaven?" said he,—"we cannot tell where it is. The Bible does not teach us that. It may be on some distant planet, where the good dwell together in everlasting felicity. It may be in the air around us; or in the far off blue heaven above us. Or, it may be in the centre of the Universe. The sun itself may be the throne of God; and around that throne may lie those heavenly plains, those golden mansions, and those fragrant gardens of delight,—wherein the redeemed of every clime and kindred, who have been ransomed by the blood of the Lamb, may dwell in eternal joy and rapture."

Caroline listened to her husband with breathless attention. Her religious knowledge and ideas were inferior to his, and he was capable of enlightening her on many points, which now assumed great interest in her mind.

"And what *do* the redeemed in Heaven engage in," said she, following the natural course of ideas on the subject.

"Heaven," said George, "is a state, or a condition, of pure and unmixed felicity. To go there, we must be purified in our natures, and made capable of enjoying holy and spiritual pleasures, for no other enjoyments can exist there. God is the centre of the delights of Heaven. The Redeemed are supremely and infinitely happy in obeying his will; in contemplating the divine perfections of his character and providence, and the glorious works which he has made. There, all the mysteries of Providence and of Revelation, which now distress or puzzle us, will be clearly understood. Our natures and capacities, here so limited and so feeble, will there be expanded, enlarged, and elevated, and we will advance from one degree of excellence and happiness to another, in eternal and unchanging progression."

"Oh! what a happy state," said Caroline, warming into holy rapture at the thought of the blessed abode she hoped so soon to enter.

"But all this happiness" continued George, "is adapted only to the good. The wicked man,—the man in his natural state, hates and abominates such happiness, because he cannot possibly enjoy or appreciate it. It would be the greatest misery to him. That is the reason the Bible says we must be converted, changed, and regenerated, in order to get to heaven. If we went there without that great change, it would bo after all, a hell of torment to us."

"I know it, George. I hope I am prepared for heaven. I am, and have been, a great sinner, but I hope God will forgive me all. Won't you pray for me," said she affectionately, as if she well knew how fervently her husband would offer up prayers to heaven for a soul, whose well-being he cherished more than the value of a world.

"I will," said he. "Let us both pray."

George knelt on the floor, by the side of the bed, and by the side of his sick wife, who had craved his prayers, and he offered to the great Father and God of all, a petition of such earnestness and impressive solemnity, that Caroline was moved to tears. George prayed that his wife might be pardoned and redeemed by the Friend of sinners; and prepared for her last great change. He prayed that God would alleviate her sufferings, and gently smooth the dark valley and shadow of Death, the rugged pathway to the tomb, which she was so soon to tread. He prayed that she might at last reach the Canaan of bliss, beyond the dark rolling waves of Jordan; and that at length, he too, his trials on earth all forever ended, might meet her there, and their dead infant, already gone before them, to inherit everlasting joys; where the fear of the slave-master,—his stripes, and blows, and curses, might never reach or harass them more.

Caroline was much edified and encouraged by these intelligent exercises of George. She loved her faithful husband still more, not as husband merely, but as her only spiritual friend and adviser. She knew it was his kind hand which would guide her trembling spirit on its last dreary journey, now begun; and conduct her, with undying affection, to the confines of earth; lead her safely, at least until she entered within that dark mysterious veil, whose heavy folds shut out from mortal gaze the mysteries of the future state.

After the prayer was ended, George rose from his knees, and sang a hymn. Caroline attempted feebly to accompany him. Her strength soon failed her, and George alone, with his strong manly voice, continued the strain. He sang in deep and solemn tones the well-known verses:

"There is a land of pure delight,
Where saints immortal reign,
Eternal day excludes the night,
And pleasures banish pain,

There everlasting spring abides,
And never fading flowers;
Death like a narrow sea divides
This heavenly land from ours.

15*

> Could we but climb where Moses stood,
>   And view the landscape o'er,
> Not Jordan's stream, nor Death's cold flood,
>   Should fright us from the shore."

As he sang these beautiful lines with religious fervor, and with that chastened enthusiasm which is so natural to the intelligent negro, Caroline experienced a religious rapture, as she listened, which seemed almost a foretaste of heaven itself. The impression produced upon her mind by the new ideas her husband had just suggested to her; her own physical condition, and her affection—undying and eternal as it was for him, whom she was so soon to leave behind her,—all combined to fill her soul with overpowering emotions. She lay in silence, and wept tears of mingled joy and sorrow. His voice seemed to her like the voice of an angel, calling to her from the heavenly spheres, to come away from earth to the abodes of the blessed.

> "Music is always sweet, but oh!
>   When loved lips sing,
> Like ring-doves' notes the measures flow,—
>   Love's murmuring.
>
> Music is always sweet—but, when
>   A loved one hears;
> 'Tis like the sounds which pious men,
>   Toll of the spheres!"

Shortly after this occurrence, Miss Julia accidentally heard of Caroline's illness. The latter had carefully abstained from troubling her young mistress, by sending her any message respecting her condition. Since Caroline had been compelled to work in the fields, and had therefore been withdrawn from attendance on the person of Julia, her absence from her work could not of course attract her attention. But she accidentally heard of Caroline's critical condition from one of her female servants.

The kind-hearted lady immediately visited the sick girl at her cabin. She entered quite unexpectedly, and found Caroline alone, weeping, upon her bed. She wept at the thought of so soon bidding her husband a long farewell. There was no other tie to bind her to earth.

"Why Caroline, they tell me you are dangerously sick," said Julia, as she hastily entered.

"I am, Mistress Julia. I don't think I shall live long. I think I have consumption," she replied.

"I hope not," responded Julia. "What is there I can do for you?" she inquired.

"I know of nothing," said she. "My husband nurses me when he comes home from the field, and during the day, I lay here, and await his coming in the evening."

Julia looked around the apartment to see what comforts Caroline might have, or want, suitable to her condition. She found in the fire-place a small teapot, with a little warm tea in it, which Caroline drank from time to time; and on a plate, some black-looking bitter gum, which Uncle Jesse had obtained from burning pine knots, and which the negroes regarded as beneficial to those afflicted with consumption. These were all the medicines which the apartment contained.

"I will send you some cough drops from the house, Caroline, and some other medicine, and something better to eat than this hard rough corn-bread," said she; "and I will get Richard to allow your husband to remain at home with you during the day, so that he may nurse you better," she added. "Be of good cheer. I hope you may soon be better." But the violent cough which racked the frame of the invalid, and her generally emaciated appearance, forbade the idea that any improvement or recovery was possible.

"Good bye! Caroline," said she, as she was taking her leave. "I hope next time to see you better."

"Thanks for your kindness, Mistress Julia. I thank you, but I have no hope," was her reply, as the graceful form of Julia vanished out of the humble room,—the image of the health and beauty which she herself had once possessed.

Time rolled on, and Caroline rapidly approached her grave. She was soon to enter within its eternal gates. One Sunday afternoon, Uncle Jesse, the preacher, and his wife Harriet, who had witnessed a year since, the marriage of George and Caroline, and several other slaves, were assembled around the bed of the dying girl. They intended to hold religious exercises in the chamber of death, for the special benefit of the departing spirit. Caroline had become much worse. She was sinking rapidly. · Her cough was dreadful, and her weakness and prostration were extreme. Her beauty had all fled. Nought told of the splendid creature she once had been, but her large dark eye, and clear, full, and finely arched forehead.

She lay upon her bed, calmly and patiently suffering from the fever which consumed her. There was no hope for her recovery now, and she knew it. Silence reigned among the sad company, who conversed around her bed only in whispers. Caroline seemed to be dreaming, and an aspect of sweet serenity and peace rested upon her features.

> "How lovely was the smile that played
> O'er thy pale cheek and forehead fair;
> No withering look, no dark'ning shade,
> All, all was heavenly radiance there!"

"Now, George," said Uncle Jesse, in a low and subdued voice, " you knows everything; tell me, does you believe dat such poor miserable niggers as we is, kin go to heaven beside white folks, eh ?"

George was not prepared to debate with Jesse any very abstruse theological questions at that moment; but the innocent sincerity of Jesse's manner convinced him that his question was honestly put for the sake of information, and he replied :

"Certainly I do, Jesse."

"Well, but what will de great white folks say, when they gits to heaven, and sits down on the t'other side of Jordan, and looks around 'em, and sees de poor niggers a sittin' there too. When they sings God's praise, and our people jines 'em, they'l be 'sulted, wont they?"

"Never, Jesse. If the white folks, our masters, ever get to heaven, they will have learned, before they get there, to love all their fellow creatures, white and black, as themselves; and when they see us there, too, if we ever are so fortunate as to get there, they will love us as brethren and equals, because God regards us all in that light, and because we are such."

"Well, den, I b'lieves that many of de white folks won't go to heaven, becase we is to have a seat dare, too. They'd rather singe and roast in hell, alone, than enjoy heaven wid de niggers. Dats what I think. Now what would ole Missus, who'se dead and gone, say, when she gits to heaven wid her silks and satins, if she was to see my old Harriet dare, in one ob de heabenly seats, with her old cotton frock on. Why, she'd skreech right out, and leave 'em."

"Well," replied George, "if the white people won't go to heaven because there are negroes there, who have been redeemed by the same blood which has redeemed themselves (if indeed they are redeemed), they will find the same black associates in the other place—the place of torment. There are specimens of our unfortunate race both in heaven and hell, as I believe," said he.

" If de white folks," continued Jesse, " kin stay in heaven with de colored folks, and worship God and de Lamb there together, I can't help but think, what a wonderful change gits into 'em, from what dey is here, eh ?"

" The grace of God makes the difference, Jesse," said George ; "that grace makes all men brothers; takes away the spirit of cruelty, pride and selfishness, and makes us love our neighbors as ourselves, whatever may be their characters, and colors, and conditions in life. You may rest assured, that whoever gets to heaven, will possess there the spirit and disposition of the Redeemer of men ; and all pride, jealousy, rivalry, and self-glory will be forever rooted out of their hearts."

" Well, den, if dat's de case," said Jesse, "I kin believe how all de good people, white and black, kin go to heaven together, and stay in de same place, widout having a partic'lar heaven for de white folks, all nicely cushioned and fixed up ; and a place boarded off for de niggers, sep'rate by theirselves, where de white folks won't come."

"No, there can be no such division there," said George.

" Then I wants to go dare. I'd like to see ole Missus,

how she gits along; and whether she likes de loud singing of de niggers dar, when dey sings,

"Jerusalem my happy home,
Name ober dour to me;"

kase she used to be so monstrous put out here, wid de
noise, when our meetin' used to sing dem words so loud
togedder."

"Ah, Jesse," replied George, " you must not think of
such ideas.   You must remember that heaven is a mysterious state, and that there are many things connected
with it, which we cannot now explain.   Now, we look
through a glass darkly, as the good book says, because
God has not seen fit to reveal everything to us.   We
must have faith, that all which we cannot understand,
he will make plain and clear in that future world toward
which we are going."

"Oh, yes! I guess it must be so," replied Jesse,
good-naturedly.

But the attention of the humble company was attracted, and their conversation stopped, by a sudden
convulsive movement on the bed.   All eyes were eagerly
turned there.   Caroline had begun to be rapidly worse,
and to the dismay and sorrow of her friends, she was
evidently near her end.   She was in great pain and
agony.   She coughed with fatal violence; and the severity of the paroxysms was so great, that she seemed
about to faint or expire under them.

"George," said she, feebly, in an interval of repose, "George, I'm dying—I'll soon be gone."

"I hope not, my love, I hope not," he replied, kissing her pale lips.

"Yes, I shall soon be at rest. It will soon be over." She took his hand in her's, and said "farewell, my husband, farewell, I'm sorry to leave you behind me here, I know how sad and wretched you will be. But you must put your trust in that kind Being, of whom you have spoken to me so often and so well. He will protect you, until we meet again in heaven!" Her tears and sobs here stopped her utterance; and George, who sat beside her on the bed, wept as if his heart would break.

He felt fully the sad truth of her words, that he would be left lonely and cheerless enough on earth.

"Farewell, Uncle Jesse," she continued, holding out her hand, "Farewell Aunt Harriet, I hope to meet you all in heaven. Continue in the right way, and you will all get there."

The groans of the humble company here became so loud and heart-rending, that her voice could no longer be heard, and she paused.

"Yes Carry," blubbered out Jesse, as well as he could. "Yes Carry, we'll try and meet you thar, in heaven."

Silence reigned around the cabin, and no sound was now heard within it, but the feeble voice of the dying girl.

"Put your trust in God," said George, "my dear

16

Caroline, and he will conduct you through the dark valley and shadow of death, and see you safe on the other shore of Jordan."

"Oh! George," said Caroline smiling, "I am so happy now. I feel that I am going to Heaven, to be at rest. I feel that I am pardoned and redeemed by the blood of the Lamb. Oh! I think I hear already the hymns of the angels in glory, singing hallelujah! glory to God and the Lamb! and I long to join them in that immortal song. And there too, I shall see my poor babe, my little boy, he who was murdered. Yes, I think I see his spirit there, among the multitude of the Redeemed, holding out his little arms to me inviting me to come. Oh! glory to God, I shall soon be there," she continued, as she kept her eyes fixed intently on the rough ceiling above her.

There was a pause for a few moments, as George did not wish to interrupt the happy trance into which Caroline seemed to have fallen. After a moment her eyes fell upon George's face, and she said to him, "George, there is a tea-cup yonder, upon that shelf," pointing to a rude cupboard in one corner of the room; "bring it to me," she added.

George did so; she took the cup in her thin fingers, and removing several spools and bunches of loose thread which were upon the top, she took out from the bottom a small plain gold breast-pin, which Miss Julia had formerly given her, in happier days; and said, "here, my dear husband, is a trifle which I wish you to keep in remembrance of me; when I am dead and under the ground, wherever you are, whenever you look at this little trinket, think of me, and believe that I love you still and forever."

George took the breast-pin, and kissed it; "I shall keep it while I live," said he, "in memory of you;" and he pinned it on the inside of his shirt, and beneath his roundabout.

"And you must meet me in heaven, George," she continued, after another severe spell of coughing. "Yes, in heaven I hope we will meet again."

The excitement of this scene had been too much for the enfeebled girl, and a sudden spasm of visible agony passed over her face, telling a fearful tale of what changes were going on within. When she recovered from it, she continued feebly; "Yes, I am happy now; the worst is passed. It will all soon be over."

George still retained possession of her hand. He placed her head as high as he could, with the help of the poor pillows on the bed. Jesse and the rest surrounded her couch, sobbing and crying, as they saw how soon her spirit was to take its flight, and the last agony be endured.

Caroline was evidently sinking rapidly; her breath became shorter and quicker. The large drops of death-

sweat stood upon her smooth, pale brow; a feeble
twitching of the nerves about the mouth and lips, be-
tokened the last agony of suffocation; there was, at
length, a long, deep sigh, and one spasmodic shudder of
the limbs, and the head fell back; the mouth remained
open; the eyeballs turned up and became fixed; and
her immortal spirit bursting its earthly cerements,
sprang upward toward its God and heaven.

> "True, 'tis an awful thing to die;
> But the dark vale once trod,
> Heaven lifts its everlasting portals high,
> And bids the pure in heart behold their God."

Farewell! thou wearied and persecuted soul! Thou
hast found rest at last. Thy short span of life,
saddened by clouds and darkness, though heaven ordained it to be one of hope and delight—is ended now,
and merged into that eternal day which knows no shade
nor setting. Thou wilt sigh and weep no more, for
ever!

As the poor weeping slaves hung around the humble
couch on which Caroline had just breathed her last,
their pent up sobs and groans broke forth without re
straint. They thought of the sad fate of her, so young,
so fair, and once so gay and happy; whose early end
had closed so sadly and so cruelly; for they well knew
all the circumstances of the case, and the many outrages
she had endured from Richard.

After Jesse had left George's cabin to go to his own, he met his master, Richard Dudley; whose attention was attracted to him by the swollen appearance of his eyes, as if he had been weeping. Richard stopped and demanded, what was the matter—what he had been crying about?

"Oh! Massa Richard," said he, "she's gone, she's gone at last!—gone to glory!"

"Who's gone, and gone to glory?" inquired Richard, roughly.

"Oh! it's pore Caroline, she just dead and gone!" replied Jesse, overcome with emotion.

"Ha! Caroline's dead, eh?" said Richard, passing on. "Then let her die, the cursed huzzy; 'tis what I wanted;" he continued, soliloquizingly. "Had she listened to my demand, and yielded to my passion, instead of marrying this worthless scoundrel, George, she'd be alive now, I warrant me, and living like a queen. Well! she was a splendid creature, when I wanted her. As my mistress, she should have commanded wealth, luxury and splendor. She should have been the mistress of my plantation, and I would have done well by her: let her go—she's got just what she deserved. And as for this George, her husband," gritting his teeth and clinching his fist, "I'll punish him yet, for his audacity in marrying that girl; I'll torment his life out. One of my victims I have already finished; the other I'll pursue

16*

with my vengeance, until he hides his head in the grave!"

By this time Richard had reached George's hut, where the dead body of Caroline lay; he entered abruptly, and without taking any notice of George, walked up to the bed to take a last, malignant look at the remains of his first victim, or rather his second, when we take into consideration the cruel fate of her child.

"You've come to that, have you?" said he, as he regarded contemptuously the emaciated form of the poor girl, as she lay extended on her humble bed. And he took hold of the hair of her head, once so abundant and magnificent, and carelessly pulled her head from side to side, in order to get a better view of her attenuated appearance.

George witnessed this act of brutality, but he said nothing; he mastered the emotion of indignation which it produced in him, and calmly remarked, "She's at rest now, Master Richard; her troubles are over!"

"Hold your tongue, you black scoundrel!" said Richard, fiercely. "Who told you to speak?" With this he gave the corpse a smart blow on the face with his open hand—the last farewell salute of the master to his slave upon earth—to his half-sister—and then turned abruptly on his heel and went out, scowling upon George vindictively as he went.

Julia Dudley soon heard of Caroline's death. Aunt

Harriet made bold enough to go to the house, and communicate the fact to her.

The sympathy and regret of this noble-minded girl were at once deeply excited. She immediately gave orders that proper material should be sent to the humble abode of the dead, with which to make a decent shroud; and she also directed the carpenter on the place to make Caroline a handsome walnut coffin.

When she had been laid out and the time of burial arrived, a few negroes on the plantation had been allowed to stay at home from work, to attend the funeral; the cabin was pretty well filled with the weeping company. Uncle Jesse preached them a short sermon after his own fashion, then sang and prayed. The grief of poor George, as they were about to carry away his beloved from the humble home which she had so cheered and illumined by her love and affection, was uncontrollable, yet he strove to confine his anguish within his own breast. Just as the funeral was about to move, and as they were going to take their last farewell of the corpse, and nail down the coffin lid, Julia Dudley came in, gracefully attired in black, carrying in her hand a beautiful wreath of white roses. She went slowly up to the coffin, gazed for some moments upon the remains of the poor girl, whom she doubtless knew to be her half-sister, though the unconquerable prejudices of education and habit had never induced her to acknowledge her as such

—and her tears began to flow. She gently laid the wreath of flowers upon the bosom of the dead, and as she turned to leave the room, said audibly, amid her subdued sobs, "Poor girl! Farewell for ever!"

Caroline was buried by the side of the little grave, in which slept the body of her murdered infant. Those poor, humble, defenceless slaves shed bitter tears, as the remains of one so young and so fair were lowered into their long home. But one heart was desolate there, beyond all the power of language to express. George was as miserable as it was possible for the unfortunate and the desolate of soul to be. He returned to his lonely hut, laid himself down upon his bed, and prayed that God would take him from this world of sorrow, to that better land, whither his wife and child,—all he loved on earth,—had now gone before him, and were forever at rest.

When reflecting upon the conduct of Richard Dudley, in reference to his slaves, and especially in reference to Caroline, whom he knew to be his half-sister, the offspring of the same father as himself, we cannot forbear to dwell for a moment upon the operation of slavery, in regard to one important and prominent phase of it. We mean the treatment of masters toward their own children, whom they beget into bondage, and whom they ever afterward retain in that position.

This is one of the most lamentable sights to be seen

on the face of the globe. By the operation of slavery, and by its *inevitable* operation, too, in a Christian land, crowded with churches, and in a republican country, the freest and happiest, in many respects, on earth,— the revolting spectacle is constantly presented in myriads of instances, of men begetting children; then retaining them through life in a state of the most abject and most degrading bondage; and in many instances selling them to distant and unknown regions, often to cruel and brutal masters, subjecting them to stripes and chains, and sometimes to death itself; all for money,— for the sake of profit.

Now we desire to ask any rational being, who has the capacity to think, where is the difference, in the light of common sense, between a man selling for money, or abusing in the most brutal manner, his own child by a white woman, and his own child by a quadroon woman, or by a mulatto woman, or by a woman black as ebony?

In all these cases alike, his children are his own flesh, and blood, and bones; and yet he sells them for gold. He treats them often with a cruelty unfit for brutes. If a man were to sell his white child for money, he would be stigmatized as the most infamous wretch that lives— as a heathen, a savage. And the law, or the institution, which would authorize him so to do, and protect him in so doing, would be regarded by the civilized world as a disgrace to humanity and to civilization.

Yet here is an institution, established and protected by law, in a Christian country, and in a republic to boot, whose inevitable operation it is to induce men to sell their own flesh, and blood, and bones, for money; simply because they are a very little shade darker than themselves. This institution inevitably leads men often to abuse, and in many instances to murder their own offspring, or their half-brothers, half-sisters, and other kindred in slavery, without any legal restraint or penalty of a preventive character whatever. Intelligent republican men do it, and the law of the land protects them, and authorizes their crime. Now where is the difference between this actual case, and the case just supposed, where a man's children are entirely white? There is no difference—none. The thing is as monstrous and as infamous in the one real case, as it would be in the other putative case.

The very act which a Turk would scorn to do; which a Persian, a Japanese, or even a Malay, would turn away from in abhorrence and disgust; that very act do thousands of American freemen every day, under the plain authority of Christian and republican law; and that too, led on by the example of some of the greatest lights and celebrities of the nation.

As this last assertion may be doubted, let us look at a few facts, which cannot be called in question.

Thomas Jefferson, the very author of the immortal

Declaration of Independence, was guilty of the infamy of having children by his female slaves, and afterwards of having them sold at public auction, in his own presence, and that before a crowd of men who knew that he was the father of the slaves there placed under the hammer. His children by his slaves were *very numerous:* but by his will, he did not manumit one of them, but left those whom he had not already sold for money, soul and body, to degradation and the cartwhip.

A daughter of Thomas Jefferson was sold, some years ago, by public auction, at New Orleans. She was publicly known as the offspring of the illustrious statesman,

"Who dreamt of freedom in a slave's embrace;"

and she brought a high premium, because she was the daughter, and carried in her veins the blood of the great Apostle of freedom.

James Madison, another patriot, almost as illustrious in the annals of American liberty as Jefferson, had no white children; but had a numerous family by his various slaves, whom he treated, living and dying, precisely in the same way as did his intimate friend, Thomas Jefferson.

A few years since, while Senator Foote, of Mississippi, was occupying a high position in the Senate of the United States, and that too, as a democrat, and the most radical of republicans, his own half-brother, a son

by the same father, was an ostler in a stable in Washington city, almost within reach of the eloquent voice
of his brother, when declaiming loudly and fiercely of
universal human freedom, and the inalienable rights of
man! That brother of the senator slept in the loft of a
stable, consigned only to ignomy and life-long servitude;
nor would the "honorable senator" have stirred a finger
to confer freedom, and social or mental elevation upon
his own blood and kindred. We say, he *would* not do
it, judging from the single and satisfactory proof, that
he *did not* do it.

Very many similar instances might be narrated.
Hundreds of representatives in Congress, of senators, of
State senators and representatives, of judges, of jurists,
to say nothing of men of wealth, and high social standing in the South, might be adduced to prove, that the
enormity in question is one of universal frequency
there; that the law protects it, and that public sentiment, poisoned by the presence and influence of the
slave power, excuses it, permits it, even justifies and
defends it.

The advocates of slavery urge, that the negro is a fit
subject for bondage, because he belongs to an entirely
different and inferior genus, or even species, from that
of the white race. And they also contend, that he is
incapable of self-government, because he is thus inferior.
But this argument must certainly fall to the ground, or

be wholly inapplicable to all those slaves, who bear in their veins the nobler blood of white men. And especially should that argument be null and impotent, when applied to those slaves who bear such close kindredship to the powerful and far reaching intellects of the author of the Declaration of American Independence, his associates, and his successors in fame, in office, and in mental supremacy!

CHAPTER XVI.

LITTLE ADA DUDLEY.

" Alas ! regardless of their doom
  The little victims play !
No sense have they of ills to come,
  Nor care beyond to-day;
Yet see how all around them wait
The ministers of human fate,
  And black misfortune's baleful train.
Ah ! show them where in ambush stand,
To seize their prey, the murderous band;
Ah ! tell them they are m)n."—GRAY.

IT is time that we should introduce to the acquaintance
of the reader, the most interesting member of the Dudley family,—little Ada.

This child, at the period of which we speak, was five
years old; and never had the innocence and happy artlessness of youth combined more successfully with great
personal beauty, to constitute an attractive and lovely
being.

Little Ada was the child of Major Dudley's old age.
Her advent into the world was scarcely looked for, and
being unexpected, her appearance, and the surprise it

created, were the more agreeable. Her parents had always regarded her with that tender and partial affection, which is generally entertained for the children of one's old age. She was pre-eminently the pet and idol of the whole family; and the poor slaves on the plantation had long esteemed her as almost a being of an unearthly and heavenly nature,—too pure and good for this sphere of sin and suffering.

And the appearance and disposition of Ada seemed to warrant such an extravagant supposition. Exceedingly gentle and affectionate, she appeared instinctively to love everybody. It did not seem possible for her to exhibit the least petulance or severity of temper; but a constant dispoistion to be submissive and pleased with everything, characterized her constant life.

Nor was she at all deficient in intelligence. Her quickness of apprehension; her curiosity to see and learn; the readiness with which she comprehended things which attracted her attention and were explained to her, proved that the child was one of more than ordinary capacity.

Her personal appearance would of itself have attracted the attention of the most casual observer. Her figure, though slight, was of perfect mould; and her countenance was intelligent and expressive in a high degree. Her large, dark, hazel eyes, proved her the daughter of a Southern clime, and indicated that she possessed a soul capable of deep and intense emotions; her forehead was beautifully rounded, and her hair, dark as the raven's wing, fell in long, abundant, and luxuriant curls over her shoulders. Her complexion was as clear and delicate as wax; and were it not for the ceaseless animation of her manner and movements, she might almost have been mistaken for a doll, or for the counterfeit resemblance of some infant angel.

Her movements were characterized by great ease and gracefulness. During the whole day, she was running to and fro through the house; and her sweet though feeble voice, might ever be heard chaunting some favorite lay or ditty. This child was, as a matter of course, a great favorite with her sister Julia; and especially since the death of Major Dudley, her affections had clustered around this fair child with renewed and increased intensity of attachment.

Ada was ever rather shy of her brother Richard; his nature was too stern and repulsive, to afford much sympathy with any one; yet he occasionally fondled with her, as a bear may be supposed to play with a kitten. She had rarely made any acquaintance with the slaves on the estate; they were too numerous, and were too far removed by their constant toils and ceaseless occupations from her usual haunts, ever to meet them; except those few, whose duties confined them entirely to the house and family of their owner. With Caroline alone, during her lifetime, Ada had been on terms of intimacy; and now that the poor girl had been removed from her society, there was no one among the slaves on the estate, with whom she felt inclined, as yet, to be intimate.

One day Richard ordered George to go into the garden, attached to the mansion house, and to work there, instead of going out as usual, to the cotton field. During the course of the day, little Ada came tripping down the large gravelled walk in the centre of the garden, and soon approached George, who was spading and raking a new bed for strawberries. Her person was no stranger to George, though this was the first time that he had ever conversed with his little mistress. After watching for a few moments the movements of the slave, she said gaily to him, "What is that bed for, that you are raking?"

"It is a strawberry bed, little mistress; do you like strawberries?" said George.

"Oh yes, very much, indeed;—I like strawberries and cream. What is your name?"

"My name is George—don't you know me?"

"No, I don't know you, but I have often seen you," replied the child.

"How old are you?"

"I will be five years old next month, so sister Julia tells me," said she.

17*

The garden on the Dudley estate was situated on one side of the house, and was a large plot of ground, of about an acre, appropriated to the production of both flowers and vegetables. It was very tastefully laid out, and well tended by several of the slaves, who were especially detailed to that work, and who possessed considerable knowledge of gardening. This had been George's special department of labor before he had incurred Richard's hatred, and had been, in consequence, degraded to the toil of the cotton field.

While the preceding short conversation was progressing, George did not cease his work, but divided his attention between that and his young companion. He was much charmed and delighted with the innocence and sprightliness of little Ada. Here, he thought, was something on earth, for him to love; his desolate heart immediately felt disposed to cling around this tender and attractive object of regard, and bestow upon it that overflowing wealth of affection which swelled up within him, and which had been deprived of its only and cherished objects by the cruelty of his master. He stopped a moment and gazed with admiration and love upon the fair being before him; who looked more beautiful from the unusual color given to her cheeks by her late exercise. He thought that just such a child as this, so fair, so innocent, and so attractive, would one day have been his; such an one would he have folded in his arms, and pressed to his bosom, had it not been for the unnatural cruelty of the very brother of the innocent creature before him.

"You are five years old," resumed George; "you will soon grow up to be a big woman."

"Yes, by and by; but not till after I go to school; sister Julia is going to send me before long. What makes you look so sad, George? I always see you look distressed; does any thing trouble you?" inquired Ada.

In truth, the generally mournful appearance of George was in consonance with his prevalent feelings, and could not escape the notice of any observer; even of a child so young as Ada.

"Why am I sad, did you say? Well, I will tell you. I once had a little child, interesting and pretty like you; but it is dead, and that makes me sad," said George.

"It is dead? Why, what made it die?" inquired the innocent child.

George started at this inquiry, as if a dagger had penetrated his heart. Yes; *why* did it die? The answer to this question opened a flood of torturing remembrances to his mind. And, if he answered truly to his questioner, how unwelcome and seve e would that answer have been! He did not, for one moment, entertain the thought of wounding the poor child's sensibilities, by telling her that her brother was murderer, and that his hands had been stained with the blood of his dear infant. He evaded the searching query, and replied: "It met with a dreadful accident, and was killed."

"Was killed!—a little child killed! How dreadful to think of it! How dreadful, if I was to be killed! How distressed my sister Julia would be, if I was killed," said Ada innocently.

"Yes, and I would be distressed too, my sweet little Ada. I hope *you* will never be killed; but live long to grow up to be a great, big, handsome woman," said George.

"Where is your little child's mother? It had a mother, hadn't it?" inquired Ada.

This was another unconscious blow struck to the very heart of poor George. Yet he subdued his rising emotions, and answered calmly; "It's mother is dead too."

"Both are dead. May be she died of grief, because her baby was killed," said Ada inquiringly.

"And so indeed she did," said George. "Her heart was broken, and she could not live, after her baby had been killed."

"How cruel to kill such a baby, and its mother too. Pray tell me, George, who killed it?" said Ada.

"I had better not tell you, my dear little girl."

"Why not?" she eagerly inquired.

"You would not like or love the person, who did it, after that. So I had better not tell you."

"Very well then. I don't want to know who did it. Why don't you rest yourself; you work too hard, don't you? See how the perspiration rolls off your face and hands."

"I am a poor slave, Ada, and slaves must work hard, else their masters will punish them; and I have already been punished very hard."

"You are a slave? Well, but you must rest too. Now don't work so hard. Stop awhile, and pull me a bunch of roses from these bushes. Won't you, please?"

"Yes, I will a little while, but I can't stop long, Ada. I must finish all these beds to-day yet, and I can't get them done before night, unless I hurry."

George went to some rose bushes, which lined the garden fence, and pulled off a small bouquet for Ada, and then handed them to her.

"Thank you, George. You are very kind. I only wish you had your little baby yet, and its mother. I'm sure you deserve to have them. You are so industrious, and so obliging. Good bye. I'm going to sister Julia now. I'll tell her that you had a little baby once, and that it was killed by somebody. Good bye!"

With these words the fair creature gaily tripped up the garden walk toward the house; soon entered the verandah; and disappeared within the lattice work.

When left alone to his reflections, George could not but dwell upon the difference between the natures of these two beings, possessing the same flesh and blood, with whom he had to do. The one had robbed him, by excessive acts of cruelty, of those whom he most loved and cherished on earth. The other seemed almost kind and tender enough to repay that loss, by filling within his heart the aching vacuum, which their loss had created there. He prayed to Heaven for resignation to his bitter fate; and for blessings on the head of the fair and lovely innocent, who had just left him.

The next day, George's work took him again to the garden; and he had not been very long engaged at his task, before Ada came tripping toward him again. Her short acquaintance of yesterday soon had ripened, between such congenial hearts, into a strong and tender friendship. The fresh morning air, with its invigorating breezes, made Ada more beautiful than ever. She possessed the appearance of robust health,—and of a hearty child, whose excellent constitution promised a long continuance of years.

George was delighted at having found a new object of affection in little Ada. They soon entered into pleasant conversation.

"You told me yesterday, George, that your baby had been killed. I told sister Julia that; and she told me never to say anything about it again to anybody, especially to brother Richard. Why did she tell me that?"

inquired Ada earnestly, and looking up to George's face, as he kept raking away.

"Well, perhaps because he lost a slave by its death, and he does not like to lose his slaves," answered George, disposed charitably to evade the true answer to the unlucky question,

"You said you were a slave," continued Ada. "What does that mean?" and she sat down upon a little bank of moss on the other side of the walk, disposed her little skirt neatly around her limbs, and prepared herself, quite deliberately, to receive the communication she expected George to give.

"A slave?" said George, resting for a moment; "is it possible, Ada, you do not know what a slave is? Well, I will tell you. Some people have a right to buy other people, if they have money enough; and when they have bought them, they are the masters, and those they buy are their slaves. And the slaves must do just whatever their masters order them."

"Have you always been a slave?" inquired Ada, apparently perfectly satisfied with the explanation of slavery which George had given her.

"Yes, I was born a slave," said George, resuming his work; "and I have lived a slave all my life, and expect now to die a slave."

"Where were you born, George?" inquired Ada.

"I was born here, on this very plantation. Here I have lived all my life, and here I expect to die."

"Do tell me when your baby was born, and who was its mother. I know you must have loved them very much, and must be very sorry that they are dead."

"My baby's mother," continued George, "was a young woman, whom you have often seen. Her name was Caroline, and used to wait on your sister Julia."

"Oh! Caroline? Yes, I remember Caroline. She was your baby's mother, was she?"

"Well, when our baby died, we dug a hole in the ground, about so long," and George defined the dimensions of the infant's grave with his spade, upon the garden walk; "then we put the little coffin with the baby in it, about so long and about so broad, down into the hole; and then we covered it up with the earth, and there it still remains."

While George was giving this simple history of his child's burial, he saw that the big tears began to flow from the dark eyes of Ada, as she eagerly watched upon the ground the marks drawn by George, to indicate the dimensions of the grave.

"Poor little baby," said Ada, sorrowfully, "to have to go down into such a dark hole under the ground. I hope I won't ever have to go into such a place; do you think I will, George; do you?" she eagerly inquired, gazing up into his face for an answer.

"Oh, no, I hope not," said he.

"It must be so dreadful!" she continued.

"Yes, but when little girls and babies die, you know that their spirits go to heaven, even if their bodies do go down into the ground. They go to heaven, Ada, and there they are happy. There is where my little baby has gone," said he.

"So my sister Julia told me. She said your little baby was in a better place; that it was in heaven. And she said the baby's mother was there too. Ain't that so?"

"Yes, I hope so, I believe she is in heaven; and I hope to meet her there some day too," said George, looking up from his work, to the clear blue sky far above him, where he almost thought he saw, among the heavenly hosts, the spirit of his beloved Caroline, smiling to him in his toil.

"You don't like to be a slave, do you, George?" inquired Ada, with earnestness.

"Not much, my dear Ada. But I can't help it; I must submit to my fate. I was born a slave, and I suppose I must die one."

"You would like to be free, wouldn't you?"

"Oh yes, I would; but that can never be," replied George, with the sad consciousness of the truth of the declaration.

"But I will ask brother Richard to set you free. I'll

18

tell him you have lost your little baby and its mother, and you would like to be free, and I will ask him to make you so. I wonder if he will do it for me? Do you think ne would?"

"I am afraid not, Ada. I don't think that I will ever be free. I have given up all hope, now."

"Now don't you do that. There, I see brother Richard now on the verandah; I will run and ask him." And little Ada ran with all her might and main up the long garden-walk toward the house, to beset Richard to set George free, especially because he had lost his baby and its mother!

How often do the innocent prattlings of childhood administer to the most desperate sinners among men, reproofs more searching and effective, than all the thundering eloquence of a Massillon or a Chalmers!

Richard Dudley was sitting on the verandah alone, smoking, and looking out over the plantation. Ada ran up to him, got between his knees, and said gaily, "Brother Richard, I want to ask you something."

"Well, what is it, Ada?"

"I want you to set George, in the garden there, free, won't you?"

Richard's brow instantly lowered at the utterance of this request. He imagined that George had suggested to Ada the absurd demand, not with any hope of having it gratified, but as an indirect reproof of the cruelties which he knew had been inflicted upon him.

"Who told you to ask me that!" he inquired rather rudely.

The child started, and quickly said: "Oh, no one, I ask it of myself."

"Did not George, yonder, tell you to ask me?"

"No, he did not, brother Richard; he never told me any such thing. He told me that he was a slave, and that was all. Won't you set him free, brother?"

"Not now, my dear, at any rate. You must not trouble me with any such requests. When you ask me again for anything, let it be for something that little girls ought to have."

"Very well, then," answered Ada, as she left her brother and ran back again to George, who was working away in the garden.

"Brother Richard says, not now; and that I mus'nt trouble him about such things. I can't help it. I wish I was your master, George; I would soon set you free; said Ada, hastily, as she reached the spot where George worked. "I should like to see the little grave where your baby is buried; won't you show it to me, George?"

"Oh yes, Ada, if you would like to see it."

"Where is it?" said she.

"It is over in the burying-ground, yonder, where all the slaves are buried;" and he pointed toward the lonely spot where his wife and child lay. "But I can't leave my work now, to go there."

"When will you take me there?" said Ada.

"Well, to-morrow is Sunday, and we don't have to work on Sunday. After dinner, to-morrow, I will take you to see my baby's grave."

"Well, then, to-morrow, when dinner is over."

"But you must not tell any body, will you?"

"Oh no, I won't, if you don't wish me to," replied the little creature, as she tripped away up the garden, and left the slave to his own sad reflections.

The next day, about four o'clock, as George was sitting in his cabin door, he saw little Ada running down the lane which led between the slave cabins, evidently intent upon the fulfilment of George's yesterday's promise, to show her his little baby's grave. As she approached, gaily dressed, George saw that she held in her hands several stems of rose-bush, with the roots still adhering to them, and also a small bouquet of flowers.

"I'm come to go with you now, George, to see the grave of your little baby over yonder," said she; "will you go?"

"Yes, I'm ready. But what is this you have here? What are you going to do with these rose bushes?"

"Sister Julia told Jane to pull them up and give them to me; and told me to plant them on the grave of your little baby; you'll help me, wont you?" said Ada.

The tears came to the eyes of poor George, as this small indication of the sympathy of his noble young mistress with his griefs, proved to him that there was some pity still left for him in the world.

"Yes, I'll help you, my love; we'll plant them together on the little grave of my babe."

The day was favorable to the presence of tender emotions in the heart of man, black or white. All nature seemed buried in calm repose; her broad surface was arrayed in her most brilliant and attractive hues. The two friends pursued their way across the fields, toward the slaves' grave-yard. Ada took hold of George's hand, and thus they passed along together toward the spot suggestive of so many sad thoughts to the poor slave.

When they arrived there, they wended their way among the humble habitations of the dead, till they came to the spot where two rather freshly made graves were dug; one was about five feet in length, with a simple rough pine board stuck in the ground at the head, which board extended about twelve inches above the surface of the ground. There were no words nor inscription written upon the board, for none was necessary.

By the side of this grave was another, but it was a very small one; it was not more than fifteen or twenty

18*

inches long, and at the head was inserted a shingle of pine wood, which protruded above the ground not more than five inches ;—a tiny infant's grave it was, with the earth still freshly piled upon its little bosom.

The grave-yard in which these graves were found, consisted of about half an acre of ground enclosed by a post-and-rail fence ; it contained probably a hundred and fifty graves, some of which were very old. Here and there might be seen an occasional head-piece of stone, which indicated that the hand and skill of the mason had been employed by some surviving friend and fellow-slave to embellish, in an humble way, the last resting place of the dead. But most of the graves were marked only by a head-piece of rough stone, or by a piece of pine board, unplaned and uninscribed. The graves laid scattered about, without any order or arrangement whatever. They were of various sizes, shapes and ages ; some, as we have said, very old—not less than a hundred years; others quite newly made. Three or four large and tall walnut trees waved their thick and leafy branches in different corners of the grave-yard ; the high grass grew undisturbed among the graves, and over the ancient mounds ; and altogether the appearance of the place was exceedingly romantic and melancholy.

Here in this secluded spot, beneath this quiet turf, the weary victims of despotism for several generations past, had laid down their heavy burdens, and found their eternal rest.

"Life's fitful fever ended, they sleep well."

Here reposed the hard-worked bodies of successive generations of the slaves of the Dudley plantation; and as the winds of summer sighed and moaned over their humble beds, the visitor, as he listened to its mournful music, could not but rejoice that their thankless and un-requited toils were forever ended, and that they should henceforth suffer no more.

"This is my little baby's grave," said George to Ada, as they at length stood beside it.

"What a tiny little grave it is," said Ada, as she bent down upon it, and placed her soft white hand upon the fresh earth.

"Below this earth lies my little baby," said George; adapting the style of his language to the taste and capacity of the child to whom he spoke.

"How quiet and still it lays there under the ground," said Ada. "How long has it been here?"

"About three months, Ada; it's troubles and miseries are over now. It's spirit is in heaven," said George.

"Poor little baby! I wish I was in heaven, too," said Ada, with unaffected simplicity. At the same time she kneeled down by the side of the grave, and took the two stems of rose bush which she had brought with her, and gently pushed the roots into the ground, until the stem was firmly fixed, and the little boughs, each with several roses on them, stood up straight and steadily above the grave. She planted one at the head and the other at the foot of the little mound of fresh earth, which covered the sleeping infant.

George looked at the proceedings of Ada, which she accomplished in that quick, busy and bustling manner in which children generally do what they are very intent upon performing—with silent interest; and when she was done, he kneeled down beside her, put his arm around her little body, and kissed her soft, smooth hand, and then her cheek.

"This is the grave of the mother of my baby, Ada," said George, as he turned to the larger hillock of earth beneath which reposed his Caroline. They both gazed with silence upon the grave for a few seconds. George could not contain his grief, and his tears began to flow. His thoughts were busy with the varied scenes of the past, its joys, its sorrows, its hopes, and its despair.

Ada sat down upon the grave, and took the bunch of flowers which she still held in her hand, and scattered the fresh roses and pinks upon the last home of the murdered girl,—murdered by her own brother's cruelty. George beheld this renewed evidence of the kind feeling of the child, with increased emotion.

" Why do you do this, dear Ada ?" inquired George.

" Sister Julia told me to scatter this bunch of flowers upon Caroline's grave," replied she. This was another proof of the compassionate spirit of that noble girl, who expressed her sympathy for George's misfortunes by the only means within her power.

George still gazed in silence on the grave of his wife.

He took from his bosom the little breastpin which she had given him, as a last dying pledge of love, gazed upon it, and fervently kissed it. It brought more vividly to his mind the experiences of the past, and his tears fell faster than before.

"Don't cry so, George," said Ada, as she observed the heavy grief of the slave. "Your little baby and its mother are in heaven, a'int they?"

"I hope so, Ada. Indeed I know they are. But I feel wretched when I think how lonely and miserable they have left me here behind them."

"Don't cry then. You'll go to heaven some day and meet them there. May be I'll be there too, and we will all be happy together," said Ada.

Evening approached, and it was time to return to the house. George conducted Ada home, and the little girl informed Julia of all that had occurred. She was much interested at the description which Ada gave of the scene in the slaves' grave-yard.

George repaired to his cabin, and prayed as it was his usual custom on Sunday evening. He found comfort only in his religious exercises, and in cultivating resignation to his fate.

But the sudden ray of hope which beamed in the breast of George, when his acquaintance with Ada began, and which promised sometimes to cheer and alleviate his gloom, was destined to be of but short continuance.

On the Sunday succeeding the one in which Ada had visited the grave-yard, she went to church to hear the Rev. Mr. Pimp, together with her sister Julia, Richard Dudley, and a visitor at the family mansion. They all rode in the large family coach. On their return from church, the horses were suddenly frightened at some object near the road, and became at once unmanageable. They commenced to run away, the driver, old Uncle Ben, was unable to control them, and they ran for half a mile at a furious rate. Here the road passed by a very deep and stony bank, and down this the carriage was over-turned. The horses broke away from the vehicle, and the terrified travellers endeavored to release themselves from the coach. They had all suffered severe bruises; but little Ada was found dreadfully mashed, several persons hav-ing fallen upon her when the coach was overturned.

When taken out, she breathed but once or twice, and then expired. It was found that most of her ribs were broken.

After very considerable trouble, the carriage was righted again, the runaway horses hitched in, and the melancholy company resumed their homeward route Richard carried the dead body of Ada on his lap, as they rode home. When they arrived there, the news of her sudden death covered the plantation with gloom, as she was beloved and idolized by all who knew and ever saw her.

To none was the news of her death more heart-rending than to poor George. He had already loved the interesting child with more than a brother's love. He had hoped often to be cheered by her innocent and pleasing intelligence, by her unbought, spontaneous, and artless sympathy. But now she was no more. Her light had gone out; her lips were sealed, her spirit fled for ever. He sighed to think that now the last link was broken which had bound him to earth. He too, was ready to go where his wife and child had gone, and whither little Ada's innocent spirit had now taken its everlasting flight, to join them in a land where the distinctions of white and black, of master and slave, are unknown.

Little Ada was buried, not in the family burying ground, in Pimp's churchyard, but in the private grave-yard of a neighboring planter, who was a remote relative of the Dudleys. This spot was about three miles distant from the Dudley mansion, and as might well be supposed, it soon became a favorite resort of the now lonely and friendless slave. Almost every Sunday afternoon, George travelled across the fields, and entering the secluded spot, would seat himself upon a stone beside the little grave of his former friend, there to weep, and meditate, and pray.

Ada's was a neatly made grave, covered carefully with fresh green turf, about three feet long, with two upright marble slabs placed at its head and foot. The one at its head was taller than the other, and briefly proclaimed her name and age. As he often gazed upon her narrow and lowly bed, he thought of the fair yet mouldering form which lay beneath that silent earth, there to slumber until the archangel's trumpet, breaking the silence of that last great day, shall reverberate through the heavens, and summon the sleeping millions from their long-forgotten graves.

There is something peculiarly affecting in the solitude and silence of a *country* graveyard. This one was a small piece of ground, separated by a low stone fence from the surrounding fields. It was placed upon the gentle slope of a hill, with three or four tall elm trees scattered here and there, whose falling leaves year after year descended gently upon the graves below. The only sound which could there be heard, was the mournful sighing of the winds, often blowing freshly from the Mexican Gulf, as they strained the waving branches of the trees, and fanned the long and uncut grass. There slept in peace the quiet dead; the rich, old, arrogant planters; the accomplished and beautiful maidens; the chivalrous and gallant young men; the innocent and artless chil dren, who for three or four generations past had died in that neighborhood, and been consigned to their long homes—life's toils and triumphs, its loves and hates for ever hushed and ended. There reposed the aching heads, the throbbing hearts, the lacerated, the exulting, the despairing beings, who once moved about so busily, and ambitiously over life's shifting scenes. Year after year quietly revolves away. Heroes and empires arise to grandeur, they convulse the trembling nations with their aspiring struggles, and then crumble into undistinguishable dust again. But these inhabitants of the grave sleep on undisturbed amid the restless revolutions of cycles and of ages. Oh, when meditating calmly at such a spot, how trivial and insignificant seem all the coveted and cherished objects of human toil and tempest! How truly enviable does then appear the unbroken and untroubled repose of the quiet, the unconscious, the forgotten dead!

Feelings such as these filled the breast of George, as he pondered over that little grave, and as he cast his eyes around him, over the larger tombs of so many who were once great, lordly, and courted, in their brief day. Tears came into his eyes, as he thought of the past; when he remembered how all his own earthly joys had been wrung from his grasp by the cruel hand of his young master; how his wife and child had been murdered, and how this last welcome and solitary light,

19

which had so suddenly arisen to beam sweetly and
brightly upon his darkened way, had as suddenly gone
out in the eternal night of the grave. He turned his
eyes upward, and almost thought he saw, far off in the
clear blue sky, the angel forms of little Ada, of his wife,
and his child, hovering gently over him, and smiling
kindly down upon him, to cheer his desolation. He
prayed that he too might soon be released, and become
one of that happy band, who had escaped from a world
of everlasting tears, and obtained a home in other and
happier realms.

CHAPTER XVII.

THE COUNT DE CLERMONT.

NOTWITHSTANDING the experience which Richard Dudley had received, of the slippery wiles and questionable qualities of the plausible Count de Clermont, while at New Orleans, he had invited that young gentleman to visit him on his estate, whenever his leisure or inclination might lead him to do so. The invitation was indeed, one merely of formal and empty courtesy; and the young planter entertained no idea whatever, that the plausible Count would avail himself of his offer.

What, therefore, was Richard's surprise, when some several months after his return from New Orleans, he saw the equipage of the Count driven up to his door. He was seated, at the time, in his verandah, enjoying the combined luxury of his Havana, and the evening breeze, as it coursed over the flat plains of Louisiana, fresh from the Gulf stream below.

The equipage of the Count consisted of a light car

driven by a young negro in livery, who sat upon the front seat. Whence he had obtained so imposing a set-out, it was impossible to say; unless he had been unusu-ally successful in some of his late gambling operations.

Richard immediately advanced down the steps of the verandah, and met the Count on his way up the walk toward the house. The latter was elegantly dressed; and the excitement of the ride had given an additional color to his features, which very considerably increased the usual beauty and attractiveness of his person. His bearing was graceful; his manner bland and affable to the last degree.

Richard received his guest with all the cordial hospi-tality which uniformly characterizes the Southern plan-ter, and invited him to enter his house.

"Quite an agreeable surprise, I assure you," said Richard, as he retained the extended hand of his visitor in his own.

"I had not forgotten your kind invitation, my dear sir; and intended, from the first, to do myself the plea-sure of complying with it," said the Count most blandly.

"I'm glad you did so,—very glad, indeed."

"What a delightful region of country you live in! As I rode along, I could not sufficiently admire the richness of the cotton crops, the abundance on the rice fields, the green freshness of the meadows, and the opulence and rural luxury of the residences of the planters," observed the Count.

"It is a very flourishing region of country; but I find the life of a planter on his estate, an exceedingly dull one. I'm dying for some excitement. I'm almost dead with *ennui*. My dear sir, your visit is most welcome, I assure you," said Richard, with earnestness and apparent sincerity.

During this conversation, the two young gentlemen had reached the parlor, the windows of which Richard now threw open; and they soon felt perfectly at home; the one in entertaining his guest; the other, in receiving the proffered hospitality of his host. Supper was soon announced; and the Count de Clermont, in being ushered into the dining-room, for the first time beheld the attractive form, and blooming loveliness of Julia Dudley, who occupied the head of the table, prepared to do its honors. Richard immediately presented the handsome Count to his sister.

The impression produced on De Clermont by the first view thus obtained, of the sister of his friend, was very deep. Accustomed as he was, to behold and scrutinize the beauties of every clime, he was able at once to appreciate the peerless and superior charms of Julia; and if he were at all capable of such a thing as love, he would most assured have felt it then. Her pale but beautifully oval features, her very large dark eyes, and her magnifi-

19*

cent luxuriance of hair, indicated too plainly to be mistaken, the ardor of her soul,—her capacity both to excite and to experience the utmost intensity of love. But in the language of Byron to Southey, it might be said of Clermont:

"Thy love is lust, thy friendship all a cheat;
Thy smiles hypocrisy, thy words deceit."

The Count de Clermont was incapable of true love. His heart was impure, hard, selfish, riven and shattered by the tempests of ungoverned and conflicting passion;—it was all callous, rotten, and hollow. Nevertheless, he experienced a sensation in beholding Julia, such as he had never felt before; and he may possibly have confounded that quickening though cankered feeling, with something like true love! He thought that the possession of Julia Dudley, would be the greatest felicity of his life; and in an instant, his future purpose was secretly and unalterably fixed. He would marry the peerless Julia; and in her attainment, he would also become the possessor of her large and independent fortune. He was, of course, in ignorance of the fact, that William Stanley was her suitor, and had already succeeded in making a deep and favorable impression on her mind. Yet, even if he had been aware of this fact, it would not have deterred him for an instant from forming such a resolution, and from making the most determined and resolute efforts to execute it.

The Count immediately began the fulfilment of his purpose, by putting forth his intensest efforts of fascination. Handsome in person, agreeable in conversation, polished in manners, possessing a large fund of general information, drawn much more from his adventurous travels through the world, than from any settled habits of inquiry or study,—there was much to favor the accomplishment of his suddenly conceived enterprise.

Julia received her brother's guest with all the cordiality which was due to the friend of one she loved. She was pleased with the graceful person, and the glittering qualities of the Count; and it required no effort on her part, to treat him with the utmost courtesy.

De Clermont, as soon as propriety would permit, began to render his attentions to Julia quite marked. Yet his unprincipled and experienced craftiness prevented him from urging matters with undue and precipitate haste. He knew too well the unfavorable impression which such a course would produce upon her mind. His approaches were therefore made with all the insidious stealthiness of the couchant tiger, who wishes with silent and inaudible tread, to approach within springing distance of his unsuspecting victim. He saw that here was at last an object, and an occasion, worthy of his most consummate efforts; and one also, which would require the adroitest exercise of all his powers of fascination and allurement. He discovered that the part which he would be compelled to play, was that of a virtuous, honorable, and high-minded suitor; for he soon discovered also, that Julia Dudley was a person of high-toned principles, of unapproachable virtue, and of very keen and sagacious insight into the hidden follies and perfidies of men's characters. His own honorable birth, and his early associations with his own excellent family, before his contact with the world of vice had debased and polluted his nature, enabled him sufficiently well to simulate an excellence which he did not possess, to commend those principles which he inwardly despised;

> To boast of beauties which he never saw,
> And fancy raptures he will never know.

De Clermont and Richard Dudley soon became inseparable friends. They hunted and fished together; their hours at home were spent in smoking and drinking; and their excursions in the neighborhood were made in constant company. There was indeed such a similarity in the tastes of the two young gentlemen, that their coalescence was a matter of moral necessity, under the circumstances of the case. What Richard thought of the attentions of De Clermont to his sister, and their ultimate results, it might be difficult to say. He probably imagined that the previous hold which Stanley had already obtained on her affections, would render it impossible for the Count to make any impression upon her; and therefore he gave himself no uneasiness on the subject.

Thus several weeks wore on; Richard found the Count's society very agreeable, and Julia was amused, perhaps even pleased, with the attractive qualities of their guest. " Tell me," said she to him, one day, as they sat alone in the parlor, " of some of your travels, Count. You must have met with some strange adventures, and seen many wonderful things, in wandering so far from home."

" Most assuredly; and it will afford me much pleasure to recount them to you, Mademoiselle," replied de Clermont, in the most affable manner. " I spent my early life at my ancestor's home, in Normandy, until I was twenty years of age. At that time I had seen nothing, scarcely, of the world. I had been but once at Paris, where I remained only a month; and during all that time, I was under the close surveillance of an old uncle who accompanied me; and I could, therefore, see little but the bare houses and streets. But when I arrived at the age of twenty, my father died. My oldest brother inherited his title, and the management of our estates. I had quarrelled with him a short time previously, and therefore it was very disagreeable for me to remain under his control. I resolved to travel, to see the great world which had so long been shut out from my ardent and inquisitive gaze.

"I had often read accounts of the strange peculiarities of men and things in Russia, and thither I determined first to go. I arranged my private affairs so as to be able to remain absent for some years; and then I bade adieu to my family and friends. I travelled directly by post to St. Petersburg, where I took up my residence. My letters of introduction to several persons of distinguished rank, at once opened to me the avenue to acquaintance with all who were most celebrated for beauty, wealth, and position, in that magnificent and imposing capital. I was presented to the Emperor himself, and he ended our interview, by inviting me to take a commission in his service. The idea at once inflamed my fancy, and flattered my ambition. I accepted the offer, and was immediately promoted to the rank of cornet in the imperial bodyguard. I was honored with the smiles and the confidence of the most distinguished ladies at the court. It would not have been impossible for me soon to have formed a matrimonial alliance with a family of the highest rank,—to have won as my bride the daughter of one of the oldest and most powerful nobles of the imperial court. But just at this critical moment, dark misfortune suddenly lowered over my brilliant path. My rapid success and promotion had excited the jealousy of my rivals, and they determined upon my ruin. At that period, a conspiracy against the life and throne of the Czar was dis-

covered; it was a formidable one, with extensive, numer
ous and powerful ramifications. My enemies accused
me of being implicated in the plot. I was arrested; I
remained for some months in prison; I was eventually
tried, but acquitted. Yet the splendor of my career
had been o'erclouded. My enemies had too well accomplished their purpose. It was impossible for me to stand
as favorably as I had done in the imperial judgment.
I could no longer behold, without pangs of the deepest
mortification, the scene of my former glory and felicity,
and that too, of my subsequent degradation and disgrace. With deep curses in my heart, at my disappointment, I turned my back forever on St. Petersburg, and
set forth to seek, in some more propitious clime, the
realization of my yearnings of ambition and of love!"

"Truly, a most romantic story!" exclaimed Julia, as
the Count concluded his long, though animated description. "You were indeed unfortunate!"

"Not half so romantic an adventure was this, as what
befel me afterward in Morocco. Will you hear it, Mademoiselle?" said de Clermont.

"Certainly! pray do go on," replied Julia, eagerly.

"I had always regarded the peculiarities of Ottoman
countries and society, as much more romantic and interesting than those of christian countries. I had just experienced a stinging proof of the perfidy and heartlessness
of the latter; and I determined to gratify my curiosity,

and visit a clime where the solemn voice of the Muezzin
called the faithful to morning and evening prayer, from
the lofty summits of tapering minarets; and where the
dark-eyed damsels of the sunny South sighed and loved
beneath the shade of the luxurious orange groves, and
amid the perfumed air of citron, and olives, and spices.
The empire of Morocco seemed to me to be an untrodden
land—at least to European and to Christian feet.　There
was a romance, a remoteness, and a mystery about that
clime and country, which powerfully addressed themselves
to my imagination.　I determined to travel thither.

"I reached Trieste by railway, and embarked in a
Venetian vessel which was about to sail to the coast of
Morocco.　I soon arrived in safety at the place of my
destination, and set foot, for the first time in my life,
upon a soil over which the standard of the crescent waved,
as the imposing emblem of power, supremacy, and super-
stition.　I immediately travelled inward from the coast
to reach the city of Morocco, the capital of the empire.
As I passed along, I beheld on every side, peculiarities
of a romantic clime, such as I had never seen or imagined
before.　The houses, the costumes of the people, their
habits and appearance, all struck me as being novel and
interesting in the highest degree.　I took up my residence in the most commodious caravansera or khan in
the city of Morocco, and spent my leisure in walking
around the city, which is eight miles in circumference,

observing its people, its palaces, its shops, and whatever
•else might interest or amuse an inquisitive stranger.
From the magnificent Mosques alone was I excluded.
No foot of infidel is ever permitted to profane those sacred
retreats under penalty of death. Yet I determined to
make the dangerous experiment of seeing even them, and
thus leave nothing unobserved, of the strange wonders
and beauties of that land. The accomplishment of this
purpose required considerable time. I permitted my
beard to grow. I industriously devoted myself to the
acquisition of the Turkish language. At length after
some months of assiduity, I found that my beard, my
oriental garb, my proficiency in the language of the land,
and the darker shade which the intensity of an African
sun had given to my complexion,—all had rendered me
an unquestionable Mohammedan, so far as my external
appearance was concerned.

"As soon as a favourable opportunity presented itself,
I entered several of the most splendid Mosques of the
city; and while apparently engaged in my devotions, I
carefully scrutinized the magnificence of the buildings.
I continued my visits undetected, to all the Mosques, for
some weeks. It was in one of the retired alcoves or recesses of a Mosque, that I one day made the acquaintance of a young Morocco beauty, whose lovely form and
features at once fixed my attention. She was a perfect
specimen of Moorish beauty, with large dark eyes, ex-

20

quisite figure, and gracefulness in every movement. I
will not disguise from you, Mademoiselle, that she made
a deep impression on my heart; while I soon learned
from her manner, that I was not displeasing to herself.

"She took me, of course, for a Mohammedan. Beneath
the lofty arches of that Mosque, we continued to appoint
our frequent meetings, until at length, while hidden behind the shadow of a great pillar, we perfected our plans
of escape from the surveillance of those who watched
her movements; and we resolved to fly together to some
remote retreat in the country. One evening, when
prayers were ended, she directed her steps toward the
spot which we had fixed upon; where a suitable conveyance was in readiness to take us to our destination.
Before we parted at the Mosque, we had sworn eternal
constancy. Nor did the noble Moorish maiden shrink,
in that decisive hour, from her plighted faith, or from
the desperate purpose which love had generated in her
heart. I knew not then the terrible importance of the
step which her attachment to me had induced her to
take. How noble was that heart, which could dare so
much, and so desperately, for one to whom she was
bound by no other tie but that of love alone!

"We fled rapidly from the city of Morocco. The
precious living burden which I thus carried away with
me, now, for the first time, exhibited on her person, and
in her attire, unmistakable evidences of unbounded

wealth. Her person was adorned with jewels of incalculable value. Her dress was of the richest and costliest texture, excepting only the rude outside garment, which she had borrowed from her nurse, in order to disguise her flight. After a rapid journey of several days, we reached a romantic and lonely village, seventy miles from the capital, situated near the base of the Atlas mountains, whose towering summits are covered with eternal snow. This village was embedded in a thick grove of orange trees; while the proximity of the mountains constantly rendered the air cool and refreshing.

"In this delightful spot, my lovely Inez and myself found a secure retreat. After several weeks had passed, she ventured to reveal to me, with considerable hesitation, the mighty secret of her birth. She was the daughter of the Emperor himself, whom the power of love had induced to descend from her exalted eminence of birth and station, to become the partner of one whom she knew and felt must be very far beneath her.

"My consternation at the discovery of this dreadful secret may readily be imagined. The harrowing dread of pursuit, of discovery, and of our terrible punishment, for my apparent presumption, and for her great imprudence, gave me now neither rest nor comfort. After endeavoring to conquer these feelings, but in vain, I resolved upon the only course which was to be pursued, and which could save her life, which I prized far better

than my own. That plan was immediately to return to
her father's palace; to conceal the real circumstances
of her flight; and to endeavor to regain her father's
confidence. This plan, though perhaps it would be
death to our love, was the only way to secure an escape
from final discovery and inevitable destruction. My
affectionate Inez pondered long and sadly over this cruel
proposition, before she could bring her mind to consent
to it. Her love for me was pure and intense; yet her
life, as well as my own, depended upon the execution
of the plan. At length she yielded. After a month of
rapture spent in our charming abode, during which time
distant and vague reports reached us, that great efforts
were being made throughout the empire, and in neighboring kingdoms, to discover the retreat of the Emperor's
daughter, we determined to return to the city of Morocco.
We travelled only by night, and halted by day. As
great good fortune attended us, we at length reached
the outer gate of the city without being detected. The
same covered conveyance which had carried us forth,
conveyed us back again. Just outside the gate, it was
necessary for us to take our last farewell; for there I
proposed to leave her, in order to escape detention; while
she preferred to pass alone, and unattended, to the
palace gates of her incensed yet afflicted father, whose
vengeance she was to disarm by some story of misfortune or of capture,—such as woman's wit alone could

devise. That parting scene was indeed a sad and bitter one. My fair Inez was bathed in tears, and hung upon my neck, as if her life depended on my presence. But fate was cruel and peremptory. We vowed eternal constancy and devotion to each other. We promised to meet again, as before, in the Mosque, and there renew the memory of the raptures we had enjoyed. And so I bid her farewell, and returned to my hotel.

"You may readily imagine that I was faithful to my appointment at the Mosque, Mademoiselle. But alas! my dear and gentle Inez never came again! I repeatedly visited the spot, so hallowed by the sad and sweet memories of the past, hoping to see again the form I loved so well; but she never afterward entered the sacred edifice, and very soon vague and terrible rumors floated through the city, that the missing daughter of the Emperor had returned, or had been discovered in her retreat; and that her cruel and incensed father had ordered the fatal bowstring to put an end forever to her adventurous joys and miseries. Such were my feelings of intense sadness at this report, that I immediately left that land of gloomy despots, and embarking on board a vessel for New Orleans, in the hope of happier days, soon arrived there; and thus it is, Mademoiselle, that I am this day honored by sitting at your feet."

Julia had listened to this romantic and impracticable *yarn* of the Count, with unbroken attention; and while

20*

he thought that he was producing a favorable impression upon her heart, by the glowing recital of his adventures *in nubibus*, he was only exciting more of her distrust, and even of her contempt. The more he talked, the more he convinced her sagacious and discriminating mind, that he was a person of very unsettled principles, a mere man of the world; and though he might not indeed be a *bad* man, yet, that there was but little sincerity or genuine honesty in his nature.

During all this while the handsome Count de Clermont was playing the part of a consummate hypocrite. He had never been in Russia in his life; he had never set foot on the shores of Morocco; nor caught the remotest glimpse of the lofty summits of the Atlas mountains; but he acted on the principle which has often proved successful with adroit adventurers in love's affairs; and hoped to interest Julia in his favor by the recital of his past adventures. As the sooty Othello had once made conquest of the snowy loveliness of Desdemona, by a narrative of his bloody adventures and hair-breadth 'scapes, in the imminent deadly breach; so thought the plausible Count de Clermont to enlist the regard, and perhaps even win the love of the fair Julia, by an interesting detail of his own pretended history.

But though he failed, and that utterly, in the accomplishment of this purpose, Julia still treated him with her usual courtesy; nor did she give any outward indication to her admirer, that he had as yet, at least, totally failed in making any impression upon her.

"I hope soon to return to France," said the Count one day to Julia, "and to carry with me thither, an American wife. I admire American women more than those of any other clime."

"You flatter us very highly, indeed," responded Julia.

"But though I admire American women, I much prefer to reside in Europe; life here is comparatively dull and tame. There is far greater enjoyment of existence in the European capitals, where the highest art, and luxury, and refinement, all combine to charm, to delight, and to gratify our senses. I think you would enjoy such a mode of life very much, Mademoiselle."

"Perhaps I might," said Julia, "but I know too little of the peculiar traits of such a life, to be able properly to appreciate it."

"That may be; but you would very soon become initiated, I assure you," responded Clermont, still pursuing the theme, and adroitly approximating its aim. "In the splendid capitals of Europe—in Paris, in Vienna, in London, the presence of the court is the source and centre of a thousand delights, which are nowhere else to be found. The nobles of the land congregate together there, and expend, in the most sumptuous luxury, the revenues of their princely estates. Court balls are the most brilliant assemblages in the world, where beauty, grace, wealth, high rank and birth, illustrious person- ages—generals, statesmen, diplomatists, men of letters, female celebrities, and all that the world can boast of are congregated together; and glittering in jewels of priceless value, almost emulate the splendor of the sun. And there, too, is the opera; they have the Italian opera in those cities constantly. Oh! Mademoiselle, you would be delighted with the opera! You cannot form the least idea of the raptures enjoyed in hearing the heavenly warblings of Sontag, of Grisi, of Malibran, of Wagner, of Mario, of Badiali, of Susini, and a host of others well known to the world, and possessors of an immortal fame. There, too, you find the most glorious achiev- ments of the arts; the productions of the pencil of the godlike Michael Angelo, of the divine Raphael, of Reu- bens, of Titian, and the wonders of the chisel of Canova, Thorwaldsen and Danecker. You have no actors or actresses in this country that deserve to be named by the side of Talma, Rachel, Kean and Deveient. In fact, all the noblest arts are in their very infancy here. European capitals, Mademoiselle, are indeed the proper abode for persons of your accomplishments and taste. There you would appreciate and be appreciated; and there alone. Think you not so?" inquired De Clermont, eagerly, while the irrepressible confidence of his manner indicated that he felt assured that he had produced some impression on the young lady.

"I doubt it very much, Monsieur," replied Julia. "My education has been too long neglected. I am entirely too domestic in my tastes and habits. I would never be able to appreciate and enjoy those things to which I have lived so long a stranger."

The count was quite confounded by so blunt and direct a denial; by so clear a proof that he had succeeded but poorly in producing a favorable impression. Nevertheless, he did not despair of eventual triumph, and waited for an opportunity to renew the attempt in some more successful way. He reflected, when alone, on the best mode which could be adopted for this purpose. He had discovered that his task was more delicate and difficult than he had imagined. What was to be done next? He was in a deep quandary. He racked his brain in vain for a long time, for some new and more effective expedient.

In one of his conversations with Richard Dudley, the latter had accidentally made an allusion to an incident connected with the history of his ancestors. The Dudleys were directly descended from a very ancient and honorable English family, and were in fact related to the great race of the dukes of Warwick, whose family name was Dudley. They had occupied prominent positions in English history, on various occasions. A direct ancestor of the Dudley family was a staunch royalist in the time of King Charles II. He and another noble cavalier named Wilmot had accompanied that unfortunate prince when he fled from England to Normandy, in 1652. Lord Dudley had defended the king with might and main from the attacks of the Roundheads; and had even personally engaged and vanquished several of their most noted champions, among whom might be named *Stand-fast-on-high* Stringer; *Kill-sin* Pimple; *Fight-the-good-fight-of-faith* White; *More-fruit* Fowler; and *If-Christ-had-not-died-for-you-you-had-been-damned* Barebones; commonly called, for the sake of shortness, *Damned* Barebones.

It is matter of history that Lords Dudley and Wilmot accompanied Charles II. during all his eight years' exile in France; remained his most faithful and trusted friends through all his adversities, and returned again with him in triumph to England, in 1660. After the Restoration, they shared between them the confidence of the king, and became the possessors of great influence and power. The family of Richard Dudley was lineally descended from this noble stock; though they had long since relinquished all claim, or even allusion, to the rank which their kindred held in England. They were republicans in principle, and were satisfied with their position in the land of their adoption, as citizen-sovereigns and no more.

The Count de Clermont having adroitly drawn the above particulars from Richard Dudley, in conversation, determined, as his only expedient, to make use of them for the purpose of advancing his suit with Julia. Accordingly, on the first favorable opportunity he introduced the subject, pretending to be as yet quite ignorant of the preceding facts.

"From what country of Europe do your ancestors come, Mademoiselle?" inquired the count.

"From England, sir. They are an ancient race; but their descendants have lived in America for nearly a hundred and fifty years."

"Ah! an English family. It appears to me that I have heard the name of Dudley before; or perhaps I might have read of it."

"Very probably, indeed. The name is not unknown in English history."

"Pray give me their history. I assure you it would interest me exceedingly," said the count, eagerly.

"Indeed! Well, my ancestors in England have always been staunch royalists and high tories. One of them was the friend and attendant of King Charles II. during his banishment from England, and his exile in Normandy."

"In Normandy! Was that Dudley who was the friend and attendant of the exile prince in Normandy, your ancestor?"

"He was, I assure you, sir," replied Julia.

"Is it possible? I am indeed most happy to know it. What a singular coincidence! How wonderfully strange is it, that I should meet the descendants of that illustrious cavalier on the far-off shores of Louisiana!"

"Why so, sir? Of what coincidence do you speak?" said Julia.

"It affords me great pleasure to answer your inquiry," replied the count. "On that occasion, the king and his two noble attendants, one of whom was named Dudley, and the other Wilmot, were the honored guests for nine months, of an ancestor of my own in Normandy. His estate and fortress, situated in that department of France, happened to afford the most convenient retreat, on their entry into the French territories; and they honored my ancestor, the then Count de Clermont, with their presence and society, during the period I have named."

"Indeed! How singular the coincidence!" exclaimed Julia.

"Yes, it is singular; but the most singular part of the story is yet to come. The emissaries of Cromwell, the usurper of the throne of England, having ascertained the retreat of the fugitives, sent over some five or six secret assassins, for the purpose of dispatching the king and the two cavaliers who attended him. They were very near accomplishing their bloody purpose, when their intention was detected by the French count; and they were arrested by his orders, tried by himself, according to the laws of the then prevailing feudal prerogatives and tenure; condemned by him to death, and immediately despatched by his own men-at-arms."

"How fortunate the king's escape!"

"Yes; fortunate for the king and his friends, indeed; but extremely unfortunate in the end to one of my female ancestors, the count's noble daughter, Winifried."

"How was that, Monsieur?" inquired Julia.

"As soon as Prince Charles ascertained that his retreat was discovered, he was compelled to remove to other quarters. During their residence at the Count de Clermont's castle, Lord Dudley had admired, and then loved the beautiful and accomplished daughter of the Count, and she had returned his passion with all the intensity of her romantic nature. They would soon have united their destinies by marriage; but the sudden departure of the Prince and his two friends, compelled the postponement of their nuptials. They parted as such lovers only can part, vowing eternal constancy; and each of them then waiting for the first propitious opportunity to consummate their felicity. But, alas! the unsettled and lowering fortunes of the Prince, postponed indefinitely the happy day; and before three years of the eight had transpired, during which the Prince remained a wandering and periled exile, the fair and

21

devoted Winifried had languished, and at length expired,
a victim to the pangs of unfortunate love, and of the
keen, exhaustive anguish of hope deferred. This true
history has long been preserved by my ancestral family,
and carefully handed down from generation to generation."

"Quite a romantic history, indeed!" said Julia.

And thus the artful Count thought to beguile the
affections of the fair descendant of the English Dudleys,
by a fabricated romance of mutual ancestral attach-
ments and vicissitudes. But it would not answer. Whether Julia believed the ready story which dropped with
such prolific and oily ease from the artful tongue of her
suitor, it were impossible to say. But even if she did
believe it, her good sense taught her, that such recom-
mendations did not, by any means, guarantee the pro-
bity and virtue of a strange and otherwise unknown
suitor. Yet it must be confessed, that the conversational
powers, and the pleasing manners and person of de Clermont, rendered his society exceedingly agreeable to
every one of the family of his host; nor had de Clermont
for one moment despaired, that he should eventually
succeed in accomplishing the object of his ambition,—
the possession of the hand and the fortune of the fair
Julia.

It was but several days after the preceding conversation had occurred, that the Dudleys and their guest

were invited to an entertainment given by a neighboring planter, who had long been an intimate friend of the Dudleys. The assemblage was somewhat numerous, comprising all the most wealthy and aristocratic families in that neighborhood, together with several strangers from abroad, who happened at the time to be visiting in the vicinity.

The company was exceedingly agreeable, and the day passed away in alternate diversions of music, dancing, and feasting. The Count was introduced by the Dudley's to their acquaintances as a friend of their's, who was then visiting them, and who at that time was a resident of New Orleans. It may readily be supposed, that the fascinating and handsome Frenchman, was not long in making himself quite agreeable to the company in whose midst he was thrown. To the gentlemen, he was affable and courteous; to the old ladies, he was obsequious and respectful; and to the young belles who glittered and bloomed around him, he was as complimentary and fascinating as he possibly could be. As a natural consequence, the Count soon became the lion of the occasion, a favorite with everybody, and the most flattered and honored person in the assemblage.

Unfortunately for the prosperous Count, one of the strangers present was a gentleman from New Orleans, named Richards, of undoubted respectability, who happened to be perfectly acquainted with his person, his history, and his real character.

"Do you know who it is, that you are honoring with your confidence?" said Mr. Richards to Miss Julia, whom he drew into a corner of the room for the purpose of private conversation.

"He is a friend of my brother Richard, who is paying him a visit at our plantation. He met the Count de Clermont in New Orleans. More than this I do not know."

"Then I hope you will permit me to inform you," replied Mr. Richards. "I know this person much better than your brother, whom he doubtless has deceived. De Clermont, I assure you, is a mere adventurer, without character, unprincipled, and of infamous reputation, wherever he is fully known. I dare not say anything more than this to you, Miss Julia; but you may rely upon it, that he is a person of abandoned character. I say this much, to put you on your guard."

'Can it be possible!" said Julia. "I thank you for your well-meant information, and will profit by it."

Julia communicated to no one whatever, the startling revelations which had just been made to her. De Clermont was still her brother's guest, and she could not treat him rudely. She had herself introduced him to the friends whom they met on this occasion, and she could not of course afterwards give unfavorable statements to them. She determined, however, as soon as possible, to get rid of the adventurer; and in the mean time to exercise additional caution in reference to his intercourse with her.

The next day after the occurrence of the party in question, the Count de Clermont determined to bring matters to a conclusion, and directly made the offer of his heart and hand to the fair Julia. He urged his suit with redoubled efforts of impassioned eloquence and of argument; and doubtless hoped to succeed in the accomplishment of his darling purpose. Julia quietly listened to the proposals of the Count, with decorous attention; and after he had concluded, she respectfully but resolutely declined the offer.

"However flattering to me I may regard your proposition, you will of course be satisfied with my refusal, when I inform you that though I respect you, I do not love you; and without love, marriage, with me at least, is impossible!"

"Ah! Mademoiselle, how cruel you are! And must I then yield to despair? If you love me not *now*, surely it might be possible for you to love me hereafter. Do not destroy all my hopes, I entreat you. I'm sure, that without you I cannot live. Not only my happiness, but my life is in your hands. It is for you now to say, whether I shall immediately die in despair, or be supremely happy."

21*

"I can promise you nothing, and you compel me to make a further declaration, by your importunity. Let me therefore inform you, that I am already engaged in marriage; and that, also, to a man whom I love, and love passionately, fervently, and unalterably. You see at once, Count, that your proposition is forever utterly out of the question."

This announcement fell like a thunderbolt from heaven on de Clermont. He saw at once, that his suit was perfectly hopeless. He could do no less, than to resign the inestimable prize which he had lost, with as good a grace as possible. For once in his life he had been signally foiled in the accomplishment of a scheme upon which he had set his heart, and exerted his best endeavors.

The very next day after his refusal by Julia Dudley, the Count de Clermont, concealing his disappointment and mortification as best he could, ordered his servant to drive up his carriage to the door. With polished and hypocritical politeness, he thanked his kind hosts for their hospitality. He eagerly expressed to Richard Dudley the hope that he would soon meet him again in New Orleans, to plunge once more into the abyss of its debaucheries; and blandly bidding them all adieu, he drove rapidly away, cursing not loudly but profoundly, the whole Dudley generation from the time of Charles II., downwards, to the present time, and execrating the folly which had impelled him to run the risk of meeting such a refusal, and of suffering its consequent mortification.

CHAPTER XVIII.

A BOLD PUSH FOR FREEDOM.

"Hereditary Bondsmen! Know ye not,
Who would be free themselves must strike the blow?"
CHILDE HAROLD.

A FEW months revolved, and the happy moment arrived, when Julia Dudley was to be received to the arms of her affianced husband, William Stanley. They were married; and the Rev. Pimp himself tied the matrimonial knot.

Julia selected from among the family servants, several of her favorites, whom she desired to take along with her to New Orleans. One of these was Sarah, the young wife of Jerry.

Sarah was one of the most intelligent, good looking, and useful women on the plantation. She was a mulatto, and next to Caroline, had secured most of the regard and favor of her young mistress. She was a very cheerful, lively, and willing girl; and having long waited on Miss Julia in person, she was the most suitable of all the slaves on the plantation, to accompany the young bride to her new home, in the capacity of waiting maid. Her husband Jerry, was also a mulatto,—an active, willing, and likely young fellow, a good hand, and in every respect a very valuable slave. He and Sarah had been married some four or five years; and they now had one child, a very interesting little girl, of about three years of age. They were tenderly attached to each other, and lived together in great harmony and affection, in one of the slave cabins; although Sarah's duties near the person of Miss Julia, frequently detained her, a great part of her time, in the house of her mistress.

Behold then, the marriage cavalcade about to set out from the Dudley mansion. The large and commodious family carriage led the way, in which were seated Miss Julia, now Mrs. Stanley, looking more beautiful and bewitching than ever; together with William Stanley, her happy husband, who was as happy as his virtues and merits entitled him to be. This carriage was driven by the old family coachman, Uncle Ben, an aged, coal black negro, with hair perfectly white, who had driven the family coach of the Dudley's, for at least the last forty years, in all their travels and excursions, from the youth of old Major Dudley, until that time. The baggage of Mrs. Stanley, which consisted of some eight or ten trunks, was fastened on, before and behind the coach; and that part of it which could not thus be disposed of, was attached to the carriages which followed. There were two smaller ones, filled with the several slaves whom Julia took with her, including Sarah, and their baggage; together with various other matters, which need not now be enumerated.

By this arrangement Sarah was to be separated from her husband. The parting between her and Jerry was indeed a sad one, as they were tenderly attached to each other. Sarah, when she first learned her mistress' purpose to take her with her, implored that Jerry might be included among the three or four slaves whom Julia intended to take with her; and Julia used her best endeavors to persuade Richard to permit Jerry to accompany her to New Orleans. But Jerry was so useful a hand on the place, having special charge of Richard's two favorite blood horses, and was so superior in that capacity to everybody else on the place, that Richard absolutely refused to listen to such a proposal. Julia, knowing the unbending obstinacy of his temper, did not insist upon it; and Sarah was therefore to separate from her husband. Their anguish at this calamity was extreme; but all remonstrance they well knew to be useless, and they separated in silent grief, after one long, and as they then thought, a last embrace. Sarah took their little daughter with her.

The marriage party arrived in safety at New Orleans. Julia Stanley was there introduced into a splendid and comfortable home, and she was happy in the love of her worthy and excellent husband.

After a few days Uncle Ben returned with the family carriage to the Dudley plantation. He had been before that, to New Orleans, with old Major Dudley, on several occasions, and therefore was somewhat acquainted with the city itself, and the incidents of travel thither and back. On his arrival home, he was beset with numerous inquiries by the slaves, who entertained affectionate remembrance and respect for their young mistress, in reference to her new home and the appearance of things there. To these inquiries he made such answers as his information enabled him to do.

Jerry, after the departure of his wife with Julia, was overwhelmed with a sensation of loneliness and wretchedness, such as he had never before experienced. His thoughts continually wandered away after his absent wife and interesting daughter; and he felt that to be forever separated from them, would be equivalent to death itself.

But he knew that he could not be in New Orleans, where they were, unless he was a slave there also; and he most ardently wished for the coming of some slave driver, who should purchase him, and thus, by taking him to the New Orleans market, give him the opportunity of some intercourse with his wife.

But time wore on, and no such opportunity occurred.

Jerry became more and more disconsolate. His thoughts forever dwelt upon his absent wife and child. At length, one evening, in conversation with Uncle Ben about his trip to New Orleans, and the appearance of things there, he inquired the particulars of the way thither. He had suddenly conceived the purpose of attempting to fly toward the place which held the beings whom he loved. He felt that he could no longer resist the mighty hunger of his soul after those dear ones, and he resolved, whatever might be the risk, to see and embrace them once more.

Uncle Ben informed Jerry of the way to New Orleans, what roads he should take, what towns and villages he should avoid, and how he should find the residence of Mr. Stanley in New Orleans, when he arrived there.

Some days were spent by Jerry in cautious reflection upon the dangers of his journey, before he could make up his mind to undertake it. But the same restless desire to see his family, which induced him to conceive the purpose, impelled him to the further execution of it. The directions he had received from Uncle Ben, would be of great service to him; and after a desperate struggle with himself, between his fear of the consequences and his affection for those whom he longed to see, he started off, travelling only by night, and hiding during the day, along the roads which Uncle Ben had pointed out to him.

We shall not follow Jerry through all the particulars of his journey. Through many hair-breadth escapes; through dangers by land and water; amid perils from man and beast; through hunger, weariness and watching, he at length arrived near the outskirts of the famous capital of the South. It was toward the break of day that Jerry first came in view of the brightly glittering waters of the Gulf, between which and himself he beheld with wonder and admiration the stately domes and spires of the Crescent City, rising proudly toward the heavens. He hid himself for the day, among the tall grass which waved around him on the spot where he stood when the morning dawned upon him.

Here he lay quietly: as the long and dreary hours passed by, he heard, wafted to him on the breeze from a distance, the busy hum of the great city; and his heart trembled when he thought that he was soon to enter within its crowded streets, a fugitive—where the power of the slave-master was supreme. But then, on the contrary, he derived a sweet consolation from the thought, that, in that great city, the metropolis of the bloody and cruel slave power, there was one faithful heart which loved him with pure affection, which would perish to serve and to save him. He passed the day thinking of the coming night, which would bring the blissful moment when he should clasp his Sarah to his

22

arms, and which would impress on his lips the sweet kiss of his young daughter.

As soon as Richard Dudley discovered the flight of Jerry, he divined the course he had taken. He had observed for some days the sadness of his demeanor, and attributed it to his sorrow at being separated from his family. He therefore suspected immediately that Jerry had fled toward New Orleans.

Summoning Robinson, his ex-Yankee slave-driver, he ordered him to mount his horse and take the road directly toward that city, to give the alarm along his way, and on his arrival in New Orleans to go immediately to Stanley's house, and use every means to overtake the fugitive. By riding all day and part of the night, he arrived at New Orleans a day before Jerry; he had proceeded at once to Stanley's house, and had communicated to them the purposes of his journey.

Of course they had seen and heard nothing of Jerry, and Robinson was somewhat non-plussed to know what to do. He concluded, however, to remain a day or two in New Orleans, and have some search made, and a watch kept for the missing slave.

As soon as Mrs. Stanley heard the purpose of Robinson's visit, she came out to the kitchen where Sarah was, and informed her that her husband had fled from his master; that Robinson was then in the house in pursuit of him; and that she must keep a strict look-out, lest, should Jerry arrive and visit her while Robinson was there, her husband would be detected, and dragged back again to his incensed master.

Sarah was almost overwhelmed at this intelligence; her rapture at the thought of so soon seeing her husband, was more than equalled by the horror she felt lest he might be discovered. She knew that he would not appear during the day; but as evening approached her apprehension increased, and she kept looking out of the back windows every moment, lest Jerry might incautiously approach, and be discovered by Robinson.

The night wore on, however, and no sign of Jerry appeared. Sarah did not go to bed, but sat up nursing her daughter in her arms. It was now eleven o'clock; the family of Mr. Stanley had retired to rest, and Robinson had been conducted by Sarah herself, to one of the spare chambers, appropriated to his use.

The silence which reigned was universal. Sarah was dozing upon her chair, when she heard a slight knock at the kitchen door; her heart leaped within her, as she sprang up to open the door; she laid down her child, raised the latch, and slowly opened the door a little way.

"It's me, Sally! it's me—it's Jerry!" said the visitor in a whisper; and in another instant the door was opened wide; the stranger had entered; and Sarah was clasped in her husband's arms, in a long and rapturous embrace.

Morning was about to dawn, when the happy slaves

began to see the necessity of providing some place of
safety for the fugitive during the day. After some consultation, they came to the conclusion that the best
thing which could be done for the present was, for Jerry
to hide himself in Mr. Stanley's stables, under the hay;
in a day or two they might, and must, be able to discover some other and better retreat.

With this purpose in view, Jerry was quietly stealing
along the path which led through the yard to the stables
in the rear, when Robinson, who, by accident had risen
very early that morning, espied the fugitive through the
window of his chamber, which looked out upon the yard.
He immediately put his head out of the window, and
cried for assistance. He screamed "murder! watch!
police!" at the top of his voice; and immediately the
whole household of Mr. Stanley was aroused. They
came running from all quarters into the passage-ways,
inquiring what was the matter?

Robinson had not entirely dressed himself when he
discovered Jerry, and it took some minutes for him to
put on enough clothing to make his appearance decorous.
Meantime his imprudent act, in giving the alarm so suddenly, had been of great service to Jerry; it had given
him some time to make his escape, and gain on his pur
suers.

Nor did Jerry fail to improve this accidental advantage. He ran with great speed through the yard, scaled

the wall, and continued his course down the lane or alley, which ran in the rear of the street on which Stanley's house stood.

This alley he pursued until, by passing several corners, it brought him to the levee. During the few minutes which had elapsed since Robinson discovered him, that worthy had done his best to secure assistance in the pursuit. But the early hour of the day, when as yet scarcely any persons were abroad, rendered it impossible for him to find any one, either citizen nor policeman, until after the lapse of considerable time; when he had lost all direct trace of the fugitive.

Jerry, on his arrival on the levee, was astonished at the large ships, and the innumerable boats of all kinds and sizes, which lay along the water. He looked around him to discover some place of concealment, which might serve him in this pressing emergency. Nobody was moving yet along the levee, and he was not interrupted in his search.

But he seemed to look in vain for any spot or retreat which appeared to suit as a hiding-place. There were piles of boards and boxes on the levee, but these would all be inspected, and possibly removed during the day, and he would thus become exposed. But he had no time to loose in idle reflection. His pursuers would soon be at his heels, and he must make the best shift in his power.

22*

Seeing a large ship laying close alongside the dock, he bethought him, as the only expedient possible, of rushing on board. He did so. The deck was clear. But Jerry saw at a glance that, unless he could get into the hold before any one came on deck, he was lost. But the hatches were closed, and it was impossible for him to accomplish that purpose.

But it was equally unsafe for him to remain on the deck. He would be visible there to his pursuers, the moment they arrived upon the levee. As a last resource, therefore, Jerry went forward, crept out on the bowsprit, and let himself down among the forechains. He climbed to that side of the ship which was not exposed toward the levee. The ship had heavy bulwarks; was a vessel of very large size; and the poor black fugitive seemed but as a speck stuck upon her mighty hull, as he hugged up as close as possible to her vast bulk.

Jerry had scarcely found himself safely ensconced in this strange perch, some fifteen feet above the water, when he heard a great tumult along the levee. It was Robinson with his pack, in hot pursuit of him. This disturbance continued for a long time. He was accompanied with about twenty persons, some of whom were policemen. They searched everywhere along the levee, but all to no purpose.

They then commenced to go on board some of the vessels lying on the dock, and to search them thoroughly fore and aft, above and below. Finding the slave on none of these, they at length came on board the very ship beneath whose bulwarks and among whose heavy forechains, Jerry was concealed. By this time the crew were mostly on deck, and aided in the search. Robinson went below, and closely examined the hold, among the cargo of cotton bales—everywhere—but nowhere could he find the absent Jerry. The latter heard from his dangerous perch, the loud and bitter curses of Robinson, appended to his name; and the direst threats of vengeance should he be discovered. After an hour's search, Robinson and his pack gave over the pursuit. Jerry was as yet invisible.

And what ship was this which had become so suddenly, and in so singular a manner, the refuge of a poor, hunted, trembling slave?

It was the good ship Lexington, of Boston, Winslow commander.

She had shipped on board a large cargo of cotton, and was ready to sail for her northern port that very day. Accordingly, soon after the departure of Robinson, Captain Winslow appeared on deck, and gave the necessary orders preparatory to clearing away.

"Cast off that line!" roared the captain.

"Aye, aye, sir!"

"Let go the mainsail!"

"Aye, aye, sir!"

The sails filled; the pilot steered the ship toward the gulf; the vessel cleared the dock, and began rapidly to cleave in twain the dark waters beneath her.

Jerry began to experience considerable astonishment, as he looked around him, at the novel position which he now occupied. No one suspected his presence on the ship. He rode the waves astride one of the forechains, and as the wind began to freshen, and the billows to roll, the motion of the mighty ship commenced to grow somewhat rough and irregular. Meantime, Jerry began to experience an internal sensation which he could not account for, but which was by no means agreeable. This sensation was new indeed to him, but perfectly familiar to old salts, and usually denominated sea-sickness. He felt so faint, and began to render his tribute to Neptune with such violence, that he was several times almost on the point of letting go his hold, and dropping into the sea below.

The ship boldly steered out into the wide waters of the gulf. Jerry had eaten something the night before with his wife, and his strength had thereby been somewhat revived. But the sea-sickness had already deprived him of some of that strength, and left him very weak.

The weather during the first day was favorable. The ship made fair headway, sailing at the rate of ten knots an hour, being favored by the wind. Jerry held fast to his chains, quietly perched under the bulwarks. He gazed abroad over the wide and tranquil waste of waters, dotted here and there with the white sails of countless ships, with admiration and astonishment. He had never seen, nor even conceived, of such a wondrous element before.

Sometimes he would gaze down into the blue, unfathomable depths beneath him, and see with terror the spotted and slimy monsters of the deep at their gambols, or in the pursuit of their prey.

These sights filled him with intense emotion. He once climbed down upon his chain, as far as he could, to be as near as possible to the water, to get a better view of the mysterious proceedings of the finny tribes. But his curiosity had nearly been a serious matter to Jerry; his black moving form caught the eye of a ravenous shark, which instantly darted out of the water at him, with gaping jaws open to devour him. But the hungry shark had not accurately calculated the distance, but shot several feet short of his prey, and fell again with a loud splash into the water some yards beyond him.

"No you don't, you cussed varmint!" exclaimed Jerry to himself, as he quickly climbed up his chain again, and hugged as close to the ship's side as possible. After that interesting adventure, Jerry confined his observations to what he could see from the safest position possible, and beheld, with horror, the furious beast which had just attempted to gorge him, swimming

directly beneath him in the sea, and every instant turning up to him his fierce and glaring eyes, as if making
ready to repeat the assault upon him.

Amid scenes such as these, the first day passed away
The time flew rapidly for Jerry, as he was too deeply interested in the sublime or impressive novelties of his position.   He began to feel hungry, and saw the necessity
of making some effort after food.   Yet he feared that if
he now made known his presence in the ship to the
sailors or captain, the latter might order the vessel to
turn about, and carry him back again to New Orleans.
He determined to wait, in his present position, during
that night, until the next morning, and then, after the
ship had progressed still further on her way, to reveal
himself and his wants to the captain, and take what
consequences might follow.

The ship sailed quietly on her way during the night,
with no incident occurring which deserves mentioning.
As the break of day approached, Jerry, who of course
had not slept a moment during the night, saw that the
heavens were overcast with black clouds, and that a terrible storm impended.   During the night he had let his
thoughts wander freely back to the beloved wife and
child, whom he had been compelled so suddenly to
desert.   He thought again and again with rapture of
that long embrace; and prayed Heaven that he might
one day possess his wife and child again, without the

fear of the taskmaster, or the dread of separation from all he loved on earth.

As the day advanced the storm rapidly approached; and such a storm! It came up suddenly; the wind blew a perfect hurricane. The waves began to roll mountain high; the poor slave in the forechains had no conception that waves could ever possibly become so immense. The surface of the sea was now white with foam. The ship pitched and rolled with terrible violence. The waves at length dashed over the whole length of the deck, and Jerry of course was frequently immersed far beneath the watery masses. Sometimes the ship made such heavy seas, and Jerry was so long immersed beneath them, that he could scarcely retain his hold for want of breath. Nevertheless, he held on to his chains with desperate resolution. It was life or death to him; nor would he give up the struggle, till the last particle of his strength had been exhausted.

Jerry heard, in the intervals of the loud roaring of the winds, the voice of the captain giving the necessary orders on board the ship; and had he expected such a storm, he would doubtless have revealed himself before its fury began. But it came on so suddenly, that it was then too late, and he was compelled to hold on to the forechains, and endure the worst that came, however disagreeable or perilous it might be.

At length, after several hours duration, the storm

abated. Jerry, though he had shipped so many heavy
seas, still survived, though very much exhausted. He
determined now to make a bold push to get on deck, and
take the consequences, whatever might ensue.

After the storm subsided, the captain had retired to
his cabin, and the seamen were dispersed about their
several duties. Jerry climbed slowly up the chains, till
he reached the bowspit. He then continued to crawl
along the bowspit till he reached the bulwarks. From
this position, with his head and shoulders projecting
above them, he had a full view of the whole deck. Jerry
stood for some moments surveying the scene, himself as
yet entirely unobserved. At length an old tar, who
had just come up from below, and was followed by
another, happened to rest his eyes on the singular spectacle which presented itself,—that of a negro, bareheaded, his woollen clothes saturated with the sea, and
head and shoulders only being visible above the bulwarks.

"I say, Jack, what's that?" said the first seaman,
pointing suspiciously to Jerry's head. "Is it a man, or
the devil, eh?"

"Devil take me, if I know," responded Jack, as he
cautiously eyed the suspicious phenomenon.

The two sailors slowly approached Jerry, and as they
drew near to him, Jack drew from his bosom a large

pistol, which he immediately cocked, and was about to take aim.

Jerry thought it was high time to declare himself, and put an end to the perils of his position; so he sung cut lustily, "Don't shoot! don't shoot! It's only me! I'm coming over." And with that, he crawled over the bulwarks, and with a bound set his feet on the deck of the ship.

"It's the runaway nigger, by the great Boot!" said Tom to his companion.

"To be sure it is," answered Jack. "Say, stranger, how the devil did you get there?" said he, approaching Jerry with the utmost astonishment.

Jerry, in a few words, recapitulated the history of his escape, and of his various adventures in the fore-chains.

"Go and tell the captain," said Tom to Jack; "he must know all about this here, at once."

Jack went off toward the captain's cabin for this purpose. Meanwhile other sailors gradually assembled around the new comer; who stood in the midst, trembling with apprehension as to what should be his fate. Their astonishment was beyond all expression; yet their sympathies were all with the poor slave. If Jack Tar had to determine the matter, slavery would soon disappear from the land and the sea.

As soon as the captain had heard the story which Jack

23

conveyed to him, he ordered that the negro should be immediately brought down to him.

Jack came up on deck and said to Jerry, "The captain wants to see you; so come along."

Jerry went below and entered the cabin, where Captain Winslow then was, working out his longitude. The captain, it may be proper to state, was a true son of New England, bold, generous, humane, and a fierce hater of the tyranny of man over man; he was a direct descendant of one of the most famous and patriotic families during the Revolution; his grandfather "fit in the Revolution," and so did several more of his kindred. The reader may easily anticipate the reception he would give to this poor fugitive from worse than British bondage, and who was making such gigantic efforts and struggles to be free.

"Well, my good fellow, how did you get here?" were the words with which the captain received Jerry, as he stood, trembling from head to foot, before him.

"I ran away from my master, Richard Dudley, in Louisiana, because he had separated my wife from me; she went to New Orleans with her misess, and I travelled to New Orleans to see her. They chased me there, and I run on board this ship, before day, and got out among the chains in front, and hung on there till this mornin, when I clum up into the ship;" was

Jerry's succinct account of his history and adventures since he left the Dudley plantation.

"And where are you going to?" inquired the captain.

"I does'nt know, master—I does'nt know," responded Jerry; for he had not yet learned the name or the destination of the vessel.

"Well, I'll tell you where you're going to; you are going to Boston. Do you know where that is, eh?"

"No sir, I does'nt know," said Jerry.

"Well, it's in New England—in Massachusetts, not very far from Canada. Do you know where that is?"

"Oh yes! I'se hearn tell of Canada; dare all de darkies is free, is'ent dey?" eagerly inquired Jerry, encouraged by the benign manner of the captain.

"Yes, they are all free there. Would you like to be free too, eh?"

"Yes, I would, master. Oh! I'd like to be free, and to have Sarah, my wife, and my little girl free, too, in Canada."

"You have a wife and child, then, eh? Where are they now?" inquired the captain.

"In New Orleans, master; I came there to see them, when I ran off from Master Dudley."

"Ah! I see now how it all is," replied the captain. "You came to New Orleans to see your wife and child, and they endeavored to retake yo , and you fled on board this ship."

"Yes, sir, that's jist it," said Jerry.

The captain gave orders that Jerry should be properly fed and clothed, and cared for; and the poor slave, who, fifteen minutes before did not know but that he should be instantly thrown overboard to the shark, which had already made one bold push to devour him, was now rejoicing in hope of security, and perhaps, remotely of freedom.

Jerry soon made a useful and willing hand on board. The captain held several conversations with him about his history, during the progress of the voyage; and really began to take a great interest in him and his fate.

Every day the poor fugitive was getting farther and farther away from the land of bondage, and approaching nearer to the shores of freedom.

He informed the captain how much he longed not only to be free himself, but also to have his wife and child free also.

At length, after a prosperous voyage of several weeks, the good ship Lexington anchored in the port of Boston. Previous to this event, Captain Winslow, who was an enlightened man, and an abolitionist, had foreseen the necessity of taking some steps to conceal the fugitive, and help him on to Canada, by means of the underground railroad. While the vessel was discharging her cargo, he kept Jerry concealed in his cabin; and during this time communicated with the proper persons on shore, who immediately took charge of him preparatory to sending him to Canada.

During the voyage, so strongly had Captain Winslow been impressed in favor of Jerry, that he took the name and address of Sarah's master in New Orleans, and promised to call upon him and inform him of Jerry's safe arrival in Canada, and his hope of purchasing his wife's freedom at an early period. Meantime Jerry travelled quietly on toward Canada, and after several weeks' journey upon the invisible railroad aforesaid, arrived there in safety.

He soon obtained a place, where he earned good wages, and by his industry, and general good conduct, became a great favorite with all who knew him; and saved every week, something of his wages toward the purchase of his wife.

Captain Winslow, on his next voyage to New Orleans, made it his business to call upon Mr. Stanley, and inform him of the fact, that he knew of the arrival of Jerry, a slave of Richard Dudley, in Canada, and wished to know on what terms he would sell Sarah and her little daughter.

Mr. Stanley communicated this information to his excellent wife, Julia, who in turn, informed Sarah of her husband's safe arrival in the land of the free.

The delight with which the poor girl received this in-

23*

formation, at once suggested a benevolent and happy thought to the mind of that noble hearted woman. Little as she could spare Sarah's services, to whose attentions she had been so long accustomed, she persuaded her husband to make out free papers for Sarah and her child, on condition that Captain Winslow, whose urbanity and benevolence had already made a most favorable impression upon her, would convey them in his ship to Boston, and thence send them to Jerry in Canada.

The captain immediately consented; and Mr. Stanley forthwith drew up the free-papers for Sarah and her daughter. Mrs. Stanley filled Sarah's trunks with good clothes for herself; and she also packed in some of her husband's clothes for Jerry. She provided a few necessary comforts for her use on the voyage; and at length sent her down to the ship when she was ready to sail. The poor slave's emotions of gratitude and delight, were far too great for utterance. She could only kiss her young mistress' hands, and weep tears of unutterable joy. Mrs. Stanley, as she saw the carriage departing with the happy woman and her luggage, to go on board the ship, experienced the rapture which the performance of noble and generous actions such as this, can only bestow upon minds as exalted as her own.

A few weeks revolve, and we must transport the reader to a flourishing village on the banks of the mighty St. Lawrence river. Among the many quiet, thrifty, and happy homes clustered together in that village, there is none more to be envied than one which lies upon the outskirts. It is a snug and tidy log cabin. It contains but several small rooms, yet each of these is furnished in a plain and comfortable manner. The cold wind and snow whistle without, and drive rudely up against the air-tight windows. A cheerful wood fire crackles on the hearth-stone. Before the fire is seated a well-dressed black man (though a mulatto); and he dandles on his knee a bright and beautiful child, with long and curly hair. Behind him, engaged in preparing the evening meal, is his wife, a good-looking mulatto woman, whose dark eye ever and anon glances from her work to her husband and child, whom she regards with intense affection.

"Sally, I have saved just eight dollars out of my wages this week. Here they are. Put them away in your trunk," said the man at the fire, with the beautiful little girl on his knee.

The wife took the money, and deposited it in her strong box. As soon as she had done so, she returned to her husband, put her soft arms around his neck, and gave him a tight hug, and a long, long kiss.

Who are these happy people?

The woman is Sarah, the servant of Julia Stanley, whom she set free and sent to join her husband.

The child is her little daughter, whom Julia Stanley also set free, and made a present of to her own mother.

The man is Jerry, who, alone in the history of man, buffeted the stormy waves, and defied the ravenous sharks of the Atlantic, in the forechains of a ship; and rode majestically out of the port of New Orleans, in a novel way of his own discovery.

There they all are, now free; and forever safe from the deadly fangs of the speculator in human blood.

CHAPTER XIX.

A BONFIRE AND A JUBILEE.

"'Tis Liberty alone that gives the flower
Of fleeting life its lustre and perfume;
And we are weeds without it. All constraint,
Except what wisdom lays on evil men,
Is evil; hurts the faculties; impedes
Their progress in the road of science; blinds
The eyesight of discovery; and begets
In those that suffer it, a sordid mind,
Bestial, a meagre intellect, unfit
To be the tenant of man's noble form."

COWPER'S TASK.

ROBINSON, the ex-Yankee slave-driver, returned from New Orleans with no very agreeable news for Richard Dudley.

He informed that amiable individual, that on his arrival in New Orleans, he discovered that Jerry had fled thither, as they suspected; that he even detected his place of concealment, and saw him as he was about taking "French leave;" but that, after looking for him high and low, and employing the assistance of the police for several days, in searching among all the usual haunts of the runaway negroes; and also after examining many of the ships on the levee; everything was to no purpose. Jerry had evidently escaped, at least for the present, in some most mysterious and extraordinary manner. It was no fault of his; he had done his best to retake the scoundrel, but it was impossible.

Richard heard the news, as he usually did all evil and unwelcome tidings, with dignified yet bitter curses. He did not know whether to blame the ex-Yankee or not. His zeal he well knew he could not censure, for he had convincing proof that *that* was ample and untiring. But he was not perfectly satisfied that he had used the necessary skill and caution to capture the runaway. For the present, however, he said nothing more on the subject.

A few days after these occurrences, by a singular coincidence, as many as half a dozen slaves, on three different plantations, ran away from their owners; and from the fact that none of them were as yet retaken, it was supposed that they must have escaped in the newly discovered mode, whatever it was, which Jerry had already practised so successfully.

These repeated escapes, all occurring at nearly the same time, and in the same neighborhood, aroused the attention, as well as the indignation, of all the planters in that vicinity. The emergency was one of more than ordinary importance. If these escapes continued in the same ratio as they had recently begun, there was no telling to what great losses of property the slave-owners might soon be subjected. Suspicions were excited against some person or persons as yet undiscovered, who must have imparted some information, or given some assistance, heretofore unknown to the fugitives, which rendered their escapes so successful. While these thoughts were occupying the attention of the planters in that vicinity, the baffled Robinson one day accidentally overheard the conversation of several of Dudley's negroes.

This conversation took place in the stables, where Jake was currying Richard's favorite saddle horse, Selim. Uncle Ben, the old family coachman, was talking to Jake, who had been ordered by his master to take Jerry's place as his ostler, after the escape of the latter. He unfortunately revealed to Jake, in the hearing of Robinson, how he had, on his return from New Orleans, informed Jerry of all the particulars of the route to that city. He told Jake that Jerry no doubt had escaped by means of the assistance he had given him ; and also inferred, that all the other negroes who had recently taken to flight, must have pursued the same course, and thus attained the same ultimate success.

The instant the ex-Yankee heard this important information, he rushed into the presence of Richard Dudley, in breathless haste. Richard was sitting smoking in the verandah, after supper.

"Sir," said Robinson, "I've found out the mystery

at last. I've discovered who it was that helped Jerry off."

"You have indeed?" inquired Richard, eagerly.

"Yes, I have. I know all about it."

"Well, who was it? Who is the d—— scoundrel? I'll hang him, d—— me if I don't;" exclaimed Richard.

"Well, sir, it's old white headed Ben, your coachman," responded Robinson.

"How did you find that out?"

"I overheard Ben talking, just this minute, to Jake; and he told him how he had taken pity on Jerry, because he was so anxious to see his wife Sarah, and that he had told him all the particulars of the road to New Orleans, where he could find his wife, and where he could conceal himself while in New Orleans," proceeded Robinson.

"Is it possible!" exclaimed Richard, rising. "The infernal old scoundrel! You overheard him, eh? talking to Jake in the barn, eh? Well, I'll punish him for it, I warrant you."

The news soon flew rapidly, not only over the Dudley plantation, but also throughout the neighborhood. Those planters, especially, who had lately lost some of their slaves, took fire at the news; swore to execute summary vengeance; and soon made their appearance at Dudley's house, to consult together as to what had best be done in so appalling an emergency.

The whole neighborhood for miles around was soon

involved in one vast and terrible excitement. A great crisis had evidently arrived in the history of the country, and the most decisive measures must be taken, to bring to immediate justice, the infamous and daring wretch who had thus interfered with the security of slave-property, and had struck so fatal a blow at the very foundations of "the peculiar institution." There was no telling where the evil would end, if not instantly crushed by some signal and appalling punishment. No ordinary vengeance would suffice in this great emergency.

Poor old white-headed Uncle Ben, the unintentional cause of all this frenzy, among the high and low magnates of the land, was still unconscious of the danger which impended over him, until the next day after his overheard conversation with Jake in the stable.

Richard then sent for him to come to the house. In a menacing tone, he inquired whether he knew anything about Jerry's escape to New Orleans.

"No, Master Richard, I does'nt know nothin' about it," was the old man's unfortunate reply.

"Did'nt you tell him how to get to New Orleans, and what roads to take, and where to hide himself when he got there?" inquired Richard in the same tone.

"No, Master Richard, I neber told him nothin' about it, I neber did, master," continued Ben, as tremblingly, he began to discover the peril of his position.

24

"You old black scoundrel, you lie; I know better,' responded his master. "Did'nt you tell Jake all about it yourself yesterday, in the stable? How dare you deny that? I overheard you myself," continued Richard.

The old man now gave himself up for lost. He trembled in every limb. He remembered his imprudence in the conversation just referred to, and knew from the accuracy of his information that Richard must have overheard him.

While he was yet standing before his enraged master in the verandah, his thin white hairs waving in the breeze which blew freshly, their attention was attracted by the loud noise and tumultuous shouts of a crowd of persons who were coming rapidly down the lane, which led to the Dudley mansion from the main road. Of these, some were on foot and a few were on horseback. They came on, cursing and swearing, and raving in the most violent manner. Many of them were evidently under the effect of intoxicating liquor,—in fact, very drunk, and consequently, very savage. Their noise and shouts increased as they approached Richard's house; and without stopping a moment, they poured through the front gate, and rushed up through the yard, toward the house.

Richard came out from the verandah, to meet the crowd, and immediately inquired the object of their visit. He saw among them, several gentlemen from neighboring plantations whom he knew very well, on horseback. He felt no apprehension therefore, and was much more surprised than alarmed at the singularity of their visit.

One of the leaders of the crowd, who was evidently a drunken overseer, a white man, and probably another ex-Yankee, if his history were known, answered in a loud and fierce tone: "We've come to take that nigger of your'n, which has been helping our niggers to run away. Where is he?"

"Who told you I have such a negro here?" inquired Richard in a self-possessed and indifferent manner.

"The whole country knows it. And the scoundrel has helped one of your own niggers off, too. We want to punish him."

"What do you propose to do with him," asked Richard.

"Oh, we're a'going to make an example of him. We'll hang him, eh? boys!" said the leader, turning toward the crowd for an answer.

"No, we'll burn the black scoundrel!" responded one, as drunk as the rest.

"Yes, we'll burn him!" chimed in several others, evidently the drunkest of the whole lot. "Burn him! burn him! burn him!" they continued to vociferate, in the most violent and excited manner.

Richard for a moment, was at a stand still. He had

intended to punish Ben in the most severe manner. But he had not determined to go quite so far as to burn his old family coachman, for the offence which he had committed, aggravating as it was. Beside, the pecuniary loss of a faithful old slave like this, was something to be considered. Ben was a vigorous old man, and might live many years yet. His loss was something, as we said, to be taken into consideration.

But the frenzied crowd were not disposed to allow the young planter any time for consideration. They became more violent and restless. They might proceed to extremities, disagreeable even to himself; for what on earth is so beastly, senseless and devilish, as a drunken rabble of ignorant, debased and infuriated men!

After a moment's hesitation, therefore, Richard pointed to poor old Ben, still standing trembling on the verandah, awaiting his dread fate, and said: "There he is; there is the old fellow who helped our runaway slaves to reach New Orleans. Do with him whatever you wish!"

The words were scarcely out of the mouth of Richard Dudley, when the whole gang of ruffians rushed past him, up to the verandah, and seized hold of the unfortunate wretch, with a violence which threatened to tear him from limb to limb.

They dragged him down into the yard, and after putting him into the middle of the crowd, they consulted together as to what was to be done with their victim. They first tied his hands with a rope, to make his escape impossible. They spent the next few minutes in closely inspecting the person of old Ben, criticising his appearance, and jesting upon his coming agonies. Ben himself was almost speechless from terror, and his eyes rolled around him upon the crowd of infuriated demons who surrounded him, seeking in vain for some friendly face to encourage him.

After a consultation of some minutes it was determined to take Ben to an exposed and barren spot of ground, about a quarter of a mile from Dudley's house, and there burn him to death, as a punishment for the heinous crime, which it was supposed he had committed, against the interests of the slaveowners in that neighborhood. In this judgment Richard Dudley at once acquiesced.

As soon as Ben heard his terrible fate, the old man burst into tears; and he implored his young master, whom he had known and served for his infancy till then, to interpose and save him from so awful a death.

Richard, however, did not pay the least regard to the supplications of the aged slave; and he was dragged away toward the scene of his sufferings, amid the ribald shouts and screams of his persecutors. Richard Dudley slowly followed the crowd at his leisure.

It took but a few minutes for them to reach the spot.
24*

designated. The old man, faint with terror, could scarcely keep up with the hurried pace of his tormentors. Arrived there, the crowd set to work, led on by several slave-drivers, or overseers, among them, to make the necessary preparations for the approaching execution.

By this time, and before their preparations were finished, the news of what was about to take place had been carried far and wide, and there might have been seen running toward this spot, from all directions, persons of various classes and colors, eager to behold, if not to take a part in the horrible and bloody saturnalia about to be consummated.

One of the crowd procured a green willow stake, which was sharpened by an axe at one end, and then driven firmly into the ground. While this was being done, others brought to the spot a large quantity of pine knots and brushwood. Twenty or thirty of the crowd were engaged in this work, for they had some distance to go, and some difficulty in procuring sufficient fuel to accomplish the tedious task of burning a human being to death.

These things all being provided, Ben was first tied to the stake. The old man besought the crowd in the most melting and affecting tones, with prayers and tears, not to punish him with such terrible sufferings; even to hang him, or to kill him first, before they burnt him.

He implored in vain. You might as well expect the

hungry and thirsty Bengal tiger to abstain from devour
ing his helpless prey, which he had just succeeded in
capturing after a long and wearisome chase, as to hope
that that assemblage of freemen, in a Christian land,
would desist from the sweet draught of vengeance and
cruelty before them.

Ben's hands were first tied behind him, and then fastened to the stake; then his feet were tied fast in the
same way. This was done so firmly, that he could not
move an inch from his painful position.

The pine wood, knots and brushwood were soon piled
around him, until nothing appeared above the surrounding fuel, except the white-haired head of the victim,
who looked around him and above him in terror, hoping
for some sudden means of deliverance from his awful
position. But he looked in vain.

The fire is now set to the brushwood, which burns
rapidly, and large volumes of flame and smoke roll upward in the air, around the stake and the victim. Unfortunately, Ben was not suffocated by the smoke or flame,
as every humane person would hope him to have been.
The wind blew to and fro in fitful gusts, so that the
smoke and flame were carried by it alternately in different directions. As the conflagration became larger,
and approached nearer to the victim, and crackled louder,
the infernal joy of the spectators expressed itself in loud
shouts and exultations.

As the flames approached the poor old man, and as he began to feel the sensation produced by the intense heat, his prayers and supplications for mercy were indeed most heart-rending. His screams of agony at length became terrific. The air resounded with his horrid and repeated utterances of suffering, which completely drowned the sound of the crackling flames.

All the brushwood had now been burnt away, and the pine logs which had been piled, end upward, around the victim, had become fairly ignited. The flames had already burnt the white hair from his head, and the lower part of his body and his hands were undergoing the slow process of roasting. Convulsive spasms of agony every now and then shook his body; and from time to time he uttered such piercing shrieks, as one would think must move to pity the hearts of cannibals and devils.

Ben's head now hung down upon his breast. The whole lower limbs of his body had been burnt to a crisp, and he remained attached to the stake only by a large chain, which had been passed tightly around the centre of his body.

At length his groans gradually became fainter and fainter, and finally they ceased entirely—the old man was dead.

But still there was considerable fuel for the flames left upon the stake; and his trunk continued to burn for some time after Ben had ceased to give any signs of life or suffering. The last evidence of this kind which he had given, was one long, loud, piercing, heartrending scream; and with it, his spirit tore itself away from his rapidly consuming frame.

During the time that the burning of Ben was progressing, which was nearly an hour in duration, the surrounding crowd furnished a singular spectacle.

We have read many impressive accounts of the orgies of the naked savages of the South Sea Islands, when devouring their murdered human victims. And we have wondered, whether it could be possible for anything human to be so debased, so savage and so beastial. We have also read of the inhuman cruelty of pirates, desperadoes and murderers, who, in the moment of danger, or of frenzied rage, have committed signal acts of vengeance on powerful, vindictive, but subjugated foes. But we have never read, in all the annals of human ferocity a parallel to this; for here were people who were comparatively enlightened and civilized, rivalling in cruelty the savages of the South Sea Islands. Here were the same people displaying more than a pirate's vengeance upon a fellow being—not upon a formidable one; not one calculated to excite their future apprehension, if unpunished and permitted to go again at large; but upon a poor, harmless, and defenceless slave, whose only crime, during a long life of useful and unrequited

toil, had been that, in a moment of incautious sympathy and benevolence, he had given a little useful information to a fellow slave, who yearned to embrace once
more a beloved wife and child, from whom he had been
cruelly and unjustly separated.

The air was filled with a horrid stench from the burning body. While the flames were doing their work, and
long before the poor old man was dead, the happy crowd
amused and exercised themselves, by throwing stones at
his head, which frequently hit him and severely wounded
him. A loud and exulting laugh would testify to the
delight of the multitude, whenever these missiles touched
the old man's head and wounded him. Laughter, inde-
cent jests, and boisterous buffoonery, were the chief
amusements of the crowd, while the burning of the unhappy slave was in progress

But at length the fun is over. The stake is burnt off
and falls to the ground, with the trunk of old Ben still
attached to it, a blackened mass of crisp; the pine wood
is all burnt away, and a large pile of ashes now covers
the ground where the wood and the stake, and the living
victim so lately had stood. Some of the crowd satiated
their curiosity by coming forward and kicking about the
ashes with their heavy boots, and rolling over and over
the burnt lump of flesh, which was now the only remains
of poor old Uncle Ben.

After loitering around the spot a while longer, and

seeing that all was ended, Richard Dudley, who had been smoking and calmly surveying the whole scene, invited the crowd to adjourn to his house, where they would be furnished with something to drink. They accepted the invitation, and amid their drunken fumes and revelries, they jested long and laughed loudly, at the excellence of the sport; at the dying grimaces and agonies of their victim; and at the justice of the severity of the punishment which had been inflicted upon him.

Richard Dudley's slaves kept out of the way of this horrid sight; they could not bear to see an aged man, so much respected and esteemed as old Uncle Ben had always been, punished with such an awful death. In secret they shed bitter tears, at the thought that so unfortunate an end had at length overtaken him. Richard Dudley inwardly congratulated himself, that if he had lost the value of a slave, he had, at least, punished his impertinence and his temerity as they deserved!*

* Lest it might be asserted that the horrors described in this chapter are the production of fancy, and not the narrative of fact, we will quote from unquestionable authority two other cases of similar, and even of greater ferocity, the truthfulness of which is beyond all cavil:

"Some time during the last week," says an Alabama paper published several years since, "Mr. M'Neilly having lost some clothing, or other property of no great value, the slave of a neighboring planter was charged with the theft. M'Neilly, in company with his brother, found the negro driving his master's wagon; they seized him, and either did, or were about to chastise him, when the negro stabbed M'Neilly, so that he died in an hour afterwards. The negro was taken before a justice of the peace, who *waived his authority,* perhaps through fear, as a crowd of persons had collected to the number of seventy or eighty, near Mr. People's (the justice) house. *He acted as president of the mob,* and put the vote, when it was decided he should be immediately executed by *being burnt to death.* The sable culprit was led to a tree, and tied to it, and a large quantity of pine knots collected and placed around him, and the fatal torch applied to the pile, even against the remonstrances of several gentlemen who were present; and the miserable being was in a short time burned to ashes.

"This is the SECOND negro who has been THUS put to death, without judge or jury, in this county."

Another case, which we quote from the narrative of a Presbyterian clergyman at the South—a Southern man with Northern principles—is as follows:

"In the county of Livingston, Kentucky, near the mouth of Cumberland river, lived Lilburn Lewis, a sister's son of the celebrated Jefferson. He was the wealthy owner of a considerable gang of negroes, whom he drove constantly, fed sparingly, and lashed severely. The consequence was, that they would run away. Among the rest was an ill-thrived boy of about seventeen, who, having just returned from a skulking spell, was sent to the spring for water, and in returning let fall an elegant pitcher: it was dashed to shivers upon the rocks. This was made the occasion for reckoning with him. It was night, and the slaves were all at home. The master had them all collected in the most roomy negro house, and a rousing fire put on. When the door was secured, that none might escape, either through *fear of him* or *sympathy with George,* he opened to them the design of the interview, namely, that they might be effectually advised to *stay at home and obey his orders.* All things now in train, he called up George, who approached his master with unreserved submission. He bound him with cords; and by the assistance of Isham Lewis, his youngest brother, laid him on a broad bench, the *meat-block.* He then proceeded to *hack off George at the ankles!* It was with the *broad axe!* In vain did the unhappy victim *scream and roar!* for he was completely in his master's power; not a hand among so many durst interfere: casting the foot into the fire, he lectured them at some length. He next *chopped ed him off below the knees!* George *roaring out* and praying his master to begin at the *other end!* He admonished them again, throwing the logs into the fire—then, above the knees, tossing the joints into the fire—the next stroke severed the thighs from the body; these were also committed to the flames—and so it may be said of the arms, head and trunk, until all was in the fire! He threatened any of them with similar punishment who should in future disobey, run away, or disclose the proceedings of that evening. Nothing now remained but to consume the flesh and bones; and for this purpose the fire was brightly stirred until two hours after midnight; when a coarse and heavy back-wall, composed of rock and clay covered the fire and the remains of George. It was the Sabbath—this put an end to the *amusements* of the evening. The negroes were now permitted to disperse, with charges to keep this matter among themselves, and never to whisper it in the neighborhood, under the penalty of a like punishment.

"When he returned home and retired, his wife exclaimed, 'Why, Mr. Lewis, where have you been, and what were you doing?' She had heard a strange *pounding* and dreadful *screams*, and had smelled something like fresh meat *burning*. The answer he returned was, that he had never enjoyed himself at a ball so well as he had enjoyed himself that night."—*See "American Slavery as It Is;"* p. 72.

CHAPTER XX.

SOUTHERN LAW AND JUSTICE.

THE cheerless and gloomy days of George's existence
still continued to wear away. Life had become a blank
to him. It was now a desolate waste, without one cheer
ing spot of hope or verdure, amid the boundless desert
of the future. Those whom he loved were dead; and
his life was spent in thankless toil, without experiencing
a single sensation in consonance with the desires and
aspirations of his nature.

Richard Dudley continued on all possible occasions to
persecute this slave. Whenever George came across
his path, his inexorable spite seemed to revive afresh
with undying bitterness; for every time his eye rested
upon George, he thought of his failure in the accomplishment of his brutal purposes in reference to Caroline. George had been the only obstacle which stood
in the way of that coveted gratification; and he was determined never to forgive him.

It is a principle of human nature, that men always

hate those intensely, whom they are conscious of having deeply injured; just as we are disposed to feel kindly towards those for whom we have performed a kind and generous action. This rule was applicable to Richard Dudley; he had injured and persecuted George beyond measure, without the least particle of just cause; and he consequently hated him in the same unlimited degree.

Dark thoughts of suicide frequently rushed upon the mind of the slave. How much more desirable would be the eternal peace and repose of the graves than this bitter life of toil, and defenceless persecution? And yet George was a Christian; and he knew that to become a suicide was an act forbidden by the laws of God, and forever subjected the offender to his just displeasure. He resisted all such temptations with abhorrence, though he did not want the courage to make his quietus, had his conscience permitted him.

George had also heard that there was a nominal protection of law for the slave, when the cruelties of the master became excessive. If there ever was a case, in which the protection of the law ought to be invoked, his was the one.* In a moment of desperation, he deter-

---

* That the reader may form an idea of what protection the law nominally gives the slaves in the South, we append the following extracts from the laws of South Carolina and Louisiana.

"The slave is entirely subject to the will of his master, who may correct

mined to see whether he could obtain any alleviation of his miseries from that quarter.

and chastise him, though not with unusual rigor, nor so as to maim or mutilate him, or to expose him to the danger of loss of life, or to cause his death."—*Civil Code of Louisiana*, Article 173.

And again:

"If any slave be mutilated, beaten, or ill-treated, contrary to the true intent and meaning of this section, when no one shall be present, in such case the owner, or other person having the charge or management of said slave thus mutilated, shall be deemed responsible and guilty of the said offence, and shall be prosecuted without further evidence, unless the said owner, or other person so as aforesaid, can prove the contrary by means of good and sufficient evidence, or can clear himself by his own oath, which said oath every court under the cognizance of which each offence shall have been examined and tried is by this act authorized to administer."— *Code Noir. Crimes and Offences*, 56, xvii. *Rev. Stat.* 1852, p. 550, § 141.

"If any person shall, on a sudden heat or passion, or by *undue correction*, kill his own slave, or the slave of any other person, he shall forfeit the sum of *three hundred and fifty pounds* current money."—*James' Digest*, 392.

"In case any person shall wilfully cut out the tongue, put out the eye, ● ● ● or cruelly scald, burn, or deprive any slave of any limb, or member, or shall inflict any other cruel punishment, *other than* by whipping or beating with a horse-whip, cowskin, switch, or small stick, or by putting irons on, or confining or imprisoning such slave, every such person shall, for every such offence, forfeit the sum of one hundred pounds current money."—*2 Brevard's Dig.* 241.

"Whereas, by another Act of the Assembly, passed in 1774, the killing of a slave, however wanton, cruel and deliberate, is only punishable in the first instance by imprisonment and paying the value thereof to the owner, which *distinction of criminality between the murder of a white person and one who is equally a human creature, but merely of a different complexion, is* DISGRACEFUL TO HUMANITY, AND DEGRADING IN THE HIGHEST DEGREE TO

Early one morning after he had received another brutal beating by Richard's orders, before the slaves were called out to the field, he started for the neighboring town of N———, which lay about five miles east of the Dudley plantation. This was an inland town of about two thousand inhabitants. He arrived about ten o'clock, and walked up the main street, toward the centre of the village, determined to inquire for the office of a magistrate.

As he approached the centre of the town, he perceived that the large building known as the Court House, was open; and that a crowd of people were entering it. It so happened, that the quarterly term of the Criminal Court or Sessions was just then being held; and if there was any justice for the slave, here then was a favorable opportunity to apply for it.

He entered the Court House. The Judge was about to take his seat upon the bench. The Court had not yet been opened, and the crowd were gradually getting

THE LAWS AND PRINCIPLES OF A FREE, CHRISTIAN AND ENLIGHTENED COUNTRY, Be it enacted, &c., That if any person shall hereafter be guilty of wilfully and maliciously killing a slave, such offender shall, upon the first conviction thereof, be adjudged guilty of murder, and shall suffer the same punishment as if he had killed a free man: *Provided always, this act shall not extend to the person killing a slave* OUTLAWED BY VIRTUE OF ANY ACT OF ASSEMBLY OF THIS STATE, *or to any slave in the act of resistance to his lawful owner or master, or to any slave dying under moderate correction.*" *Ibid.*

25*

seated.   George walked up to the bar in front of the
Judge, who was sitting, unoccupied, and waiting for the
crier to open the Court.   He stated to the Judge in a
plain and respectful manner, that he was the slave of
Richard Dudley, and that his master was so excessively
cruel to him, that he had been driven by necessity to
make a complaint against him.

The Judge heard his complaint; ordered the clerk to
make out a warrant for Richard Dudley, which he placed
in the hands of an officer, with orders to ride immediately to the Dudley plantation, and bring Mr. Dudley
into Court.   Meanwhile, he committed George to the
county jail adjoining, to prevent his running away, and
for safe keeping until the hearing of the case could be
had.

While the officer is serving the warrant upon Richard
Dudley, let us take a look at the Court which is to try
the merits of this case, and dispense Southern justice to
the slave.

Judge Rotten was the distinguished individual who
held the important office of county judge, in the town
of N———.   He was comparatively an old man ;
and had attained his present position under somewhat
peculiar circumstances.   His personal appearance was
not very much in his favor.   He was a very lean man,
of medium height, with black hair, and immense black
whiskers.

His history was as peculiar and questionable as his appearance. His origin was among the dregs of the populace; but being very ambitious, and having some talent, he soon aspired above the mechanical trade of carpenter, to which he had been very judiciously apprenticed in his youth; and at the age of forty, without any liberal or classical education whatever, commenced the study of the law. Admitted to the bar, he became the most thorough-going demagogue in the land. He was a great politician; always ready to speak, upon all occasions, and upon any side of any question, which might offer. He rode every hobby that presented itself. There was no town meeting, no political assemblage, even no religious gathering, in which Judge Rotten was not present, and did not manage in some way or other to have something to say.

The consequence of all this assiduous pursuit of popularity was, that he gradually wormed his way forward. Judge Rotten having luckily, and to the surprise and disgust of all respectable citizens, attained the office of county judge, each day more clearly exposed his utter incompetercy for his position, and imparted to that position the disgrace reflected from the deformities of his own character.

About twelve o'clock the officer returned, and Richard Dudley entered the court in company with Robinson. In the first interval of business, Judge Rotten called up the case of George against his master. The court room was crowded with people. Some eight or ten lawyers occupied the bar. The table was covered with books, papers, and green bags, and quite an appearance of business pervaded the court room.

As soon as Richard Dudley approached the bar, he was discovered by a legal gentleman, who rejoiced in the name of Lawyer Snake; who, judging from his appearance that Richard was a man of respectability and property, instantly approached him, and blandly volunteered his services as his attorney, in case he should need one.

The matter was quite indifferent to Richard, and he accepted the offer.

Lawyer Snake was a fearfully tall, lean, and hungry-looking individual, whose only talent was a small degree of superficial cunning. He had not been very successful at the bar, and was usually somewhat short of funds. Nevertheless, he was very foppish in his dress; wore a wig to cover the baldness of his head; sported a formidable quantity of second-hand, inferior jewelry, much to the astonishment and admiration of the lower class of litigants in the court house.

He introduced Richard to a seat within the bar, and next to himself. Judge Rotten called up the case, and Counsellor Snake rose and informed the Court, that he appeared as counsel for the defendaut, the gentleman sitting at his side; at the same time pointing with some pride to Richard, his very respectable looking client.

Judge Rotten ordered George to take the witness stand. The latter did so. Novel and trying as his situation was, George was not in the least degree confused or disconcerted.

In answer to the inquiries of Judge Rotten, he gave a clear statement of the facts in his case. He described all the punishments of whipping, ducking, fettering, and so on, to which he had been so long subjected; and declared that he had ever exerted himself to serve his master faithfully, and to the best of his ability; that all was to no use; his life was a continued scene of suffering, ignominy, and despair. He implored the Judge, in conclusion, that if there was any protection for him in the law, that it might be extended to him, and his master be compelled, under some bond or other, to treat him hereafter with at least common humanity.

While George was giving in his evidence, Richard Dudley sat eyeing his slave with a malicious scowl of contempt and defiance.

As soon as Judge Rotten had finished examining the poor slave, Lawyer Snake proceeded to cross-examine him with great severity, and at considerable length.

Snake. What is your name, sir?*

* These questions are about as relevant as most of the questions which are frequently put in courts of justice; especially when the object is to

George. I am called George Sanford.

Snake. How old are you, sir?

George. I am about twenty-six or seven years old.

Snake. Where were you born?

George. I was born on the Dudley plantation, about five miles from here.

Snake. Is your father living?

George. No, sir, he is dead these many years.

Snake. Is your mother living?

George. No, sir, she too is dead this long time.

Snake. You are sure she is dead; are you perfectly sure?

George. Yes, sir, I was present when she died.

Snake. Have you any brothers?

George. No, sir, I have none.

Snake. Have you any sisters?

George. No, sir, I have neither brother nor sister.

Snake. You are sure you have no sister, are you?

George. Yes, sir, I am perfectly sure.

Snake. Well, can you read?

George. Yes, sir, I have learned to read.

Snake. Can you write?

George. No, sir, I am unable to write.

Snake. Are you married?

---

evade the true issue, and conceal the real weakness of a client and his cause. It is for the purpose of illustrating this subject, that they are here introduced into the text.

George. "I have been married, sir, but my wife is now dead," answered George, a pang of agony shooting through his heart, as he thought of his murdered wife and child.

Snake. Have you any children?

George. No, sir, I had one, but it is dead, too.

Snake. Have you enough to eat?

George. Yes, sir, I am seldom hungry.

Snake. Do you ever get drunk?

George. No, sir, never; I never drink liquor.

Snake. Now, are you perfectly sure that you never get drunk? Remember, you are on your oath.

George. Yes, sir, I am perfectly sure.

Snake. You think yourself as good as a white man, don't you?

George. No, sir, I am nothing but a poor slave.

Snake. You think slavery wrong, don't you?

George. Yes, sir, I do, but I am willing to submit.

Snake. But you would much rather be free, I dare say?

George. Yes, sir, I confess it, I would like to be free.

Snake. Ah, that's very singular, you're quite dainty. Do you not sometimes preach, too?

George. Yes, sir, I sometimes preach to my fellow slaves.

Snake. And teach them to read, eh?

George. I have taught several of them to read.

Snake. And you tell them slavery is wrong, do you not?

George. I tell them they must submit to the fate Providence has designed for them.

Snake. Ah, that is very good of you, indeed. Well, you say that Mr. Dudley abuses you, and treats you cruelly, do you?

George. Yes, sir, I have said so, and it is the truth.

At this moment Lawyer Snake solemnly arose, and moved the court to rule out the whole of George's testimony, *as incompetent and inadmissible, on the ground, that by the statute a negro can never be allowed, under any circumstances whatever, to give testimony against a white man!*

Judge Rotten at once admitted the validity of the objection, and George was rudely ordered to stand back from the witness box.

With an air of great triumph, lawyer Snake then informed the Court, that he would now call a witness, who would give the true facts in the case to the honorable Court.

Snake, (loudly). " Mr. Robinson, take the witness stand, if you please." Robinson came forward, and inserted himself into the box appropriated to the witnesses.

Snake. Where do you live, Mr. Robinson?

Robinson. I am overseer for Mr. Dudley.

Snake. You know this slave George, do you?

Robinson. Yes, sir, I know him very well.

Snake. What is his character as a servant?

Robinson. He is very stubborn and sulky, and sometimes he is very disobedient, and hard to manage.

Snake. Does his master ever treat him with cruelty, as he has represented here?

Robinson. Never, sir; I never knew any thing of the kind.

Snake. If there had been any thing of the kind, would you most certainly have known it?

Robinson. Yes, sir, I would have known it. The slaves on the plantation cannot be punished and I not know it.

Snake. George is treated well then by his master, is he?

Robinson. Yes, sir, very well, much better than he deserves. His master is very kind and gentle with him, gives him but little work to do, and feeds and clothes him better than any of the rest of his slaves.

After this conclusive testimony in rebuttal of evidence which had been entirely ruled out, lawyer Snake observed to the Court: "If your Honor please, you have now heard the true facts in this case, and I ask, in behalf of my client, that the complaint be dismissed."

Judge Rotten. There is no evidence before me whatever, to implicate Mr. Dudley in this charge of cruelty to this slave. On the contrary, the evidence is all entirely the other way. The complaint is therefore dismissed. "George!" continued the judge to the complainant, who had retired and had sat down upon one of

26

the benches in the rear of the building, "George, don't you come here again to trouble the Court with any more such unfounded complaints. If you do, I shall punish you severely !"

Poor George justly thought to himself, that such a court, and such a judge, were very fit and suitable subjects for contempt, and that they deserved to be regarded with no other sentiment.

. As soon as the case was dismissed, Richard ordered Robinson to take charge of George, and drive him back to the plantation. He himself determined to remain in town for a day or two.

At three o'clock the Court adjourned for the day; Richard handed Lawyer Snake a handsome fee; and that evening Judge Rotten, Richard and Lawyer Snake spent nearly the whole night together in a boisterous carouse.

The next day Richard Dudley rode home, exulting in the utter defeat of George's complaint against him, and admiring the even-handedness with which Southern law dispenses perfect justice between the master and the slave.

CHAPTER XXI.

A REPRESENTATIVE OF CONGO.

"OLD HANNIBAL" was the name of an aged negro, who belonged to the Dudley plantation, and had lived upon it from the earliest recollection of the oldest inhabitant.

He was a person of colossal size, as black as ebony, and must have been at least a hundred years old. His hair was perfectly white, though from its usually tangled condition it looked like the head of a Gorgon, intertwined with snakes; or, to use a more modern, and less classical allusion, his head resembled a birch broom in fits; his nails he permitted to grow to an immense length, and he had other personal peculiarities which rendered him every way a very remarkable individual.

Hannibal had never been married, and was not known to have any relation or kindred of any degree, living on the earth; he was born in Congo, in Africa, and in early life he had been captured by a Spanish slaver; was brought to America and sold as a slave at New Orleans, at a period prior to the abolition of the African slave-

trade. He had been purchased by an ancestor of Richard Dudley; had been brought by him to the Dudley
estate; and there he had remained ever since, with the
exception we will mention, during a period of at least
seventy-five years. He had outlived three or four generations of his master's family.

During the revolutionary war Old Hannibal had been
a soldier, and "fit," not exactly in the ranks, but he had
served among the Continental army; sometimes as a
keeper of the tents and baggage; sometimes as a body
servant to his then master, Richard's grandfather, a
colonel in the Continental troops, under the heroic
Marion; and in any and every capacity in which he might
make himself useful. And he had been very serviceable
on several critical occasions; one of them may be briefly
mentioned.

The small army of patriots under Marion had made a
long and very fatiguing march, to effect a surprise upon
a portion of the British troops stationed in Alabama.
Late at night they had arrived at a short distance from
the foe, whom they proposed to attack unexpectedly,
early the following morning. The troops were excessively weary, and to save the men, such faithful followers of the camp were stationed as picket-guards, as could
be relied upon. The post of greatest danger being
nearest to the lines of the enemy, was assigned to Old

Hannibal, in whom Colonel Dudley always placed the greatest confidence.

The guard was quietly set. Old Hannibal boldly assumed his post of danger, and kept it with wakeful vigilance. But the approach of the Americans had not been as hidden from the foe as they expected; the British and their allies, the Indians, had been informed by their spies of the arrival of our troops in their vicinity, and they naturally inferred that an attack was contemplated early the next day.

They knew that our troops being fatigued with a long march, would by midnight be sunk in deep slumber, overcome by weariness; and they determined to take advantage of the opportunity, and make a midnight attack. Such an attack, effected by such an union of civilized and savage ferocity, would doubtless tell, with fatal effect, on the Americans.

The night advanced, and Old Hannibal kept up a vigilant outlook. The wearied Americans were soon sunk in deep slumber; their camp was pitched in a thick forest, and the British lay about a mile distant, on the outskirts of the cleared country. As the hours advanced, the watchful Hannibal thought that he heard some sounds of suspicious activity wafted upon the midnight breeze, from the adverse camp. These sounds became more and more distinct; and yet they were of such a confused and mysterious character, that it was

26*

impossible for him to detect the real movements which they indicated. At length, in the darkness he thought he saw a black form stealthily approaching him on all-fours; something which seemed to resemble a large black bear. It was in truth an Indian disguised in a bear's skin, who was attempting to approach him, and in an instant, before he could give any alarm, stab him to death; and having thus despatched the guard, the foe could spring unheralded upon the sleeping camp.

The vigilance of Old Hannibal, however, saved the Americans; in an instant his rifle was raised to his eye, and he shot the pretended bear through the heart. The instant this was done the attacking force advanced in a body; but the report of Old Han's rifle had already aroused the Americans; they sprang to their arms on the instant; Hannibal rushed into the camp to confirm the news of the impending attack; and the British received such a fierce reception that they fled after a short conflict, leaving a very large number of dead and wounded on the field.

The intrepidity and vigilance of Old Hannibal, had saved the American army from a most destructive defeat.

In consequence of this eminent service, he had always been treated with more than usual lenity on the Dudley plantation; and having long outlived the time when negroes are expected to serve their owners, his superfluity of age and life had been pretty much given over to his own use; and now, at the period of which we write, Old Hannibal was allowed to do very nearly as he pleased.

He was still a heathen, however; having obstinately adhered, during his long life, to the idolatrous usages and opinions which he had learned in his youth, among the fragrant groves and plains of Congo. He still kept up, from time to time, the observance of some of the idolatrous rites of his native country. Not all the missionary efforts of all the preachers to whom he had occasionally listened during his long life, though always with no other feelings than those of contempt, had ever produced the least conviction upon his mind.

He still dressed himself on general training days, in two valuable remnants of his Revolutionary uniform, which·still survived the lapse of years; these were a glazed hat, with a faded red cockade stuck into the front of it; and an old coat, with very short tails, and striped with a few red pieces of tape sewed over the breast and shoulders. He uniformly took his place in the ranks, on all occasions of militia training; and his great age, his revolutionary services, and the general eccentricities of his character, gave him the privilege of mustering along with white people. On these occasions the old man walked proudly erect; kept time with the drum and fife with questionable accuracy, and exhibited a laughable, though vain determination, to keep step with the music.

Old Hannibal usually occupied his time in fishing, and in tending his corn and potato patch. His sight was still good; and it was amazing to see, with what vigor his aged frame had borne up against the attacks of time. Once, in a long while, he would get drunk on raw whiskey. On these occasions, however, he was quite harmless, and gave offence to no one, confining himself entirely to his hut. He subsisted almost entirely on the product of his fishing, and of his vegetable patch.

He had built with his own hands, across the creek which ran about a mile from the Dudley mansion, a stone dam, for the purpose of driving the fish into a large wooden fish-trap, built as such contrivances usually are, of long thin slats of wood placed in a slanting position, by which they caught the descending water, and with it, the fish which might be driven into the trap by the force of the current. Among his other peculiarities, he would eat snakes, of that harmless sort known as water snakes, which were caught along with the fish in his trap.

The stream was bordered on each bank with tall trees, and thick brushwood. Near the fish trap, on one of the banks, was a smooth open space, overshadowed by the trees, where the only sounds which greeted the ear, was that of the winds sighing among the limbs above, and

the everlasting murmur of the waters of the stream below. Here, on this open spot of ground, was the place
where Hannibal performed, from time to time, the idolatrous ceremonies which he had carried with him from
his native Congo, and which, for nearly a century, he
had religiously observed.

One Sunday afternoon, as George Sanford, overcome
by the loneliness and sadness of his situation, wandered
abroad toward the spot which we have just described, he
came suddenly upon old Hannibal, while he was engaged
in his religious ceremonies. He saw that the aged
idolater had not discovered his approach, and he determined to watch, unobserved, the religious mummeries
of the old man. The latter was bareheaded, his long
white hair was wafted idly to and fro in the breeze.

In the centre of the bare spot of ground was placed
an altar, in the shape of a single large square stone.
Upon that stone was placed a very small image, carved
in wood, which was of circular form, and resembled a
ball more than anything else, though flat at the sides,
and covered with strange figures. Before it, were deposited on the ground, the contents of the fish-trap
which Hannibal had just visited, and cleared of its victims. The old man first approached the image, got down
on his knees, and bowed himself repeatedly to it, uttering aloud at the same time a string of unintelligible jargon. He then rose from his knees, and danced wildly

three times around his god, accompanying his movements
with short, quick screeches and shouts. This done, he
returned again to his first position, bowed himself repeatedly to his image; then held it high above him in
the air, while he gazed upon it with exultation; and then
placed it back again with the greatest care and reverence upon his altar. After this, he took up one fish
after another from the ground, and laid it upon the stone
before the image. Then he danced again three times
around it, as before, accompanied by the same chanting
of the same mysterious words; which were a religious
song of Congo, which he had remembered and cherished
during his long life.

Various other ceremonies followed, too senseless and
absurd to bear repetition. One of these, however, may
be mentioned. Old Hannibal frequently held up his
image directly between his eye and the sun, gazing upon
the former, and uttering mysterious shouts of enthusiasm
as he did so.

The image in question was one which the old idolater
had brought with him in his youth from his native land.
It remained suspended around his neck during all the
fearful horrors of the middle passage; and had then
escaped the notice and the violence of the Spanish
slavers. He had preserved it ever since, with the most
profound reverence, as an infinitely precious god; and
for seventy-five years he had continued to worship it.

He always carried it suspended around his neck; and as soon as his mummeries on this occasion were ended, he carefully took it up from its pedestal, and hung it by a cord in its accustomed place.

Old Hannibal was about filling a small basket with the fish he had caught, preparatory to returning home, when George came forward and discovered himself.

"How do you do to-day, Hannibal?" said George.

"I'se middlin', George, how does you do?" said the old man, looking up toward his friend.

"What is that you've got around your neck?" inquired George; for Hannibal had always tried to conceal his idol from the vulgar gaze of the people; and long as George had known Hannibal, he had never before seen the curiosity in question.

"Hush! honey, hush! Musn't ask ole Han about dat ar," replied he.

"Why not? is it anything so wonderful? Let me see it, won't you?"

"I neber shows dat ar to anybody. Dat come from Congo wid me,—long, long ago," chuckled the old man, as he put his hand inside his shirt and took hold of the treasure, to grasp it more safely.

"Come, sit down, and tell me what you have been doing here, Hannibal. I've seen all your manœuvres here this afternoon, without your knowing it. Come, tell me what it all means," said George, and he led the old man back again to the spot where the large square stone lay, and they both sat down upon it.

"What does all this mean? this dancing, singing, and so on, in which you have been engaged?"

"Dat's my religion, George. Dat's de true religion. Dat's de way dey worships in Congo, whar I cum from, honey."

"Who is it that you worship? Is it that little image which you carry around your neck?"

"Yes, I worships dat little image; but dat image is a god, and he is mighty pow'rful. He is de broder of de sun, yonder; dat ar sun. I worships de sun, honey. De sun is de true God. He makes ebryting; he makes eberyting grow. He is de only true God. He made us, and de world, and ebryting."

"Are you sure of that, Hannibal?"

"Yes, I is sure of dat. I learned dat in Congo, whar I was born. I knows it is true," said Hannibal.

"Did that god ever do you any good?"

"Yes, many times," replied the old heathen.

"Where did you get it from?"

"It dropt down from de sun in Congo, and it is a oroder of de sun, or may be a piece of de sun." With this he ventured to pull out his treasure from his bosom, and showed it to George; though he would not permit him to touch or to handle it.

"What good has this god done you, Hannibal?"

"Why doesn't you see? Here I is, most a hundred years .:1. All de oder niggers which I knew in my time, is dead. I've seen hundreds of niggers die in my time. And yet, here I is. I fit in de Rebolushun, and was neber wounded nor kilt. De Injuns and de British couldn't tech me wid deir long rifles, kase I had dis here 'around my neck. No, dey neber could tech old Han, no how. He! he! he!" and the old man chuckled at the thought of his many hairbreadth escapes—all through the protection of his Congo god.

"Hannibal," said George, "did you ever hear of Jesus Christ, our Saviour?"

"Yes, I often hearn of him. He's nobody. He's nothin' but a man. He's dead dis long time, and here is my god; he aint dead, not he."

"What do you know about Jesus Christ, Hannibal?" inquired George, solemnly.

"Dey tells me dat when he lived he wanted to be somebody, but he couldn't. Dey kilt him at last, so dey all tells me."

"Yes, they murdered him. But he was God."

"A mighty pore God he war den, to be kilt by de people. You couldn't kill my God dere," pointing upward to the sun. "No, you couldn't do dat."

"Yes, but he died by his own consent."

"Den he must a liked dyin' better dan de most of folks does; dats all. He! he!"

27

"But he died to redeem us fallen creatures."

"He must a had mighty leetle to do, to die for oder people. He gits mighty little thanks for it, I reck'n."

"That's true, Hannibal. Mankind are ungrateful. But he is our true God and Saviour."

"Is he? I wouldn't swop mine for yourn, den, no how," responded the aged infidel.

"Are you prepared to die, Hannibal?"

"Yes, I is. I wants to go. I'se a hundred years old now, most, and I wants to go."

"Where do you expect to go to, when you die?"

"Go to? Golly, I goes right back to Congo when I dies; dat's sartin. De moment I is dead, I flies 'cross de big waters, to de happy shores ob Congo. Dare is all my people. Dare we dance and sing, and play de banjo. Dare is my sisters and broders; and dare we gits gold and big elephants' tushes ob white ibory. Dare our little huts is bilt among de palm trees, and de bananas, and de spicy grobes. Dare is no work, nor nothin' to do. Dare too, is my young sweetheart Abo, dat 1 left there seventy-five years ago. She's as young and purty now as eber, and waits for me. Oh, I'll soon go back to Congo! I'll go back to Congo!" and the old man broke out into a frenzied song of rapture, at the thought of going back again to his beloved Congo.

"I'm afraid you are a great sinner, Hannibal, like

myself," said George, trying to do the old man some good, if possible.

"I aint no sinner. I does nothin' wrong. I'se never done nobody any harm, and I'se done a great deal of good in my time, and 'tic'larly in de Rebolushun. Den, beside dat, I'se worshipt my God here, eber since I was in Congo. I neber missed a day since I came across de big water. Now you neber worshipt de true God in all your life, honey; kase you don't know nothin about him. You'se a great sinner and heathen, not me. I goes strait to Congo when I dies," continued the old man. "You neber git dar."

"Alas, Hannibal! you have worshipped a false god all your life. The true God is he who made all things, and ourselves," said George.

"No, my God made eberything, not yourn."

"How will you prove that, Hannibal?"

"How will you prove dat your God made eberyting? You wasn't dar when eberyting was made; neder was I dar. I hab jes as good proof dat my god made eberyting, as you have dat your God made eberyting. Beside, I see my god; he is de sun; but you neber seed your God. You wouldn't know de critter if you was to meet him."

"But my God, Hannibal, is invisible to mortal eyes, in the very nature of things," said George.

"Ob course he is inbisible. You neber yit seed anyting what neber was, dat was inbisible. If anyting *is*, you kin always *see* it. If you can't see it, why den it isn't at all; and dats de way wid your God. He isn't nowhar—he! he!—and you can't see him, no how."

"I see it is not much use to reason with you, Hannibal, I'm afraid you are an obstinate unbeliever," said George.

While this conversation was progressing, evening approached, and with it the evidences of an approaching storm. George asked Hannibal if he was ready to go home. Hannibal replied, that he believed that he would stay awhile, and worship his god again.

George left him to return to his hut, and as he departed from the spot, he saw the old man return to the stone altar, take out his god, and place it upon its accustomed pedestal. He soon heard him singing, shouting and dancing around his Congo deity as before, and one of the last sentences he distinguished was, that he'd go back to Congo soon again.

George hastened home, for the storm was coming up with terrific fury. The thunder roared, and the dark heavens were torn with the forked lightnings. The wind swept with the fury of a hurricane over the land, tearing up trees and bushes, and oversetting fences, outhouses and cabins. The tempest still raged in all its fury, as dark night settled down upon the earth.

The next morning Old Hannibal was found dead, laying by the side of his Congo god.

He had been struck with lightning, while engaged in his heathen worship, during the storm of the previous evening.

He had, at last, gone back to Congo!

CHAPTER XXII.

....HERN FIELD SPORTS.—THE SLAVE HUN...

The stars and stripes, immortal let them wave,
O'er freedom's home, and fetters of the slave!

GEORGE SANFORD had now lost his only friend, and
he felt homeless and desolate on the earth. He longed
for the hour which was to set his own spirit free, and
release him from an existence which he now felt to be
blasted in all its legitimate aims, and made only a source
of misery and degradation to its unfortunate possessor.
But death was not yet allowed to come to his relief; he
had still more calamities to endure, before he received
his deliverance from bondage.

Richard Dudley still pursued George with a cruelty
and hatred which seemed to be inexorable,—to know
neither cessation nor relaxation. By Richard's express
orders, to George were assigned the most burdensome
tasks, and if his strength failed him to execute them, he
received the most cruel punishment, sometimes from the
hand of Robinson, and sometimes from the hand of

Richard himself. These punishments were of several sorts. Terrible whipping was one of them; fastening a heavy iron ball to his leg by a chain and ring around his ankle, was another. The ring once happened to be too tight, and being rough and rugged, it so lacerated his flesh as to produce mortification, and being of thick iron, it was almost impossible afterward to remove it, without tearing the bleeding flesh, and inflicting the greatest agony on the sufferer. At another time George was " ducked" in a tub of water, by his unfeeling master. The latter took peculiar pleasure in the infliction of this punishment. He ordered a large tub to be filled with water; taking George by the neck, he forced his head under the surface, and held him there, enduring all the pangs of suffocation, for a minute or more ; and if George struggled to release himself, he held him by main force beneath the surface, till life was well nigh extinct. Robinson stood by to aid, in case the resistence of the poor wretch became desperate. On one of these occasions George struggled fearfully under the water, but the more he struggled, the tighter was the grip with which his two tormentors held him under ; and when they released him, he seemed to be dead, and was unable to raise himself. Robinson instantly jerked his head from the water, and it was some time before George was restored to his senses.

Savage vengeance such as this, and the desolate condition in which he was placed, at length induced the poor, persecuted slave to think of running away, with the dim hope of traversing the vast area of bondage which he knew intervened between Louisiana and Canada. He watched the north star in the heavens, and determined at length, after long and bitter misgivings, to attempt the great and desperate task, upon the event of which hung all his future destiny and career. It was after one of the most savage and brutal " duckings" which he had ever endured, that he made up his mind to commence his flight. To remain where he was, was worse than death; but if he made the venture who could tell but that, like many more, as miserable and as desperate as himself, he might perchance succeed. He could but fail, and even perish in the attempt; and in that result, he could not be more miserable than he then actually was. He had never been informed of the success of Jerry's expedition.

It was a dark and stormy night, upon which this persecuted and friendless slave mustered courage to leave the scene of his miseries. Tying up two or three articles of clothing in a bundle, he took the precious keepsake which his murdered wife had given him, kissed it fervently, and pinned it carefully next his bosom. He then knelt upon the floor of his humble cabin, and implored the blessing of heaven on the attempt he was about to make, to escape from bondage, and the vengeance of the taskmaster. His strong heart trembled within him, as he sat upon the side of his bed, and for a few moments pondered over the immense hazards of the die about to be cast. But he was desperate, and desperation at length gave determination to his will. He uttered another short prayer, gave a last look around his rude cabin, the scene of so much rapture and of such deep woe, and then glided silently from the door in the rear, across the cotton fields which adjoined the slave huts, and ran for the swamp, which was situated some five miles to the north of the Dudley plantation.

It was about ten o'clock at night when George left his cabin, and the grey tints of morning began to appear in the East, as he approached the outskirts of the well-known swamp in which he was about to take refuge. On his way thither, he had passed near the buildings of several plantations; but as the night was dark and stormy, and the wind blew violently, and the rain decended in torrents, he managed to escape observation.

Silence rested over the Dudley plantation on the next morning till a later hour than usual. There was no work to be done on the day succeeding George's flight. Nor was that day Sunday. What then could be the reason for such a strange divergence from the usual prevalent custom? Can the reader forget that American freemen have a political Sabbath, as well as a religious one? Can he forget that there is one day in the year, which is observed with pride and acclamations from Maine to California, from the Atlantic shore to the Pacific wave?

The day after George's flight was the immortal Fourth of July, the birthday of American freedom!

As the slaves were not called out to muster for the cotton-field, the absence of the fugitive was not discovered until about ten o'clock in the day.

Uncle Jesse called at George's cabin after he had eaten his breakfast of corn cake and fat pork; but he found the cabin empty, and its inmate gone. He at once informed his wife Harriet of his discovery. She told the news to a female negro friend of her's, who happened to be in the hut at the time; but under solemn promise that she would not reveal it.

Nevertheless, by twelve o'clock, the news had become generally known among the slaves on the plantation, that George Sanford had fled; and it was not long after, that the information reached the ears of Richard Dudley. His rage knew no bounds. He raved, stamped, and cursed. His fury was indeed appalling to look upon. He came out on the verandah, and there pacing to and fro, he immediately summoned Robinson; and fiercely demanded of him, what he knew about the escape of George.

"Nothing at all, sir;" replied Robinson, with much surprise.

"We must hunt him out instantly," said Richard. "I wonder which way the black scoundrel fled?"

"No doubt, toward the swamp," responded Robinson.

"Have we any dogs near the plantation?" inquired Richard.

"Not one; but we can get a pack not many miles off. I saw in the Monroe paper yesterday, a pack of hounds advertised. I think I have the paper here in my pocket, now." Robinson fumbled about his person for a moment, and then produced a newspaper, from which he read the following advertisement.

"NEGRO DOGS

"The undersigned would respectfully inform the citizens of Ouachita and adjacent parishes, that he has located about 2½ miles east of John White's, on the road leading from Monroe to Bastrop, and that he has a fine pack of Dogs for catching negroes. Persons wishing negroes caught will do well to give him a call. He can always be found at his stand when not engaged in hunting, and even then information of his whereabouts can always be had of some one on the premises.

"*Terms.*—Five dollars per day and found, when there is no track pointed out. When the track is shown, twenty-five dollars will be charged for catching the negro."

"Order Jake to ride over to the writer of that advertisement, and engage him instantly to hunt up George," said Richard. "I will send another advertisement to that paper, so that the whole neighborhood may be on the look out for him. Come in the house, and I will write one for Jake, to take to the paper,"

and the two gentlemen went into the sitting-room, where
Richard opened his secretary, and taking pen and paper,
wrote the following advertisement:

"FIFTY DOLLARS REWARD.

"Ran away from the subscriber, living in ―――― county, Louisiana,
on Tuesday, July 4th, my negro boy George, a bright mulatto, about
six feet high, and stout built, twenty-seven years old, and very intelligent. His hair curls; he is very light complexioned; and might
easily pass for a white man. Has a deep scar over the right eye. I
will give the above reward for him, if alive, or for satisfactory proof
that he has been shot or killed.
                                    RICHARD DUDLEY."

Jake soon rode up to the door, ready to carry the advertisement to its destination. Robinson brought the
paper out and gave it to him, with strict orders to ride
as fast as possible, and to engage the pack of hounds for
immediate service. Jake started off at a gallop, and
was soon out of sight. Richard was restless and uneasy,
pacing up and down the room, and cursing the unfortunate fugitive in the bitterness of his hatred. "If I
catch him, I swear, I'll whip the black scoundrel to
death. He shan't live a day longer. I hate his bold
and defiant nature, and I'll conquer him, I warrant me!
I'll crush him! I'll tear him limb from limb with the
dogs, rather than let him live any longer." Thus he
raved, while Robinson sat by him, overawed and in
silence.

It was the first time George had ever been in "The

Wild-Cat Swamp." As he penetrated deeper and deeper into its dark and gloomy recesses, his mind was over-awed by the loneliness and desperateness of his condition; he thought he was travelling northward; but he knew that the land of freedom, after which he sighed, lay thousands of miles away; and how was he to travel so far, how to subsist so long, and how to elude so many perils? His prospects were gloomy indeed.

After the storm, had come one of those delightful days, for which all nature seems to give thanks to heaven; the birds chirruped upon the trees; the innumerable insects hummed in the atmosphere. But except the countless tribes of the minute creation, which swarmed around George's path, the pervading aspect of things was that of the most terrible loneliness and desolation.

He had not travelled more than five miles into the swamp, before he entered a large open space in the jungle, in the centre of which was a sheet of water of considerable extent, filled, as George could readily perceive, with immense alligators. The lake, by its branches, penetrated into the swamp in different directions. When he observed the natural solitariness of the spot, the smoothness and immobility of the lake, the heaviness of the foliage, and the loftiness of the pine trees, it was not strange that a feeling of intense loneliness came over the poor fugitive. He sat down to rest himself near to the margin of the lake; he watched the move-

ments, the gambols, and the conflicts of the wild and
dangerous animals, disporting in the water before him.
He began to feel hungry, and for the first time since he
left the plantation he had leisure to think of the necessity of having something to eat. He began to search
around him, and after a little while he had picked berries
enough to satisfy his immediate cravings.

But the fugitive had something else to do beside observing the movements of the alligators in the water;
the swamp which lay before him, was fifty miles in
width; it was difficult to travel through it, and his progress was slow. Sometimes the brushwood was so thick
it was with great difficulty he could penetrate through
it; at other times he had deep stagnant lagoons to cross.
If logs lay over them, he had less difficulty; but sometimes he had no such facilities. Reptiles, some of them
very poisonous, often beset his path and glided around
his feet. Several times he intruded among a nest of
rattlesnakes, which would have attacked him, had he
not fled with the greatest expedition from their poisonous fangs. During this first day he had a conflict with
an alligator, which, coming out of a lagoon suddenly,
made after him with great fury. He only escaped his
jaws by climbing quickly up a pine tree, which his foe
could not ascend. Every now and then he travelled by
the bleeching bones of some poor fugitive like himself,
who had died of hunger in the deep shadows of the

forest, and from whose bones the vultures and turkey-buzzards had picked the last remnant of flesh.

Amid scenes such as these, George travelled onward during the first day. As the shades of night approached, the awful stillness of nature, and her desolate appearance amid those untrodden wilds, almost overcame his spirits. He had gone about fifteen miles during this first day, from the plantation of Richard Dudley. The shades of evening were setting over the earth. It was his first night in the swamp, and his stout heart might well have quaked within him as he reflected upon his condition. He first sought to allay his hunger; all the food that he could find, were the same kind of berries which he had eaten in the morning; there was but little nourishment to be found in them; yet he was forced to be content with them. No water was to be found except the stagnant water of the pools, in which the snakes, toads and lizzards were to be counted by hundreds. He looked about him for a bed whereon to repose during the night; there was no safety upon the ground. He now began to hear the distant howlings of the panthers and wolves, which come forth by night from their haunts to prowl around for prey.

There was but one thing which George could do to secure his safety during the night, and that was to climb a tree and sleep among its branches: he did so. He scaled a tall pine tree, which had no branches within thirty feet of the ground; and about twenty feet above the lowest limbs he found several large boughs which projected from the body of the tree at such an angle, and across each other, in such a way, as to form something of a seat, or nest, for him to repose upon.

He slept little during the long, tedious night; the moon shone brightly down upon that poor desolate heart; and as he looked up at her calm and far-off disk, while she sailed through the clouds, he wondered whether she, too, was a world of sorrow and sadness, such as this; or whether all were happy and holy there! During the night he could see the wild beasts bounding along beneath him, in pursuit of their prey. From his lofty eyrie, he could hear the distant roaring of these beasts, of ravenous panthers and wolves; and he could hear the screams of the vultures and the hootings of the owls. The swamp seemed alive with new orders or races of beings from those which had peopled it and made its gloomy recesses more hideous still, by their presence in the day. Toward morning George managed to sleep some, and when the sun arose he threw his beams upon the wearied fugitive, still perched high among the branches of the pine tree, and still sunk in blessed unconsciousness.

George awoke and descended; but before he recommenced his journey, he breakfasted again on berries as before. He began to feel very weak; his food imparted no nourishment to his system. He felt faint and sick; but there was no remedy for his sufferings. He had a long and almost endless journey before him, and with a sad heart, he resumed his onward march.

This was George's second day in the swamp. He was impeded in his progress, as before, by fallen logs, by the thick brushwood, and by the deep lagoons of water which frequently lay across his path. It was about the middle of the day, and the sun poured down its scorching rays with the most fearful intensity. He was picking his way along a part of more than usual difficulty, when his attention was suddenly attracted by a loud moaning which fell upon his ear. It was evidently the voice of a human being, but the spot from which it came he tried in vain to discover. He looked first to the right, then to the left, both before and behind him; but he looked in vain. Still the moaning continued; it seemed to be that of a human being in the utmost agony and prostration; a cadence of the deepest despair seemed to be mixed with the groans, which made his heart shudder at the sound He advanced a few steps and listened again. The groans were still more and more distinct. At length he looked upward, when lo! a most horrible object was presented to his view.

Upon a large limb of a pine tree, about twenty feet from the ground, was suspended, by a chain, an iron cage, which dangled to and fro in the wind; and in that

cage was confined the most horrible spectre of human
misery that eyes ever beheld. It was a large, coal-
black negro, quite naked. His form was reduced to a
skeleton by starvation. His back was raw with bloody
welts. The flesh on his arms was actually eaten and
gnawed away by himself, in his horrible agonies of
starvation. The cage was about five feet square, and
three feet high, so that its inmate could not stand
upright, but usually remained in a sitting posture. His
eyes stood out in horrid prominence from his head; his
large and thick lips hung loosely down upon his chin.
When George first saw him, he was leaning his head upon
his hand, and every now and then, amid his groans, he
would snap at the flesh on his own arm, and actually
tear it away, shred after shred, chew it with savage
eagerness, and then swallow it. He would then relapse
again into his plaintive groans of despair, which were
thus aggravated from time to time by the fresh lacera-
tion of his flesh. He was also beset by myriads of mos-
quitoes, which he endeavored in vain to drive away.
About half a dozen hungry turkey-buzzards were patiently sitting on different branches of the tree above
him, awaiting their expected feast, while as many more
of them might be seen slowly sailing around in circles
and eddies, in the far off heaven above, preparatory to
a descent upon their expected victim below.

George was appalled at the sight, and he gazed long

in silent horror at the scene. The cage was suspended by an iron chain, and swung idly and loosely to and fro in the wind. It was open on all sides; the floor only was made of boards. This poor wretch had been placed there by some fiendish master, to perish from hunger, far away from the reach of human succor; and probably his tormentors had visited him from time to time, to gloat upon the spectacle of such indescribable misery, and to taunt and jeer him in his last agony.

George approached nearer to the cage. Still the unhappy wretch, intent upon his own miseries, and the awful doom which awaited him, observed him not. At length George spoke; his voice broke the almost audible silence of that scene of primeval loneliness, and immediately the poor wretch raised his eyes, and looked searchingly around him. Soon his glance fell upon the stranger below, and for a moment each gazed in mutual silence on the other.

"What are you doing up there; you seem to be fast in that cage, are you?" inquired George.

"Yes, I'se fast here. My massa's fixed me here, I reckon, to die. I'se most dead; I'se starvin' to death. Can't you help me?" said the prisoner, in a tone of pitiful despair.

"I would if I could," responded George; "but who is your master, and what have you done, that he has inflicted such a terrible punishment as this on you?"

"Oh! I'se run away three times. He was so cruel to me, I couldn't stand it. My massa is old Kernel Sarjint; he lives 'way over on t'other side de swamp. He catched me here twice, and he swore dat I should die on dis spot. He had dis cage made for me, and hung me up here to die. Oh! I'se so orful hungry! Haint you got nothin' to eat?" he eagerly inquired of George.

"No, I've got nothing. I'm almost starved myself. But I'll try to pick you some berries, if I can find any. What is the matter with your arm, the flesh seems torn off?"

"I'se eat it off, myself; I'se so hungry;" and the poor wretch looked through the bars of his strong cage, like some imprisoned wild beast, glaring his eyes around him, restless, keen, desperate, earnestly looking for the berries which George had promised to hunt for him. After some little search, he succeeded in procuring a few, but in consequence of the height of the cage from the ground, George had to throw them up, one by one, through the bars. The dying wretch caught the berries, and devoured them with intense avidity. It was a sad sight indeed, to see him thus tampering with his impending doom, and striving to put off the last agonies of his inevitable end.

"How long have you been there?" inquired George.

"Dis is de fifth day," he responded, licking his emaciated jaws, and looking eagerly around him, like a hungry panther, for more prey. "Git me some more—some more berries—quick!" he added, holding out his skinny hands through the bars. The wind had freshened a little, and the cage was now swinging to and fro. George complied with his request, and threw him up some more berries.

"Can't we get you down from that dreadful cage you'r in? you'll soon die there," said George.

"Yes! I'se soon dead here. Git me down, can't you. I'se most dead now!"

George, although fully conscious of the perils of his own situation, as well as of the difficulty of releasing the wretch suspended before, or rather above him, felt it his duty to try to rescue him from his impending fate, if he possibly could do so.

While he was pondering upon some way by which he might accomplish this purpose, a distant, horrid sound fell suddenly upon his ears, which seemed like the knell of doom to him. It was the deep baying of the blood-hounds echoing through the swamp, which, by this time, were upon his track, had succeeded in discovering the direction of his retreat, and would soon overtake him.

> "In the dark fens of the Dismal Swamp
>   The hunted negro lay;
>   He saw the fire of the midnight camp,
>   He heard at times the horses tramp,
>   And the bloodhounds distant bay."

The common instinct of self-preservation at once compelled George to seek his own safety, in flight. He might, perhaps, succeed in hiding himself, or throw the bloodhounds off their scent. But he well knew the difficulty of the attempt, and the consequences which would follow his failure.

Without saying another word to the poor captive in the cage, he darted off in the opposite direction from that in which the sounds were heard. He ran swiftly about half a mile, till he reached what seemed to be a thick and almost impenetrable jungle. It was the best retreat he could find under the circumstances. He entered it after some difficulty. It was a thickly tangled brushwood, which had grown up around and under some very large pine trees. Vines and briers were so thickly twined among the brushwood, that it was almost impossible to make any headway through it.

At length, after much difficulty, he succeeded in getting within the limits of the jungle, and toward its centre. He was torn and scratched by the thorns until the blood flowed over his face and hands. He hoped that the bloodhounds had lost scent of him, or that they would be unable to see him, or to penetrate his retreat.

Vain hope! Soon he heard their approaching yells. They came, straight as a line, upon his track. They soon reached the outskirts of the jungle. There were four of them, and they were followed by Richard Dudley, Robinson, and Jake, all on horseback, who urged them on with loud shouts and screams.

So dark and thick was the jungle, that it was impossible for his pursuers to see the fugitive. But the infallible scent of the dogs made them as certain of his presence, as if they saw him in the clear mid-day light. At first they made the circuit several times of the jungle, deeply baying, and searching for the most suitable place for entrance. This was no easy task. Richard and Robinson rode round and round, to aid them in their endeavors. With fatal sagacity the dogs at last discovered the spot by which George had himself entered, and they slowly began to thread their way through its complicated intricacies.

The poor slave saw his enemies slowly approaching him. He heard their yells for his blood. To fly through the thicket by the opposite direction was impossible. He knew not what to do. To destroy the four dogs was an impossibility without any weapon; and even if accomplished, he would not be protected from his infuriated master, who he knew was doubly armed, and would shoot him down without a moment's hesitation.

While debating with himself what was to be done in this extremity, the foremost dog espied his victim. His red eyes glared upon the poor slave through the thick foliage. Onward the wild beast fought his way, regardless of the thorns which tore his skin, until at length he

came within a few feet of his victim. George heard his
heavy breathing. He saw him glaring, with open mouth
upon him; and he discovered in the rear of the foremost,
the remaining three, worming their way through the
thicket, and laboriously advancing toward him. He
gave himself up for lost.

At length the leader succeeded in penetrating the last
intervening obstacle, and bounded fiercely with a loud
yell at the imprisoned slave. George fought him off with
his fists; and with a heavy blow knocked him down. But
the dog soon recovered; and in a few moments the other
three reached him, and though he manfully fought the
whole troop, with repeated blow and kick, he soon became exhausted, and his resistance was more and more
feeble. They sprang upon him in succession, sunk their
teeth deeply into his flesh, and tried in concert to drag
him from his hiding-place. Seeing that all further resistance would be vain, he determined to escape their
further fury by retracing his steps out of the thicket,
as he came, and submitting at once to his master.

But the bloodhounds did not seem to comprehend his
purpose. At any rate, they bit his flesh, hung on to his
body, and tore it in the most cruel manner. They dragged him by main force through the thick brushwood, so
that his flesh was lacerated by the thorns and briars as
much as by the teeth of the bloodhounds. At length,
after being most cruelly bruised, and suffering heavy

wounds, the dogs, hanging on by their teeth, dragged him out of the brushwood.

"There he is! There's the black scoundrel!" exclaimed Richard Dudley, as George, bleeding and almost exhausted with terror and loss of blood, emerged from the thicket. Richard had his pistol in his hand ready to fire, in case George attempted to fly. But he had no disposition to do so. He immediately resigned himself to the possession of his pursuers.

Richard descended from his horse, and with the aid of Robinson he tied the hands of the fugitive behind him. George declared to his master that this was not necessary, as he would return willingly and without any resistance.

"Tie the d—— scoundrel! tie him fast!" exclaimed Richard, first laying the rope heavily over the shoulders of George, and then proceeding to finish the operation. They tied his hands behind his back securely; fastened the dogs together in their leashes; mounted their horses, and placing George before them, commenced the homeward drive at a brisk run.

Now and then the thickness of the woods in the swamp compelled them to reduce their pace. George ran on for miles without flagging. His pursuers carried heavy whips, with which they lashed him severely, whenever he failed to keep up his accustomed pace. Their progress was diversified by various curses and ejaculations,

29

sometimes fierce, sometimes jocular, between Richard and Robinson, usually at the expense of the panting and exhausted fugitive running before them, as it were for his life.

At length they reached the outskirts of the swamp. During this part of the journey, George's strength was gradually diminishing. He felt that he was becoming weaker and weaker. He hoped, nevertheless, that he might yet be able to reach his master's plantation alive; and that, whatever punishment might await him there, he might still be able to survive it.

After leaving the swamp, they struck into a road, which led along between the plantations. On all sides they heard the joyful shouts, the vociferations, and the pyrotechnic explosions, which usually characterize the celebration of the Nation's glorious birth-day, from Maine to California. On that very day, and while this fainting human fugitive was being driven back to a bondage worse than death itself, twenty millions of freemen were sending up to Heaven acclamations, long and loud, sober and drunken, in honor of the immortal fact, that theirs was the home of the free, where no tyrant dare ever set his foot; the only land on earth where man could live and die, in the full possession of all those rights with which the Creator of all had endowed them!

Poor George, as he ran faintingly along, thought within himself, how strange it was, that bondage so cruel, and so despotic, as that which he and three millions of unfortunate beings such as himself endured, should be tolerated in this boasted land of the free and the brave.

But the poor wretch had little time for reflection. As Richard rode along after the runaway slave, he himself repeatedly discharged his pistols in honor of the immortal Fourth! While engaged in the very act of forcing a man back into bondage, he lavishly exploded powder in honor of the very day which proclaimed to the whole world, in tones of thunder, that *all men* are born free and equal, and are entitled to life, *liberty*, and the pursuit of happiness.

But we may well ask, was his conduct in this respect more absurd than that of the shouting, spouting, exulting, and carousing millions around him, over the broad land? We think not.

The pursuers still rode rapidly on; but the strength of the poor slave was rapidly diminishing. As soon as his pace diminished for an instant, Richard and Robinson both laid on the lash furiously.

Only once, George turned to his pursuers to implore their pity. Their only answer was fresh blows and curses. They had yet five miles to travel before they reached the Dudley plantation. The afternoon had already far advanced, and Richard was determined to get home before nightfall.

By this time George's strength had nearly become

exhausted. He had tasted no food for two days, except the berries in the swamp. He had lost much blood from the wounds the blood-hounds had given him in the thicket. His laborious journey through the intricate mazes of the swamp, and his brutal whippings, and driving on his return, combined with the intense heat of the day, without water or refreshment of any kind, all combined to overcome him.

His pace now became much slower; nor could the heavy blows from Richard's lash enable him to increase it. At one time he was compelled to walk; but after a short distance he resumed his former dog-trot. They were now some three miles from Dudley's house. As he approached his plantation, Richard seemed determined to make the best of the remaining time and space, and laid on his lash upon the already bleeding back of his victim, with greater frequency and cruelty than before.

His plantation was bounded, in the direction in which the party returned, by a creek, very muddy and very deep. They had reached this creek, which was about a mile from Richard's house. Exhausted and almost dead as he was, George could scarcely drag himself through the soft and muddy soil beneath its waves. Richard whipped him up. The whole party were in the water, about the centre of the stream, when George found himself fainting, and fell. Richard immediately set the bloodhounds upon his body, who dragged the dying

wretch, with their teeth, through the water to the opposite shore. He was at first unable to stand. The lashes
of his drivers for a moment brought him to. He struggled to rise and ascend the muddy and slippery bank.
He fell heavily, with his face to the earth. The lash
was again and again applied, but in vain. He stirred
not. The drivers descended from their horses to raise
him up. He was insensible; the blood rushed from his
mouth and nose; he had fainted.

Richard seeing the condition to which George had
been reduced, ordered Robinson to lift the almost
lifeless body of his victim on Jake's horse, and thus
bring him home. Robinson and Jake together lifted
George across the neck of the horse which Juke rode,
and the latter mounted up behind him. Richard, rode on
rapidly home; while Robinson and the negro slowly
pursued their way with their insensible burden. They
at length arrived at George's cabin. They tumbled
off their burden on the ground, and then carried it into
the hut, laid it upon the hard and humble bed, and
each went to his own quarters to rest himself, after the
fatigues of the SLAVE-HUNT.

29*

CHAPTER XXIII.

THE FINALE.—DEATH OF THE VICTIM

IN the course of a few weeks after the preceding field sports, Richard Dudley began to weary of the monotonous life of the plantation; and he determined to make another visit to New Orleans.

He did so; and soon, by frequenting his former haunts of dissipation, fell in with his old associates in vice. Among these was the accomplished and fascinating young French Count de Clermont.

Seduced by the affable blundness of his manner, Richard was disposed to forget the evidences of his treachery, which he had detected on a former occasion; and the two young gentlemen were soon on the same terms of intimacy and attachment which had characterized their intercourse when they previously met. The consequence of this state of things might readily be anticipated. Clermont was in league with several of the professed and most expert gamblers in New Orleans. They had again baited a fat victim, and they did not leave him till he was completely ruined. This process did not require more than three or four weeks for its accomplishment.

During this period, Richard Dudley lost by gambling about forty thousand dollars; after he had spent all the ready money which he had brought with him to New Orleans, at the instigation of the Count de Clermont he raised large sums of money on his notes; and the sum total of these when he left New Orleans, amounted to the full value of what he possessed of the Dudley plantation.

He knew that unless he immediately paid these claims his estate would be sold, and probably sacrificed; and that he would, in the end, gain nothing by his refusal to pay. He therefore determined at once to sell out, liquidate his debts, and, with whatever surplus might remain, remove to New Orleans, and there fall back for a subsistence upon the dishonorable means which had already proved his own ruin, by accomplishing the ruin of others.

In pursuance of this purpose, soon after Richard's return to the plantation he advertised his property for sale; it was sold—land, slaves, stock, crops, and everything. Richard made no reservation, and left the estate and the home of his youth and of his forefathers without much regret; his habits and his nature had been completely altered by his adventures in New Orleans; he had lost all relish for the quiet, rural scenes of his earlier existence. He delighted in nothing now but the hot-bed excitement and debauchery of one of the most dissipated cities in the world.

Poor George, who had recovered from his late wounds and sufferings, had hoped, when he heard that the estate was to be sold, that he would at last change masters, and that, as his condition could not possibly be worse than it then was, a change might perhaps produce some alleviation of his miseries.

Alas! no such good fortune was to be his. When he most earnestly desired to be sold, he could not be! Richard had determined to retain George alone, among all his slaves, as his body servant, to accompany him to New Orleans. He had discovered that George desired to be sold, and his malignant spite against him, which seemed to be deathless and unchangeable, determined him to deprive his victim of that poor gratification. Beside, he now took an habitual pleasure in tormenting George; it had become an indispensable luxury of his daily life and gratification, to inflict cruelty upon this unfortunate and wretched being; and he could not think, for one moment, of depriving himself of his accustomed indulgence in the new home to which he was about removing.

Having sold the plantation, Richard removed to New Orleans. He took with him the large sum of money which had been realized by the sale; and upon his arrival in that city, he paid off a part of the debts which

he had previously contracted. But before he had liqui-
dated all these claims, a portion of his money had been
lost as before, at the gaming table, and the rest of his
debts remained unpaid.

Upon his arrival at New Orleans, Richard determined
to hire a separate, furnished house for his residence.
After some searching, he selected a large stone building, situated in a somewhat remote location, though in
a respectable quarter of the city. It was in a neighborhood which had long been appropriated to the haunts of
gamblers, and to men of dissipation and fashion in the
city. It was a very old house, and indeed had a somewhat suspicious reputation. It was said to have been
built many years ago, by an old Spanish pirate and
African slave trader, who resided in it for some years,
after he had ceased his infamous pursuits, and came to
New Orleans to spend his old age in the enjoyment of
his ill-gotten gains.

Beneath the house he had built a large and deep stone
vault. It was thickly walled all around; the floor was
composed of large flat stones; and an iron door of immense strength and thickness had been fastened at the
entrance. The roof was composed of several arches,
built of heavy stones; and there was no aperture for
light or air, except at the iron door, which was usually
closed by heavy bolts and padlocks. In this dark, deep
and strong vault, it was reported that the old pirate had

kept hidden his treasures; the gold and jewels, of immense value, which he had plundered from many a murdered victim; which had been the spoil of many a captured ship; and were the product of the sale of hundreds of unfortunate slaves, whom he had stolen in Africa, and sold in the various slave-markets of the world. The old pirate was long since dead; and the house had passed through many hands since his day.

The first story of this house Richard Dudley fitted up as a private gambling saloon. It was elegantly furnished, the first room as a private parlor, for the reception and entertainment of visitors, with a large sideboard, well stocked with liquors for their use. In the adjoining back room, was a far table, and several other appliances of gambling. The second story was appropriated by Richard to his own use as sleeping apartments, and were occupied by himself and his mistress; for we need scarcely add, that it was not long before he supplied himself with that necessary and customary appendage, to a person of his questionable pursuits.

George exerted himself with his usual readiness, to be as useful as possible in this new situation. But the mind of Richard Dudley had become deeply poisoned and exasperated by his losses, and by the constant and harassing vicissitudes of a gambler's life, to which he was now subjected, and to which he had never been accustomed. His temper became exceedingly irascible, and though his rooms were visited by a considerable number of gamblers, and he usually had on hand a sufficient quantity of funds, for carrying on the operations of his faro-bank; yet sometimes his violence became outrageous; and as he had no one else on whom to wreak his fury with safety, it usually fell in all its intensity upon the defenceless head of George.

One day, Richard took a special offence at George, and he ordered him down, for the first time, for confinement, in the old pirate's vault under the house. George, accustomed to Richard's vengeance, instantly obeyed. His master followed him down the slippery stone steps which led to the vault, and in his rage, locked and bolted the iron door upon his prisoner, and then left him to his reflections.

Upon entering this cheerless dungeon, George was at first overcome by the utter darkness, and could see nothing. After a few minutes his eyes became accustomed to that darkness, and he could barely distinguish the horrid outlines of the place. The vault was circular, and sank some twenty feet deep beneath the surface of the ground. In consequence of the dampness of the soil on which New Orleans is built, the very thick walls which surrounded the vault, could scarcely exclude the dripping dampness, and the water fell in large drops from the rocky roof of the vault, and from the sides, upon the large flat stones which composed the floor.

George soon saw the nature of the spot in which he was confined, and though he expected that his imprisonment would be but of short duration, his heart, broken by so many sorrows, and by such long and bitter persecution, sank within him, as he looked around. His once vigorous frame had now lost its manly beauty and vigor; and though tall and of a large frame, he was reduced to a skeleton, and was, in truth, but the wreck of what he had formerly been. In the vault, he searched in vain for anything to sit upon. Even no stone could be found to serve him as a stool; and he was compelled at last to sit down upon the floor.

In this position, George soon began to discover, that though the circular vault in which he was confined, had long since been completely emptied of all its contents, by the old pirate and his successors, yet, that he had living associates of his solitude. The flag-stones which composed the floor of the vault were not very closely laid together; and through the interstices had crept various vermin and reptiles; which soon approached and surrounded the new comer, to claim a share of his horrid habitation. George had not been two hours in the vault, before he was surrounded by rats, toads, and lizards; some of which he felt crawling over his person, and disposed to commence the preliminary steps toward a more intimate acquaintance.

The poor wretch, placed in so horrid a situation, employed himself in fighting off his numerous assailants. He was encouraged by the hope, that his master would soon come down to release him. Hour after hour rolled by however; and George began to suffer from hunger, fatigue and fear. But he listened in vain for the approaching footsteps of Richard. Night at length arrived; and he heard, overhead, the boisterous sounds of hilarity and mirth, among the gamblers who had assembled to engage in their usual pursuits. George knew from this, that it must be about eleven o'clock; for that was the time at which Richard's company usually arrived. At length, comparative silence gradually ensued above, and George then knew that the gamblers had become earnestly engaged in the absorbing vicissitudes of the game.

The poor captive began seriously to suffer from hunger. He had been confined in the vault since the morning, and of course had not eaten a morsel through the day. He felt disposed at length to sleep; but before he extended himself upon his hard bed, he knelt down upon the stones, and addressed his prayers to heaven, as was ever his wont, commending himself to the protection of his Maker. He prayed for himself and for his master, and hoped that all would yet turn out for the best.

That was a singular and unusual sight,—the brilliant saloon and gambling table above, with the eager worshippers of mammon there, and the dark, damp and

30

gloomy vault beneath, in which an humble slave, in solitude and in tears, upon his bended knees, was addressing his prayers to the God of heaven!

His devotions ended, George laid down upon the stone floor, and tried to sleep. He could not sleep at first, for the vermin disturbed him, gnawed at his face and hands and bare feet, and gave him little rest. Nevertheless, toward morning he obtained a disturbed slumber for an hour. And while he thus slept, his head laid low upon the hard rock, his thoughts took flight to happier scenes; and he dreamed of her, his departed and loved one, who had already fallen a victim to his master's vengeance, but whose freed spirit was now happy, in a better world. He thought that she came to him in his dark and lonely dungeon, and bending over him, impressed upon his hard and parched lips, a soft, sweet kiss of love, such as she had been wont to do in other days. Alas! it was but a dream! He awoke, looked around him for her heavenly form, and saw and felt only the "darkness visible" of his cheerless abode.

It is probable that when Richard Dudley first ordered George down into the vault, the idea had not entered into his head, of *starving him to death*. It was a momentary impulse then,—a novel punishment, which he had not tried before, and which the presence of the old pirate's vault had suggested to him. Richard's subsequent conduct toward George was evidently an after thought, and one which gradually developed itself to his savage and implacable mind.

The whole of the next day passed away, and the captive saw and heard nothing of his master, or of his other servants. George was still suffering the pangs of hunger, and for the first time, toward the evening of the second day, the horrid thought rushed upon his mind, that it might be his master's intention to finish his long series of cruelties, by actually starving him to death From his damp dungeon he could hear the rumbling of the wheels upon the street, and the other multitudinous sounds of life in a large city. Toward evening these sounds gradually diminished, and then entirely ceased. From his own feelings, George knew that it was the evening of the second day. He approached the immense iron door, and tried to move it; it was as immovable as a mountain. No strength of man could force back or break in twain the immense bolts which held it. Escape was impossible. He was buried alive, and entirely at the mercy of one of the most cruel and implacable of men.

The hours of this second day passed by, silently and cheerlessly, to the poor captive. He was kept busily employed in fighting the vermin which, emboldened by familiarity, now attacked him on all sides. He was surrounded by immense and formidable rats, which had burrowed holes through the soft earth, and had reached the vault through the floor; toads and lizzards also found their way thither; and being barefooted, and without weapon of any kind, his condition was a defenceless one.

The third day, after a night of indescribable horrors, George awoke with a nest of toads and lizzards resting heavily on his bosom. His dreams had been of a fearful nature; and his excruciating hunger and faintness, together with the awful apprehension that Richard Dudley had locked him up there, to perish by starvation, all combined to make his agonies unspeakable.

About twelve o'clock, George heard the footsteps of his master approaching. He slowly descended the steep stone steps, which led to the door of the vault. When he reached the iron door, he unlocked the bolt, and opened the door a very short distance. He put his head in, and gazed for some seconds into the darkness, seeking to find his victim with his eye, and to make an observation of the general appearance of the place.

"You black scoundrel, I have you fast now," said Richard, fiercely. "You'll not run off to court, or to the swamp again, I warrant you!"

"Master Richard," said George, "pray have pity on me, I'm almost dead with hunger. Please master, let me come out of this place. I'll try never to offend you again," he continued, in a mournful strain, which might have moved a stone.

"No sir. I'll not trust you. You'll not come out of this, until I'm ready, you worthless vagabond," was the reply which he received.

"Well then, my miseries will soon be ended," said George, with a sigh. "I'll soon be dead. It will soon be over with me."

"Die then! You deserve no better fate. I'll punish you, now I have you here, for your impertinent stubbornness in marrying Caroline, when I commanded you not to do it, you d—— scoundrel you," replied Richard with fierce vindictiveness, as he violently slammed the door shut, locked the bolts carefully, and retraced his steps up the steep stone stairs, to the light of day.

The feelings of poor George after his master had left him in this manner, may better be imagined than described. Despair took possession of his soul, and he gave himself up for lost. But the agonies of his mind were much less excruciating than those of his body. He was now literally and gradually starving to death.

It was three days since he had tasted food. The sensation in his empty stomach was one of agony, such as he had never before experienced, and was beyond the reach of imagination. He could no longer suppress his moans, and at length, short screams of suffering were forced from him. He laid upon the damp, slippery stones, and rolled about in inexpressible agony.

But though it was impossible for George, by any con-

30*

trivance, to alleviate the miseries of starvation which ho
was enduring, he at length found some consolation for
the distresses of his mind, in the solemn exercises of his
religion.

As he lay upon the ground, he prayed. He resigned
himself to the mysterious will of heaven, whatever it
might be. He asked for strength to enable him to
endure to the end, without murmuring; and to be pre
pared for that future state, toward which he felt that,
through awful agony, he was now rapidly approaching.
He endeavored to collect his thoughts and centre them
upon reflection on spiritual things; but ever and anon
the terrible and piercing sensations of his stomach re-
called his thoughts to the physical miseries which he was
now enduring. Compared with these, the pain which ho
suffered from the attacks of the vermin and reptiles in
the vault, was almost nothing.

During the whole of this night, George could not sleep
an instant. Its long hours seemed to him an endless
age of agony. He thought that the sounds of returning
day would never recommence again. At length the
fourth day of his imprisonment dawned. The poor
wretch was almost entirely overcome with protracted
suffering and weakness. His groans became deeper and
more frequent. Such were his sufferings that it was
impossible for him to suppress them.

At length, they attracted the attention of Richard,

who on that day rose late, having spent the previous night in a drunken debauch. About the middle of the day he went down to the door of the vault, unlocked it and looked in. George was laying on his side, in the middle of the vault, and now almost unable to rise. As Richard opened the iron door, and let in a few straggling rays of light, there was a general scattering of the vermin, which had collected around and settled upon the body of the unhappy wretch.

George tried to raise his head and look up. "I'm most gone, master; pray have pity on me! Please to give me something to eat,—something to drink!" he said, in an utterance so feeble, as to be scarcely aubible.

"Lay there and die, you scoundrel!" was the only response which he received. Indeed, Richard had by this time deliberately made up his mind, that George should die in the vault by starvation!

This answer shut out forever all hope from the soul of the poor wretch. His groans became heart-rending; and lest they should become audible in the street, Richard closed the iron door, and listened with infinite gratification to the horrid sounds from within, while standing on the stone stairway.

"Suffer, you villain! Ha! your screams are music to my ears. They are sweet music! They convince me that my revenge will now be complete! Die there, you wretch!" After enjoying himself in this way for

some time, Richard left his victim to his fate, and returned to his gambling saloon above.

And still the awful agonies of the unhappy victim
continued to increase in intensity, during the long and
cheerless hours of the night. The power of language
is impotent, to convey any idea of the horrors of his
situation. Impelled by hunger, he began to eat some of
the loathsome vermin which swarmed around him. But
his strength was almost gone, and in the darkness it
was nearly impossible for him to secure any of them.
But of the little of this revolting food that he could
capture, he found himself able to eat only a small portion.

The fifth day of this horrible scene had at length
dawned; but its ascending sun brought no ray of hope
to the poor, dying slave. In the morning he became
delirious. His reason at length sank beneath his intense
agonies. Sometimes, as he rolled wildly to and fro over
the floor of the vault, he raved fiercely at his master, and
cursed the cruel author of all his woes. The next
moment, he wept, as would a child. Then again, a gentler
mood would come over his perturbed spirit. He thought
he was back once more at the Dudley plantation, and
that the scenes of his innocent and happy childhood, and
riper youth, surrounded him. He thought he was playing with the beautiful and affectionate Caroline, among
the cabins where their youthful days had been spent.

Then again he imagined that he was strolling with her in delightful converse, in some secluded spot, and drinking in the sweet accents of her uttered love. Then he imagined that he was laying his aching head upon her faithful and devoted breast, after some bitter scene of his master's persecution. Then he thought he stood beside her early and cruel grave; and then again, that he held his murdered infant in his arms, and was about to deposit it on its mother's bosom, e're they filled up that grave and hid her forever from his sight. It was then that he wept bitter tears, at the imaginary renewal of these sad scenes of wo.

And when the delirious fit had passed away, he only returned to a consciousness of the horrid realities which surrounded him.

About four o'clock that day, Richard Dudley again visited his victim. As he heard his tormenter approach, a sudden impulse seized the dying wretch, to inflict upon him some signal vengeance for his cruelty. But aside from the fact, that his strength was now gone, his religious convictions deterred him from such an act. He had been taught to believe, that it was his duty to love his enemies, and bless them who persecuted him.

Accordingly, when Richard opened the door of the vault, his victim was silent, still laying in hopeless agony upon the ground. Richard addressed him with taunting words as usual.

"I forgive you, Master Richard," said George, "and I hope God will forgive you; it will soon be over; I will soon be out of misery now. I have always tried to serve and obey you, and to deserve better treatment from you. God knows I did the best I could."

"Hold your tongue, you black villain! You've always been a disobedient, worthless fellow," responded Richard.

"Ah! you did not think so, Master Richard, when we were boys, and young men together. How long was you my friend, then? How many days have we played, and fished, and hunted together, when we were young? Then you did not think me so bad: but it's no difference; it's almost over now," said George, feebly.

There was no pity in the soul of Richard; and after watching the convulsive spasms of the poor slave for a few minutes longer, he slammed the iron door shut, locked it, and went his way, whistling as he went.

George now earnestly prayed to heaven that his end might quickly come. During the succeeding night, the fifth which he had spent without food in the vault, his mind was calm; he was engaged in prayer, and his devotions had a powerful effect in cheering his soul, so soon to enter the dark valley and shadow of death. But he looked for the grim monster without dread. He had made his peace with heaven, and he expected to be admitted soon to a happier world, where he would meet those whom he loved, and who had gone before him to try the unknown mysteries of that future state. He endeavored to sing one of his favorite hymns; but it would not do. After a few words, his voice failed from his excessive weakness, and he ceased; he had sung his last on earth.

The succeeding night passed away between delirious fits and spells of unconscious agony; the sixth day dawned, and the poor slave was still alive. At this time his cell presented a horrible spectacle; the vermin had increased in number and fierceness. Unable to rise, scarcely able to move, the hungry rats tore his flesh, his feet, his face, and he no longer possessed the strength to drive them away.

George felt the last agony at length approaching. He had been reduced to a perfect skeleton; the air of the place was now most foul and fœtid. George had offered up his last prayer, and was rapidly sinking; he could no longer move; bent together with agony as he lay, he could but suffer and wait until he had uttered his last gasp, and was no more.

At this moment, as George was about expiring, Richard Dudley approached his prison, unlocked the door, and entered.

"Are you alive yet? I thought you'd be dead by this time, you black carrion, you!" said Richard, rudely.

"I am almost dead, master," said George, feebly; "I'll

soon be gone, yes, I hope I'll soon be in heaven. I hope
soon to see my poor Caroline."

"Damn your Caroline, you villain!" interrupted
Richard, fiercely, before George could finish the sentence; at the same time drawing out a bowie knife, and
stabbing his slave to the heart, as he lay before him.

George instantly expired, without a groan.

In a moment or two, after taking a last look at his
victim, and kicking his emaciated corpse over and over,
several times, Richard locked the iron door of the vault;
carefully hid the key, where it would be impossible
to find it, and left the remains of his poor murdered
slave—his third victim—to rot and moulder away, and
return, undisturbed, to its kindred dust.

Thy spirit is at rest at last, in heaven, thou persecuted, tortured slave! Yonder, in Elysian realms,
where everlasting joy and rapture reign; in the society
of the good of every clime, and every age; in sweet converse with her whom thou lov'dst so well, and who, with
thy young innocent, awaits thy coming;—there thou
wilt pass an eternity of security and peace; and there,
that noble nature which God had given thee, fitting thee
for the pursuit and attainment of the highest aims of
human existence, will have a propitious sphere; thy
powers will be enlarged, elevated and expanded; and
there thou wilt attain the great purpose of thy being, in

knowing and comprehending truth; and in serving Him, who is the great author, source and end of Truth!

Thus ends the humble history of THE PLANTER'S VICTIM. It may, perhaps, interest the reader, to learn the fate of the several other persons who have figured prominently in the pages of this history. Their tale is told in a very few words.

About four months before the death of George, Julia Dudley had been united to William Stanley, the New Orleans lawyer, as already narrated. The noble girl had confided her happiness and her fate, to a man who was worthy of her confidence. Occasionally, her brother Richard visited her, after his removal to New Orleans; but he became so much absorbed in his pleasures, and in the habits of dissipation which he had contracted, that he seemed to have little time or disposition to cultivate any domestic intimacies. Julia Stanley enjoyed many years of conjugal felicity, and probably still lives, to adorn and enliven the elevated circle in which she moves.

But a terrible Nemesis hung over the doomed head of the murderer of poor George. He did not survive long, to indulge the bloody retrospect of his sated vengeance upon his victim. After two years spent in those pursuits to which, as we have said, he had prostituted his

31

existence, he at length quarelled with another debauchee, as abandoned as himself, respecting a female favorite. The quarrel was followed by a duel, in which, at tho first fire, Richard Dudley was mortally wounded. After three days of intense agony, during which, the remorse of his mind for his unparalleled cruelties to his three victims, was more excruciating even, that the sufferings of his body—he expired; and thus, at the premature age of thirty-one, he ended his inglorious career.

There was but one being on earth, who bent in benevo- lent sorrow over his dying bed, or who shed tears of regret over his early grave. There was but one heart in all the world, whose affection for him was strong enough to resist the revolting effect produced by his base passions, his degrading tendencies, and his infamous deeds. She ordered his burial to be prepared, and his grave to be dug. And when his bloody corpse was de- posited in its last shallow home, *her* tears were the only tears which fell upon his coffin. That mourner was his sister,—the noble, the incomparable Julia. Richard Dudley died, and passed away from earth, as all tyrants, great and small, deserve to do, and inevitably will do, followed only by the disgust and execration of every virtuous and benevolent mind.

Our simple tale is suggestive of many reflections: we will give utterance to but one.

The fair Genius of American liberty was born in the midst of the storms and desperate struggles of the Revolution; and as Minerva stepped forth fully armed from the frowning brow of Jove, so did she emerge into light and glory from the bosom of immortal Heroism and Virtue. But we have often observed, that the fairest and noblest of earthly things, are ever accompanied by some unfortunate and base alloy; and thus too, when the Genius of American liberty was born, there was the germ of a deadly canker deposited in her very heart, which has ever since grown with her growth, and will eventually, we fear, devour her very vitals. That fatal canker is Slavery.

At precisely the same period, when the ineffable blessings of rational liberty were first attained, upon the rugged rock of Plymouth, and thence spread abroad throughout this virgin continent, diffusing over its boundless surface, the blooming loveliness of a "Paradise regained;"— at that same period, the malignant curse of Slavery, the powerful and direct antidote of the other, was introduced at Jamestown; and has ever since striven to extend its deadly blight over the beauteous domains which freedom had won. It is a mortal virus, nestling in the very heart of the nation. It increases with its extension, its growing magnitude and greatness; undersapping, enervating and poisoning its vitals with ceaseless and insidious power; and as the doomed victim of consumption carries

about within himself the ineradicable source of his own
coming dissolution; so does the mightiest Republic of
ancient and modern times, bear within her bosom the
poison of Slavery which appears not to rest in its destructive agency, till it will destroy this fair fabric; till it in-
troduces civil war and bloodshed; till it rends asunder
that which now constitutes a beauteous and majestic
whole, and till it scatters its dissevered and dishonoured
fragments abroad, like hideous wrecks, to the distant
quarters of the continent.

Conscience and principle on one side, and self-inte-
rest, not unmixed with inhumanity, on the other, cannot
permanently harmonise, as fundamental elements in the
same body; but like the fierce and imprisoned winds of
Eolus, they will rage and rave around the huge caverns
of their detention, until at length they irresistibly break
loose, and carry desolation and ruin over these fair
plains of freedom's chosen home.

This canker, of which we have spoken, ceaselessly
gnaws at the national unity; and will yet illustrate the
truth of the maxim, *gutta cavat lapidem, sæpe cadendo*,
—drop after drop will wear a rock away. Even now
that canker is spreading its poison throughout the system
of the body politic; it traverses every vein and artery;
it seizes on every member; it disorders every function
and faculty; and we fear it will at length drag down to
the long night of endless dissolution, the most glorious

fabric of political power and beauty, which has ever yet floated, arrayed in peerless majesty, upon the tempestuous tide of time! And, to recur to our first figure, though reversing the relative positions of the despot and the patriot, we may safely predict, that when hereafter the Genius of American liberty expires in the capitol, lying at the feet,—not of Pompey's statue, but of Washington's,—she will point her finger to the grinning and exulting spectre of Slavery, and exclaim in her dying agony, *Et tu quoque Brute!*